The Red House

a&b

The Red House

EMILY WINSLOW

Allison & Busby Limited
12 Fitzroy Mews
London W1T 6DW
allisonandbusby.com

First published in Great Britain by Allison & Busby in 2015.

First Edition

ISBN 978-0-7490-1895-5

Typeset in 11/16 pt Sabon by
Allison & Busby Ltd.

The paper used for this Allison & Busby publication
has been produced from trees that have been legally sourced
from well-managed and credibly certified forests.

Printed and bound by
CPI Group (UK) Ltd, Croydon, CR0 4YY

For Samuel and Westcott, my choirboys

PROLOGUE

Highfields Caldecote, Cambridgeshire

The digger's caterpillar rollers stopped short of its target, a peach-coloured house with uncurtained windows and an unlocked door. Services had been disconnected; saleable materials had been salvaged. There was nothing left to do to prepare the building for razing. Erik was tempted to start the job today, to get a jump on things, but he hesitated.

Listless brown and grey rabbits dappled the field, dozens of them. They should have tensed as the digger's vibration spread through the ground; the noise of it should have set them sprinting. But these rabbits – lumpy, swollen and blind – meandered. One headed towards the digger and Erik pitched forward in his seat as he stopped short of it.

It lolloped past, limp and with little spring.

It would have been a mercy to crush it, but *too fucking disgusting* Erik thought. Sweat slid from under his hard hat down the side of his nose. He jumped down from the seat. From the boot of his car he got his shotgun.

He didn't like to shoot rabbits. Healthy ones scampered off when approached, and that was good enough for him. His garden at home didn't have anything in it that he didn't mind sharing.

Myxi rabbits needed killing. They were dying already, but dying in pain.

Fucking Aussies, he thought, loading a shell. They had purposely introduced myxomatosis for the express purpose of rabbit genocide. Then, *fucking French*. By the fifties it was in Britain and running wild.

The rabbits were stupid from pain and moved slowly. One even came towards him, labouring to push itself forward in awkward spurts. It was as if it wanted it.

The repeating noise of the gun covered the shouts. It was only in the pauses that he made out the words: 'Stop it!' and just 'Stop!' and, eventually, a wail.

Bitch should be grateful, he thought.

It was her decision to remain. The other homeowners had given in and sold. If she wanted to hold out while construction cleared and drilled and poured and hammered around her, that was her choice. She'd been made a good offer. She refused to leave.

She continued shouting at him from a window in the bright red barn. He knew that no one was home in the white house beyond the barn; it was school hours and work hours. He continued shooting.

Her fence was meaningless to the rabbits. He counted six of them on her side. He loaded and took aim. The sick ones took their deaths gratefully; the few healthy ones scattered. One dived into the blackberry bushes at the back of the barn, twisting between stems and thorns, then plunging into the soft earth, through groping roots, until it scrabbled against something hard: a pelvic bone. Nestled in that bone's crook, a smaller, more curled skeleton was shifted upwards by the rabbit's churning movements.

There was a flash of movement in a window of the barn, but Erik couldn't see the old woman's face. She must be tucked behind the curtain.

Afraid of me? Stupid cow, he thought, tears tumbling down his cheeks. He hated to shoot anything. He'd kept a rabbit when he was a boy: *Milly*, he remembered. She'd been soft, long-haired, fat from treats, and glossy from brushing.

He replaced the shotgun in the boot of his car and returned to the digger's seat. He ignored the furry bodies now under his treads and scooped into the bucket; they weren't really rabbits any more, now were they. Like Milly, they were elsewhere. Peaceful. *Fuck streets of gold*, he thought. His heaven was all grass.

In the ground next to the red barn, the rabbit kept digging, nudging the bones up towards the surface.

The woman kept touching Maxwell. She was pretty, prettier than any other woman he'd been with, and more affectionate; she leant close and her shiny hair overlapped his shoulder. Muriel squirmed watching them.

The couple pressed their cheeks together, ostensibly to share the screen, but there was room enough around them to show the interior of his apartment behind: full bookshelves, a propped bicycle with a dangling helmet, a busy, bright watercolour. No, *their* apartment now; no longer just his. The watercolour hadn't been there the last time Muriel had visited. The bicycle was shaped for a woman. For *her*.

'Mum,' Maxwell said, grinning. The woman, Imogen, giggled, squeezing his shoulder.

Muriel knew what was coming. Maxwell had convinced her to install Skype for this call. He wanted to be face-to-face. *Not badly enough to visit*, Muriel noted, but that was supposedly excused by work.

'We're getting married,' he said, as Muriel had guessed he would, even though she hardly knew the woman. It was only weeks ago that Muriel had learnt that Imogen had moved in with Maxwell months before.

Imogen echoed Maxwell just a beat behind: 'Married!'

Muriel posed her face correctly. She said the right words: 'I'm so happy for you.' Her voice was a papery rasp, so she had to say it again, louder, if more briefly: 'I'm happy.'

Maxwell nodded. The movement of his head must have tickled Imogen. She nodded too, not to agree, but to rub in response, like a cat. 'We're happy too,' he said needlessly.

Muriel craved a cigarette, but Maxwell didn't know that she'd started smoking again. She nudged the ashtray and lighter well out of sight of her computer's camera, fingers twitching for the box in her handbag. 'When?' she asked. 'You know I have that trip to the Galapagos next May . . .'

'Maybe we'll elope,' Maxwell joked. At least, Imogen laughed, which turned it into a joke.

'Of course not,' Imogen corrected him. 'We're moving to Cambridge. Once we're settled, we can make firm plans.'

'Cambridge?' Muriel asked, while at the same time Maxwell said, 'Imogen, we'll see if they want me.'

'Who wants you?' Muriel said, making herself heard.

'There's a possibility of a job at one of the colleges. But . . .' He didn't finish the sentence.

'But what?' persisted Muriel.

Imogen answered: 'Mrs Gant, Maxwell's just being modest. Of course they'll want him. It's a wonderful opportunity, a choir for girls. And Cambridge is a beautiful city. I used to live near there.'

'That's exactly the—' Maxwell began, but Imogen intervened.

'I lived in a village in a peach-coloured house. It was beautiful, tucked away with a handful of other houses, all different colours: lavender and yellow and red and white. Lots of grass and rabbits. All of it was beautiful, Caldecote and Cambridge.' Imogen was incandescent with memory.

Maxwell cautioned her, 'Things may not be the same now, Im.'

'Cambridge has been there for eight hundred years. I should think that it's doing just fine,' Imogen snapped.

It was the first discord Muriel had observed between them, and it gave her a shudder of satisfaction that inspired genuine goodwill.

'No sense arguing before you're even married,' she said lightly. 'There's plenty of time for that after.'

Maxwell looked embarrassed. 'We're not arguing, Mum, we're—'

'Don't look so aghast, Maxwell. I know your father and I were no good example, but you don't need to fear that a single disagreement will turn you into us. I'm simply advising not bickering. Imogen, are your parents still married?' She took it for granted that they would have been married to start with.

'My parents are dead,' Imogen said. 'But they were married when they died,' she added, precisely, pathetically.

'Mother, that was really unnecessary,' Maxwell defended Imogen, stroking her hair.

Muriel stammered, 'How was I to know? It was a question. I couldn't have known until I asked, could I?'

Imogen said, 'It's all right, Mrs Gant. They died a long time ago. But they were special, very special, and I was incredibly lucky to have them for as long as I did. Eight years. I was eight years old when they died. That's why I left Cambridgeshire. We all did. We—'

'All?'

'There were four of us. I—'

'Mother, this is just about the wedding. That's all this call is. Let's talk about that.'

Imogen said, 'No, it's all right, Max, I don't mind . . .' But her expression had drooped.

Maxwell faced her. Their foreheads touched. Their noses overlapped. Maxwell spoke to Muriel, but his words breathed into Imogen's mouth: 'You're the first one we told,' Maxwell said, half flattering Muriel, but also half chastising her for her tepid response.

'There's someone at the door,' Muriel announced. It was only half a lie; the cigarettes in her bag by the door were indeed calling her.

Imogen straightened and threw a bright smile across her face. 'I'll be good to him, Mrs Gant. I promise.'

'Don't take any shit, Imogen. That's the advice I needed when I was younger. It took me years to learn that. Don't take any shit, even from him.'

Maxwell and Imogen held their smiles politely, while his head tilted and her eyes squinted in surprise.

'I won't give her any shit, Mother,' said Maxwell carefully. 'You know I'm not like Dad,' he added.

How would he know? Muriel wondered. *He hasn't seen the man in twenty years.* 'Sorry, the door, I said.' She clicked the icon of a little red phone. The screen blanked.

She retrieved her bag, lit a cigarette and sucked on it. She opened a window. She closed the laptop, as if it too were a window, still connecting them; as if Maxwell could see her through it, guiltily smoking; as if she could see him – them – climbing all over one another on their cheap sofa.

'No,' she said out loud, putting the image firmly out of mind. She set herself a mental timer: for ten minutes she would pretend this wasn't happening. It would be only a tiny respite, but she needed it. *One,* she counted, blowing smoke, as the minute hand on the clock flinched.

Detective Inspector Chloe Frohmann looked up from the file on her desk. *Today's the day,* she thought, steeling herself.

She could see him across the room, the new face in a crowd of familiar ones. *Familiar, but not friendly.* Not to her, anyway. But this new man was already one of the boys.

13

Their heads were bent towards one another. Hands were shaken, and his back was clapped. He looked young; he was ginger-haired; he smiled quizzically when he noticed Chloe staring at him.

The man on his right said something close to his ear, nodded towards Chloe and laughed. The new man's smile faltered. Smirks all around.

Chloe pushed back from the desk to heave herself to standing. Her pregnant belly preceded her, forcing a waddle. She resisted the urge to fulfil the stereotypical pose of hand-on-back, and kept her arms swinging by her sides.

The others drifted away as she approached. The new man tried smiling again, though more cautiously now. 'DI Frohmann?' he asked, as if the room were full of women detectives launching towards eventual maternity leave, as if his new partner could have been one of any number of them.

Chloe nodded and shook his hand. 'DS Spencer?' she confirmed. He was taller than Morris, just a bit, and leaner. He looked nervous, which she couldn't imagine Morris ever having looked, not in such a puppy-like way, even on his first day. *It wasn't nerves on his face when he left*, she recalled of their last case together. *It was* – she had to think carefully, grope for just the right word. *Grief*, she realised. *Mourning for his old self.*

A bark of laughter from the other side of the room hit her in the back. She would have told herself it wasn't necessarily aimed at her, but Spencer, who could see over her shoulder, looked embarrassed.

She leant close, flicked her glance towards their

colleagues round the coffee machine, and said, 'Aren't they a bunch of arseholes?'

Spencer hesitated, then his smile cracked wide open. 'Fucking arseholes,' he agreed.

Chloe nodded. 'Let's get to work.'

SIX WEEKS LATER

The shower water hits Morris Keene like needles. Every muscle aches; every reach and stretch is compromised. His new stab at exercise is supposed to make him stronger but he feels humbled, simultaneously childish and old. The months he's spent sulking since leaving the job have only exaggerated his reasons for leaving in the first place: his body, his confidence, and any courage there once was, are all weaker now than then.

He turns the knob to raise the temperature. Gwen wanted to change it to a handle for him; she wanted to change everything around the house, like years ago when their daughter Dora had been learning to crawl and they'd put locks on all the cabinets and drawers, and tucked pads around sharp corners. Gwen put on a hurt look at his absolute refusal, but this challenge was his adjustment to make. If he can't, he reasons, then he deserves to do without.

He manages. His left hand is fully functional, if clumsy in the normal way that non-dominant hands are, and his right hand isn't as useless as it had seemed at first. The severed tendons prevent his fingers from curling in any sort of grip, but his thumb still works. Sometimes, as with this shower knob, pressing his palm and hooking his thumb are enough. Despite his adaptations, everyone still focuses on the hand, to be polite, as if difficulties with driving and writing were enough to take him off a job that's ninety percent thinking. It wasn't the hand that took him down, he knows. It was the panic attacks, hesitation and cowardice. Those aren't things you can proof a house against.

He turns off the water. He grabs a towel off the rail. Both of these actions are now effortless gestures. He's had to insist that Gwen stop praising his little victories, otherwise she coos as if he should be proud that he can wash himself, that he can dress himself. He pulls clothes out of drawers and off hangers.

He allows accommodations in some areas. He doesn't wear shirts with buttoned cuffs any more. He wears shoes without laces. *It's not as if I have a job any more to dress properly for,* he thinks as he sits to pull socks on and to push his feet into loafers.

This is his side of the bed now; he and Gwen had switched so that his left hand is on top and free when they face one another.

It's late afternoon but he hasn't bothered to pull up the covers or plump the pillows. Gwen's side is still mussed from when she'd dressed that morning, wriggling into a fresh new suit and bemoaning having to wear tights in August. It's her first offsite for her new job; she'll be away a few days. It's just Morris and Dora and the dog now, and Dora is at summer orchestra in Cambridge, just like Morris had done when he was a teenager.

16

He glances over at the clock. Gone five. *Actually, Dora should be home.*

He finishes dressing and calls out into the corridor, 'Dora?' He glances through the open door of her unoccupied room; he calls her name on his way down the stairs. No backpack or flute case dumped by the front door. The dog is still asleep in her basket in the kitchen.

Jesse, he reminds himself. The dog has a name.

Jesse was a 'gift' from Gwen, to ensure that Morris gets out of the house at least twice daily. She worries that he's becoming depressed and hopes that sunshine and exercise might do something about it.

Jesse dances around his feet, panting. He leashes the eager spaniel, and tamps down an absurd flash of pride at his left hand clicking the little hook to the collar on the first try. *A lot has to be wrong with a person to be proud of leashing a dog,* he chides himself.

She wriggles like a puppy but she's an old dog. Like Morris, Jesse isn't useful any more. *At least Gwen didn't get an injured dog, three-legged or blind or limping. That would have been a bit too on-the-nose.*

They go outside.

Lower Cambourne is just about Dora's age, fifteen. It was built when she was small, all of it new when they moved in, the whole town new, not just the house. It's convenient and comfortable and practical. Cambridge is near enough that there's no need for charm or history or character; they can commute for that, just like they do for shopping, and music. The next day, like today, Dora will take the bus in for orchestra and *a cappella* group. Morris will . . . take Jesse for another walk. It feels fitting to him to live in a town made of loops and cul-de-sacs. *Around and around I go.*

He calls Dora's phone as he walks. No answer.

He stops so that Jesse can squat, and fiddles a plastic bag out of his pocket. He's not sure what other numbers he can call. She'll have already left the concert hall. She's probably with friends. *Gwen knows their numbers.* No, he decides. Gwen's working. And everything is fine. Dora's a teenager. She doesn't need the level of fuss that's tempting him.

Gwen would agree with that, he knows she would. Two months ago, Dora and a friend had bunked off school for the day, and he and Gwen had decided together not to overreact. The girls had only taken a bus to the mall at Milton Keynes. The mother of the other girl – Fiona, he recalled; a mousy friend that Dora probably wouldn't make now but has known since she was little – had got hysterical over it. She'd sworn at Gwen on the telephone when they didn't join in her outrage. *No wonder her daughter is so timid*, Morris had thought smugly. They'd congratulated themselves on being better parents than that.

Jesse leads him around their usual route. She pauses automatically in front of a certain house, looking to him for a decision. He considers ringing the bell, but knows that he ought to head back home.

His phone vibrates in his pocket. He pulls it out, and would have automatically hit the green button if his thumb hadn't been needed to hold on to the phone at all. He's glad that he hasn't answered when he sees that it's not Dora; it's Chloe.

As far as he's concerned, she hovers worse than Gwen. Ever since his replacement . . . *No, not replacement,* he corrects himself. The new man is a Detective Sergeant, young and fresh, not someone at his level. *Former level,* he corrects again. *Detective Chief Inspector.* Gwen had thrown a party when he achieved that rank, surprised him at a restaurant. Dora had been proud of him.

The phone quivers again. Chloe, again. He turns it off. He ties Jesse's leash to a lamp post. His pace quickens up the front walk. A frisson of anticipation travels up his back.

Later, breaking into a light jog to compensate for Jesse's boredom from having been tied up, he recognises Chloe's car as it drives towards him, coming from his house. She pulls up alongside, flops the passenger door open, and tells him, 'Get in.'

Morris hesitates.

'It's Dora,' she says.

He scrambles into the car, dog on lap, and slams the door shut as Chloe peels out towards Highfields Caldecote.

It's just the next village over. Dora's friend lives there; Fiona, the timid girl. Dora used to spend hours a week there. Since skipping school, she hasn't been allowed to associate with Fiona, but Chloe says that Dora's there.

The long private road dead-ends at Fiona's family's houses, a white house and a red barn, on an island of grass. *No, not an island.* That's what it would be if it were in the middle of all the dirt – dirt which used to be lawns and neighbouring homes – but Fiona's family's land is on the edge, more like a cramped beach of grass. The dark, churned-up earth adjacent is so vast and so uneven that it gives the sense of a sea about to break on that grassy shore, swamping the last two houses, the resisters of development.

Two little signs are redundant to the view: they say, 'The Red House' and 'The White House'. Police cars are parked in front, and an ambulance. Morris dashes out before Chloe has fully parked.

Dora's on the steps of Fiona's white house, not in the ambulance, not in a police car, though an officer stands nearby. Her knees are drawn up, and she's hugging them. Morris runs right over. He wants to scoop her up but stops short. She looks different to him: older, haunted, matured by trauma. Then she sucks snot back up her nose and wipes her eyes, ageing backwards towards being his baby again.

He crouches next to her on the step. 'Are you hurt?' he asks.

She shakes her head.

'Good, good,' Morris says, trying to keep it together. His good hand is squeezing in and out of a fist. Jesse licks Dora's fingers. Dora pushes at her, so Morris shoos the dog off.

Chloe has told him that Dora had been in the barn. Not with Fiona, but not alone. She'd been in there with one of her music tutors, a new one. Someone called Maxwell Gant. Morris had demanded on the drive over, *Who is he? How old?* Chloe hadn't known anything yet. Morris stretches his neck to see who Chloe's talking to now, but it's just a paramedic. Morris turns and looks around the other way. He wants to see this man.

The dog starts barking. Morris shouts, 'Jesse!' She doesn't stop, though. The yaps are sharp and persistent. He goes after her. Dora follows him around the barn.

Jesse's around the back. She's got her nose in the blackberry bushes. She stops barking when Morris picks up her lead. She lies next to the bush and won't budge, even when he pulls and commands, 'Up!'

Then he freezes, and he and Dora both remember at the same time. Chloe too; she steps in, hands on hips, belly in silhouette. She tells Morris to get Dora home, *now*.

This is the thing that has them all still and staring, at the bushes overheavy with ripening fruit: Jesse's a retired cadaver dog.

CHAPTER ONE

Four days ago

MAXWELL GANT

Summer, Jesus College, Cambridge

Instead of students, the college was hosting conferences. Everyone we saw wore a corporate name-tag or a serving uniform. A wheeled trolley was pushed along the pavement. Ten o' clock – must have been time for morning coffee in some Tudor-timbered parlour. *That sort of thing could be for me someday*, I thought. Not yet, though. That day, we'd slipped in the back gates behind a delivery van.

We weren't the only ones out of place there. I patted the tyrannosaur's rough, rusting flank. 'Seb would have loved these,' I offered.

'They're new. They weren't here then,' Imogen said.

The sculptures were fully life-sized but childishly abstract, made of steel slabs slotted together like the stands of paper dolls. They were hulking, cartoonish monsters, somehow cheerful in their arrangement. A football pitch spread out before them, as if their habitat. Around the sports fields, the stone walls of the college penned them in.

I turned in a circle. The older Cambridge colleges are all like this: walls, lawns, courtyards. I breathed deep. When I got back to the dinosaurs, I smiled.

Imogen stood stiff, back against the belly of the stegosaur, looking down. Brown hair fell across her cheek. In Spain, her hair had been slicked back, wet from the sea. In London, it was usually held back in a clip for work. In Cambridge, it was down. It shadowed her. I reached out but she turned her head away.

I tried a joke: 'Maybe you just didn't notice them back then . . .'

It didn't raise a smile. Even if the dinosaurs weren't enormous and unmissable, there's nothing from then that she doesn't remember. Im's memories are so sharp that they'd cut themselves into my mind too.

I tried to be logical. 'Of course things have changed, Im. Twenty years . . .'

'Twenty-three,' she said. Every year counts with her. Every detail, no rounding. 'You're right. He *would* have loved these,' she said, running her finger along the spine of a sloping tail.

Her arm stretched out, which pulled her summer dress taut. She doesn't show off her body in obvious ways, but she must have known how the thin fabric moved around her. She would never let a bra strap show, or wear leggings without a skirt, but she knows how even conservative clothes hang on her. She knows where they catch and where they flow. She knows what she looks like.

I stepped closer to her. '*I* like the dinosaurs. Do you?' *Surely the present matters more than the past. Surely.*

'I do like them,' she said. 'I do. They're wonderful.' Her

26

voice wobbled. Tears glistened in her eyes, threatening to overflow.

Frustration crackled inside me, but I forced my hand to reach out, and my mouth to form a comforting 'Shhhhh . . .' I knew that it was my fault, for bringing her here. I put my hand on the small of her back and guided her away.

That's why we came by car instead of on foot: in case of needing a quick escape. We slipped out through the gate, as it swung open for a college vehicle. We cut over to King Street, where my Mini was squeezed in along the kerb. I opened the doors to release the accumulated heat.

She faced me over the roof. 'We'll try again tomorrow,' she said, and I accepted it as an apology.

I'd been offered a job in Cambridge, at St Catharine's, one of the University's other colleges. Their music director was about to take an emergency leave of absence and I'd been asked to cover this coming year. It was a good offer. It's a new choir, starting its own traditions with its own liturgy, based around an ancient Greek hymn and candlelight. It's Cambridge; of course I wanted it. I'd downplayed my excitement, but Imogen knew. The college needed a commitment by the end of the week.

'Only if you feel you can manage living here,' I insisted. It wasn't a lie; I would give up the job for her if need be. It was the calm smile that was a lie. I wouldn't be happy about it. We got in the car and lowered the windows.

'You're so good to me,' she said, snuggling up as much as she could over the gearbox.

'I'm the lucky one,' I said in reflex. It's true. Imogen is impossibly lovely: wavy hair, swimmer's body. She regularly beats me at tennis, reads six books a week, and can speak four languages. She's a wonder.

'No, me,' she said, squeezing my thigh with her hand. 'I'm the lucky one. Let's get back to the hotel.' She breathed deep. The heat had made our clothes stick. The seatbelt emphasised her perfect breasts, a small peak on each side of that diagonal slash. I started the car.

I'm the driver; Im's too used to London life. She promised to practise when we move out of the city. There was a lot that she had become ready to try. For six years, she'd been an hour away, and she hadn't even visited Cambridge. But with me, she insisted, she could face it.

'Tomorrow, we'll slip in the back again,' she decided. 'I don't want to explain myself to the porters.'

Fine with me. The colleges don't mind visitors; I saw a fair few tourists when I interviewed at St Catharine's. But if she wanted to sneak up on her past instead of confronting it, what would it cost me? 'Shall we vault over the wall at dawn, then?' I joked.

Hand off my thigh. *All right, it wasn't funny.*

'I want our wedding to be at the college,' she announced.

'St Catharine's?' I asked, hopeful and purposely obtuse.

'Don't be silly. Jesus College, dinosaurs and all.'

I didn't think that that was a good idea.

'I've made an appointment with the chaplain,' she continued.

'Before you've even managed to walk in past the porters?' The favourite hours of her childhood had been spent at this college, tagging along with her older brothers to choir. While they'd practised, Im and her little brother Sebastian had been a pair, collecting conkers off the lawns

and running wild in the cloister. Seb hadn't been old enough
to join yet, and she was a girl. Only boys sing at Jesus. Seb
would have left her and joined in with the music when he
got old enough, but it never came to that.

We drove over the hump of a bridge.

'Max, I want Jesus College to become an *us* memory.
You and me. We're better than the past. We can make it
ours.'

Can we? I wanted it, too, but . . . It niggled at me, the
question of what made her approach me when we first
met. It was on a beach; she was wet and tan, a bright scarf
tied around her waist over a sleek red bathing suit. I'd
looked over my shoulder, thinking at first that she'd meant
someone else.

She asked me everything, even about my family and
childhood. My answers were boring, and a little self-
pitying: my dad ran off when I was small and my mum and
grandmother raised me without him. It was only later that
Im said why she'd needed to know so much about me.

She always had to be sure, she'd explained, before she
got involved with anyone. Her parents had died when she
was eight, and she and her siblings had been adopted out
to different families. She'd found her older brothers when
she turned eighteen, but Sebastian, the little one, was still
unaccounted for. He could be anywhere. She had to make
sure he was never across the table from her on a date.

She'd presented it like a compliment. She wanted me,
and so had to vet me first. But I know that that wasn't all.
There was something else she wouldn't admit.

I knew why she'd approached me in the first place. I
knew why this perfect woman – in the car with her hand

on my thigh – noticed me on a beach of hundreds. Still, I drove her back to our hotel, for lunch or maybe sex before my afternoon commitment at the University concert hall, assisting at a week-long summer music course. I accepted the situation.

She's said that she loves me for me; she loves my music, my cooking, my talkative, welcoming friends, and my collection of well-loved, cracked-spine paperbacks. She's said that she loves us as a pair: for our shared tastes and serious talks and fun in bed. But she hadn't known any of that on the beach in Spain. She'd only known that I looked like him, like Seb. She approached me then because I look like the grown-up version of her lost brother.

In the car, my leg tensed inside her grip.

She snatched her hand back to her lap. 'You're angry, aren't you?' she flung at me. 'I know how much you want this. I want it too, for you. You say it's up to me, but we both know that you'll take the job. You *should*. The real question is, will I be able to cope with coming with you?'

'Im, you know I—'

She put up a hand to stop me. 'Let me try. I may be hard to be around while I . . . while I find my footing. But I'm willing to give it my best. Are you willing to let me?'

She lifted her chin; her lips opened just a little. *Beautiful.*

'Of course I am,' I said, dragging my gaze back to the road.

'It'll be fun living in a university town. It will remind me of my youth.' She's thirty-one, five years older than me. We'd got into a habit of joking about the age difference to stop others from doing it for us.

I hate having to do that. No one would say anything if

our ages were reversed. 'When exactly is this meeting with the chaplain?'

'Tomorrow,' she answered, casually, as if that weren't a little soon. She leant her head back against the headrest and closed her eyes. Her chest lifted with breath.

I'm aware that our relationship has an element of the practical about it. I'm the man that she happens to be with when she's decided she needs a baby, so I'm the one who gets to marry her. I could worry about it, and wonder if she really loves me better than everyone else, but it seems easier to simply consider myself fortunate.

'All right,' I said carefully, as the car rolled us forward.

Are we supposed to admit that we live together? I'd had a brief fling with devout Christianity when I was a teenager, and half-remembered youth-group soundbites panic me when I encounter clergy. I reminded myself that, despite the blunt name that had been assigned to Jesus College more than five hundred years ago, it's fundamentally secular.

I tried to relax in the chaplain's office, but felt too warm despite the open window. The room was made up like a lounge in someone's house, with soft sofas and throw pillows, and I felt like I was sinking into the seat and wouldn't be able to get up.

Imogen answered the chaplain easily. 'We're both in London at the moment, and looking for a home here together.'

The chaplain didn't fish any further than that, asking: 'And what attachment do you have to the college?'

I wasn't sure how much Im would want to get into. *Do we need a reason?* I wondered. Surely lots of people

31

marry in a college just because it's a grand architectural backdrop . . . *But would that offend the chaplain?*

'My brothers were choristers,' she answered simply.

She was at ease. Not just with wedding talk but with the college in general, after a brief initial stiffness. She'd greeted the dinosaurs this morning; they're part of her memories now, she said, her *new* memories of Jesus College. A friend of mine once worried to me that Imogen lives in the past, but he'd got that wrong. Im lives in the future too. She choreographs the present as memories for future Im. It's as if all these years leading up to her old age are just the packing of the suitcase instead of the trip itself.

'Max?' she prompted me. I'd missed what the chaplain asked.

'Do you have any special preferences for the service? Are you content with the use of the Book of Common Prayer?' the chaplain repeated for my benefit.

'I am,' Im said, a love of ceremony flashing in her eyes.

'I don't mind,' I said, then immediately worried that I sounded indifferent. I added, 'I don't want her to obey me, if that's all right.'

'If you choose the 1662 vows, "obey" is part and parcel. But the 1928 and 2000 revisions provide an alternative,' the chaplain reported, precisely, like a schoolboy determined to get full marks. He looked too young, younger than I had expected.

'How old are you?' I asked.

Imogen apologised on my behalf, but the chaplain overrode her and answered. 'Thirty-four,' he said, still smiling, still unperturbed.

Older than me, so I couldn't really complain. He's older

than Im as well, by three years. I nodded. 'I just . . . expected a fatherly figure, is all,' I over-explained.

'Will your father be coming to the wedding?' he asked, cutting right to that soft part I didn't realise I'd exposed.

'No, I . . . I only meant that I expected you to be older than me. A generation older, not just a handful of years.'

'If you're uncomfortable . . .'

'No,' insisted Imogen, raising her eyebrows at me in warning.

'No,' I agreed. *There, I lied to a priest for you.*

He walked us to the chapel, explaining the history of the college, really selling it. I'd made it clear that we hadn't settled on a venue yet, so he was making sure that we knew every advantage the college has to offer.

The outer chapel is a large, echoey space that rewards looking up with an elaborate ceiling. It wasn't exactly as I'd pictured it from Im's stories, but it was recognisable in that dream-way where a place doesn't look like, say, your old primary school, but it *is* your school, it just is, and you know it despite the visual mismatch.

Imogen sucked in a breath. She looked around, all sides, clutching her hands tightly in front of her stomach.

At first I'd thought that she was mad to suggest having the wedding in Jesus chapel, but I suddenly saw that it was a necessary hurdle. She had to prove that she could do it. If we sidestepped it, married at St Catharine's or a random church or the Register Office, the chapel would always hang over her. It would be heavier than a memory – it would be a 'might have been'.

The chaplain led us through a doorway cut into a carved wooden screen, into the inner chapel, a small, tight jewel-box of a room. In it, two long stalls faced one another, each with three rows of bench seats, ascending. It was a fashion, once upon a time, for worshippers to face one another instead of facing the altar. He described the options of the current daytime sunlight, shining through the stained glass and smearing coloured light across the stone walls, versus the more dramatic evening candles and pin-prick spotlights.

I slipped into one of the rows, testing it out. It had a long wall along the back of it to lean against, as did the row in front, so anyone sitting on the middle bench is completely hidden while sitting. This middle row is the kind Im and her family had always sat in, so that any whispering or fidgeting from her or Seb wouldn't be noticed. And, I discovered, if you're at all tall, the kneeler cushions press up against your knees without you having to bother leaning forward. I felt vaguely violated, as if forced into prayer.

The chaplain asked us how we met. I popped up to tell it: on a Basque beach while we were both on holiday with friends; then discovering our proximity in London, where she worked and I'd just completed a master's degree. I didn't mention Sebastian.

While telling the rote story, I imagined Im's older brothers here. The middle third of the stalls must be for the choir. I could tell from the lack of service books: the ledges in front of those seats were left empty for their music. The boys would be positioned in the first rows, then the college men tall behind them.

The pipes of two distinct organs were visible in the archways up above. One set was a modern, asymmetric cluster; the other a classic arrangement between the flung-

34

open doors of an elaborately painted case, spread like wings. Imogen noticed the organs too, and pointed up. 'That one's new,' she said, indicating the modern one. She moved her finger to the other, the winged one, and clapped her other hand over her mouth. 'Oh!' she said through her fingers. 'I loved that one.'

Imogen had told me that she and Sebastian used to draw pictures of it, making up stops not just for different sounds, but also for anything in the world. She drew birds, hearts, even fire flying out of those pipes.

She doesn't play organ. Neither do I; only piano. I didn't start early enough to feel I could ever play organ really well. The good ones start as soon as their legs grow long enough to reach the pedals. If I take the job at St Catharine's, the two Organ Scholars will technically answer to me, which is intimidating. I'm supposedly qualified by my speciality in conducting voices and in medieval music, though, unlike their current Director of Music, also not an organist, I don't even have a PhD.

The chaplain was telling Imogen that the music director here at Jesus is a prodigy who had become organist at St Paul's Cathedral at what I quickly calculated was five years younger than I am now. I started sweating. *Whatever made me think that I belong here, among these bright, special people?*

Imogen saw the look on my face, and tilted her head in concern. 'I'm fine,' I mouthed. She relaxed immediately, always quick to believe the best possible version of anything.

'Do you want an organ played at your wedding?' the chaplain asked, apparently keen to make practical use of Imogen's reminiscence.

'I'm not fussed,' I said to the chaplain. 'Whatever she wants. If she's happy, I'm happy.'

Imogen beamed. *That smile.* What was my problem, being jumpy with the chaplain earlier? That's the man who might marry me to that smile, that voice, that body. It was real summer this week, hot at last, and Imogen had made the most of it, bare armed and bare legged.

The chaplain described the various options for music. In term time we could have the choir, and pay the boys in pocket money. Im's smile slipped. Her brothers, who'd joined when they were both nine years old, spent their choir money on model aeroplanes and chewing gum. Their mother always secretly matched the amounts to Im and Seb, and they'd bought chocolate cake slices with it while the twins were in rehearsal. Im, in the chapel, looked as though she might cry.

I reached for any change of subject. 'What about those dinosaurs?' I asked, steering back into the outer chapel. My comment sounded ridiculous without context. 'I mean, those sculptures on the lawn. They took us by surprise yesterday.'

'The college has pursued a collection of contemporary art in recent years,' the chaplain explained. 'As for the dinosaurs, technically they're only on loan. But I don't imagine the artists will find a better place for them, do you?' He allowed himself a chuckle. I couldn't tell if he approved of the dinosaurs or not. He had that blank demeanour some counsellors have, a neutrality and habit of answering every question with a question. 'Some couples like to have photos taken in front of them . . .' *Bravo.* His skill at linking everything back to wedding plans made me want to test him with more and more outlandish non-sequiturs.

But the man had moved on to talking seating with Im. Not much room for guests in the stalls, but one could use the outer chapel instead, where there's ample room for chairs and . . .

'No,' she said definitively, unwilling to give up the stained glass and candlelight of the inner chapel.

'No need,' I agreed. Our families aren't that big. *And my mother* . . . I don't know what's gone wrong but she's not been the least supportive. *It's probably my fault.* I hadn't gone home since my grandmother's funeral, haven't even been to see Mum's new house since she used the inheritance and new freedom to 'start fresh' with a downsized move to Exeter. Mum's had to come to me. Imogen has taken all of my attention, and Mum's no doubt felt that deeply.

'Well,' said the chaplain, leading towards the main door to usher us out. 'Do contact me when you've made your decision, to discuss dates. Will you want to arrange any pre-marital counselling as well?'

Im said 'No' at the same time that I said, 'Yes, sure.' The chaplain gave us a photocopied questionnaire to fill out for a future session.

We all three exited into the cloister, which is a square, covered corridor surrounding an open courtyard in the centre. 'What was that about, wanting counselling?' she asked me when the chaplain was out of earshot, the clicking of his footsteps receding.

'I thought you would want to.' I had felt happy, generous. I'd thought she wanted me to say yes.

'I already know what I want our marriage to be like: like my mum and dad's.'

I was unable to stop the automatic flick of my head from side to side. Her eyes darkened.

'I only mean,' I explained quickly, 'that I want our marriage to be like us, to be ours, not like anyone else's.'

She accepted that, and her face lit with forgiveness for my faux pas. She leant into me against the wall, her mouth on mine.

'Not in a church,' I said, wriggling out from between her and the wall.

She laughed, her London laugh, her Spain laugh. It was a surprise to hear it. It must have been the first easy, happy laugh since we'd arrived in Cambridge. 'This isn't church. Church is inside,' she chided, but she let me get out of it.

'This is churchish,' I explained. The college had started as a twelfth-century convent. It looked like it.

I shook myself. I had to get to the concert hall, to prepare for the teenagers' *a cappella* group. I had to do well with it; people from St Catharine's were coming to the performance on Saturday. I urged Imogen towards the exit at the opposite corner.

'Do you really think you can do it, Im? Are you sure this is a good idea?' Last night I hadn't thought it would be possible, but this meeting had been all right. Emotional, but that's to be expected. I felt the job near, so near that I could graze it with my fingertips.

Of the University's choirs that take children, St Catharine's is the only one for girls. King's College has their boys in Eton suits and top hats, and their annual televised Christmas service. St John's College boys wear thick cloaks and flat mortar boards, and sing regularly for the radio. Both of those colleges board their choristers, working them long hours. Jesus College boys come from local schools and have no special uniform, just ordinary black trousers and white shirts, with red and gold ties under their cassocks, but they have their own long tradition. St Catharine's girls' choir, in contrast, is just a few years old. I smile to think how easy it is to create an illusion of history at a college; a third of the population is new every year and assumes that anything that happened before they got there has been happening forever.

It's a fashion now, girl trebles. Cathedrals all over the UK are starting up girls' choirs, in place of or complementing their boys. It doesn't work as well to put them together; their sopranos clash, the girls with more vibrato and ageing up into a fuller sound, while the boys have a brief, pre-pubescent flash of hollow, light, flute-like treble. There's a pressure with boys, as their voices grow towards the peak that comes just before the inevitable break. A pipeline of trained younger probationers must be vigilantly supplied, to prevent a gap. Girl voices, on the other hand, steadily improve. You can start girls later and keep them longer. One needs to manufacture an excuse, usually an arbitrary age, to make room for the next wave, while the boys are hit by puberty, earlier and earlier now, with little warning except perhaps a growth spurt that leaves their cassocks dangling mid-calf instead of around their ankles.

I believe in it, in girls like Imogen once was, getting their chance to participate instead of just tag along. And I'm not blind to the opportunity for myself. Girl trebles get attention, for their novelty and the media angle of too-long-delayed girls' rights. The St Catharine's job could set up my career.

Before Im could answer my scepticism of her readiness, we turned a corner. Facing us was what must have been another of the college's art acquisitions: a full-sized bronze horse, plump and calm, hoof raised.

'Marco,' I said, unthinking.

Im grabbed her neck. She made a sound like choking.

'Im,' I said. 'It's all right.' But it wasn't. She was shaking. That was her answer for me, then. That was her answer. She wanted to do this for me, but just look at her . . .

She stepped forward, reaching towards the horse's nose, stopping just short of the lawn on which it stood. 'Yes, Marco,' she echoed. 'Seb loved him. He wanted to ride him. Of course, that's not allowed. The statue was new and the porters even warned us. I suppose they saw the look in his eye.' She grinned, desperately. 'He never got to do it,' she said. 'There's so much that he never got to do.' She covered her eyes.

'He doesn't want to any more, Imogen. He's an adult now.' *There are plenty of things I didn't get when I was young. I wanted a place on the cricket team; I wanted to see Blur play live. People grow up. People get other things. Sebastian, wherever he is, isn't stuck as a child who wants to ride a bronze horse, except in her memory.*

She blew out a pent-up breath. 'I'd forgotten that Seb called the horse that. I haven't thought about Marco in years. Well, I must have done. I told you, obviously.'

Obviously, because I'd known the horse's name, but I couldn't place the story. She must have mentioned it just the once, in passing, on the way to a better story, a longer one. That's why I knew it even though I didn't remember her telling me. There's a lot that I don't remember,

40

and that's normal. It's a man thing, my mother says. Certainly, in my experience, remembering every little thing to fling back at people as evidence in arguments is a woman thing.

No, that's not fair. Im only does that when I make assumptions. I put my arm around her shoulders. Maybe she will be all right. It was just a surprise is all, like the dinosaurs. 'We'll come back and try again tomorrow.'

We exited past the porters' lodge. No one questioned us. It was as if we belonged.

I looked back over my shoulder, at Marco, riderless. The statue is just the shape and size to make anyone want to jump on its back.

The urge to spring coiled in my stomach.

Living in one small room with someone is a lot different from sharing space in a flat. For once, I was grateful for Imogen's long baths. They gave me the only privacy I got.

St Catharine's had offered me a room in college for this week, but it was a single. Im and I booked this hotel together instead. While she soaked in cool water, I looked up the bronze horse online by typing, *horse statue jesus college.* Lots of hits, with pictures. I tried this: *horse statue jesus college marco.* Again, lots of hits. I wanted to crow. It wasn't a name that Seb had made up; it wasn't a private joke. It was the horse's name. That was how I'd known it. It had come up in the research I'd done about the University. It must have done.

I looked more closely. *No, not just 'Marco'.* It was 'San Marco', in reference to the more-famous horse sculptures

41

in Venice, which had partly inspired this one. I searched with *'San Marco'* excepted.

Only a handful of results. One stood out, on an adoptees message board:

I'm looking for my sweet baby brother, who I love more than anyone in the world. We were separated when our parents died in a car crash and you may not even remember the rest of us. You were almost three years old in 1989. Do you love music? You used to sing all the time. You hated ice cream; it was too cold for you. You loved playing statues but not hide and seek; you didn't like being alone. You had a toy horse called Marco, and you slept with him every night even though he was plastic and the spindly legs must have poked you when you rolled over. We lived in Cambridgeshire, and we spent a lot of time at Jesus College. Do you remember any of this? Do you remember me, your big sister?

It was dated years ago. I searched again, for *brother jesus college adopted 1989*. These keywords brought up other message boards, where she'd posted similar pleas. The responses were all support from fellow searchers; no answer from Seb.

Again, I looked at the dates. They spanned a wide range; she'd been obsessed with this for years. But there was nothing this year, and only one post last year. That one was in May, before her summer trip to Spain.

She'd stopped searching for Sebastian when she found me.

It was a compliment, I knew. It was an immense flattery and an evidence of maturity. What had she said, exactly? That she wanted Jesus College to become an 'us' thing, a present thing, not a monument to her past. But, I knew from experience that her past has a way of asserting itself.

The first time we were going to sleep together, she booked us a weekend room at a country house hotel. The formality of the arrangement seemed unnecessarily complicated. She had a roommate; that I understood. But my place was fine. It was clean and comfortable. I just wanted to be with her. I just wanted to not stop. But Imogen likes to make things special. She makes events.

So she booked us into a room with a curtained bed and outsized bath. She showed me the pictures from the website on her phone. I drove, distracted by her obvious anticipation beside me. She was practically bouncing in the seat, singing along with the radio. Her exuberance had halted when I signed the guest register for us. I'm left-handed, something I'd never hidden but it had not yet come up in front of her.

I took the key and smiled, but her anticipation was gone. Instead, she stared, mouth slack, and her hands clutched one another, whitening the knuckles.

She bolted. I chased her into the car park, but she was gone, somehow gone, despite the wide lawns and the low flowerbeds, without walls or hedges or thick trees near enough to have hidden her. I found her between two vehicles, sitting on the ground, back up against a wheel. Her head rested on her knees.

'You never told me you're left-handed,' she accused.

I didn't answer. What could I say?

'Sebastian's left-handed. I taught him to write an S myself.'

'Lots of people are left-handed,' I said, far too reasonably for her.

'We can't . . .' she began. 'We have to be sure.'

'I'm sure,' I said. I was born in Durham. I'm named after my Aussie grandfather.

'I want a test.'

'A test? What kind of test?' My mind had gone to a quiz of some sort. A pub quiz, about my childhood and family. Or an exam, requiring quotes from supporting documents, maybe footnotes.

'A DNA test. There are places that do them by post.'

It sounded shady to me.

'I need it,' she insisted. 'I need to be sure.'

She knew the drill. It occurred to me then that she must have done this before.

We ordered a kit, and swabbed our mouths. We sent them away in the post and parted. She said she didn't know how to be with me, what kind of love she was supposed to have for me. It was the first time she had said 'love' meaning me. We didn't see each other while we waited.

When the results came through she waited for me at work. I ran a teenagers' choir as an after-school activity. We were just finishing a Handel finale, bellowing out grand chords over the tinny school piano. I saw her over the heads of the children, smiling, beaming. *Good news, then*. Of course it was. I had never expected it to be anything else, but the reality of it having finally arrived made me, in that moment, giddy.

At rehearsal's end she pulled me to her. 'Take me home,'

she'd said, without any preamble. 'Now. Quickly.' That's how I'd learnt that we aren't related. That's how I knew we were free.

Here, in the Cambridge hotel, she emerged from the bathroom in her dressing gown, wet like on the beach in Spain. She posed in the doorway, that same happy look on her face as on that day, the day she'd got back the DNA results, like she had a present for me, like she had good news. Her face glowed.

I'd never asked to see the results for myself, I suddenly recalled. From her behaviour, the results had been obvious.

Something knotted in my gut, but I ignored it. How could I receive that look with anything less than gratitude? 'Hello, beautiful,' I said, forcing my mouth into an appropriate answering smile.

All couples have more or less the same ingredients to their relationships: the first spark, first sex, declaration of love, decision to commit, in some order or other. Telling someone else your own love story is as boring as telling them what you dreamt last night. But those similarities – that uniform structure – make the few true differences pop. *First DNA test*, I reminisced wryly. How many people share that?

I stifled a laugh.

Imogen pulled her wrap tight around her chest, embarrassed.

'Im . . .' I said.

She rallied. 'If you love me come get me,' she dared me, letting the neck of her dressing gown fall open again.

I hesitated.

'What's wrong?' she demanded.

'Nothing,' I lied.

'Come here then,' she said, but I couldn't move. 'Is it because I proposed?' She calls it a proposal, but it hadn't been formal or even planned; one morning two months ago she'd blurted out, '*Let's get married*,' and I'd agreed that that was a wonderful idea.

'Of course it's not because you proposed,' I snapped. She's become paranoid about it, as if she'd violated the proper order of things and bad luck will follow. 'Of course I want to marry you,' I'd said then, and said again in the hotel. 'It's just the church,' I threw out there, as explanation. She knows that I was briefly devout.

'You know it's not the religion I want for the wedding,' she said, snuggling up against my chest, only her thin dressing gown and my T-shirt between us. I held still. 'It's the music, and the memories and . . . it will be like my family is there with us.' She stroked my arm; my hands hung still, unresponsive. She pushed me and went to cry in the bathroom. I heard her through the door.

I wanted to comfort her. I wanted to embrace her. But not . . . It didn't feel right. Not there, not then, with her suddenly a young girl again in her mind. She was too fragile. That was how I justified it to myself.

Well, which is it? Her fragility, or the church? I seemed to be full of excuses.

She came out of the bathroom, holding the skimpy hand towel with which she'd wiped her face. 'You're right,' she said. 'We should do the premarital counselling. Where are those forms?' She upended her bag. Receipts and tissues wafted. The folded papers hit the bed and fanned out, leaving little room for the two of us.

* * *

Last night we'd read the questions and agreed to sleep on them. Now we were in a dimly-lit indie coffee shop near the college. I hadn't thought anything of the name until we stepped inside.

Paintings, drawings and photographs of clowns' painted faces, exaggerated costumes and contorted poses covered the wood-panelled walls. They looked down at us, beyond us, pointedly away from us. Im and Seb used to come here to Clowns Cafe often with their mum, while their brothers practised.

Imogen reminisced about the sung services in the chapel. I already knew what she'd say, because evensongs follow a set liturgy at churches all over the world. Most of the words, even the prayers, stay the same, repeated each evening beside a rotation of Bible chapters and psalms. It's the musical settings of the words that vary, a wide repertoire shared by thousands of musicians. I relaxed. Imogen and I come from a similar class and culture; of course we would share similar memories and understandings. Any seeming déjà vu shouldn't surprise me.

'I'd like hot milk with chocolate on top,' she ordered. 'That's what Sebastian and I always got, because it looked like Mum's coffee,' she told me. I, more in keeping with the weather, got a fresh orange juice. Imogen insisted on a tiny round table in the back where she and Sebastian had always sat. It felt too small for us.

We hunched over the counselling questionnaire together. Round clowns' eyes read it over our shoulders.

What are you most looking forward to about married life? How do you expect it will be different from your present life?

47

*What does a happy marriage look like to you? What
would you most like to avoid?
How do you feel about your parents' marriage or
marriages?*

I read them out loud, and stopped there, thinking, *That
one is going to release floodgates in Im.* This is the sum
of it: Im's father adored her mother. Im's mother adored
her babies. Imogen worships their perfection. We'd been
hashing this out for months; I'd been trying to persuade her
to release her parents as an ideal.

She put her hand on mine. 'This one's going to be hard
for you, huh?'

That's right; I have parents too. 'There's not much to say.
I can't recall ever seeing them in the same room together so
I really can't comment on their marriage.'

'This isn't a joke,' she pouted.

'No, but a sense of humour is helpful, don't you think? I
lack marital role models; fine. That doesn't funnel me into
a replay of whatever-it-was that happened between them
when I was too young to notice.'

'No!' she said. She smacked the table and her cup
jumped on its saucer. 'You weren't too young to notice.
You were too young to put it into words in your mind, to
make conscious memories of it, but you *noticed*. Children
notice . . .'

'I know, I know . . .' *Back to her, I see.* I cut to the
real point: 'Sebastian remembers you, Imogen. Perhaps not
your name, but he remembers the happiness and the love
and the safe feeling. I should never have implied otherwise.'
I sighed; I leant back in my chair.

48

'Why do you keep bringing him up?' she asked me.

The conversation at the next table lulled and the milk steamer behind the counter stilled at the same moment. I ducked my head and lowered my voice. 'Me? Why do *I* keep bringing him up?' *That's a joke, right?*

She looked at me, unblinking. 'Are you jealous of him?'

'Jealous? Of . . . of whom?' She couldn't mean what it sounded like she meant.

'You're an only child of a single mother. You're used to one-on-one devotion. But love isn't finite, Maxwell. I can love my brothers and love you. Like we'll love our babies and still love each other.'

'Obviously,' I sputtered.

'This whole week you haven't let a conversation go by without bringing up Seb. But that's my job. I'll bring him up when he comes up; you don't have to.'

'You're the one who brings him up.' I had to take a stand on that.

She shook her head. We'd both pushed back from the table, leaning away in perfect symmetry.

Imogen was the first to crack. 'Look at us. It's as if we're going to upend the table and wrestle on the floor.' She forced her mouth into an apologetic smile.

I answered with a nod. We leant in again, cautiously and consciously. I looked over my shoulder, but no one in the cafe was paying attention. *This only matters to us,* I reminded myself. *No one else is going to care if we fall apart.*

My voice cracked. 'I'm worried about you, Im. This city is bad for you.'

'No,' she said, wagging her head back and forth. 'Just

because something is difficult doesn't mean that it's bad.'

'Fine. This city is *difficult* for you. Why put ourselves through it?'

She covered one of my hands with one of her own. 'This isn't just for you. I know you want the job; I want you to have it; but you're not the only reason why I'm here. It's time, Maxwell. I need to face this place and all that it stirs up in me. I'm lucky to have you with me. Can you imagine if I'd tried this on my own? I'd have done something crazy. I'd have ended up riding the horse statue, or ringing the chapel bell by swinging from its rope.'

I snorted a laugh. 'You're far too elegant to do either of those.'

She raised one delicate eyebrow. 'Is that what you think of me? "Elegant"? Hello, remember me? We live together.'

'You do snore sometimes, after wine,' I admitted.

'I don't!' she protested, laughing and covering her eyes with her hands.

I reached and touched her cheek. It was wet.

'I'm happy, Max. I am. It's just that big emotions come out of me in the form of tears. Bad feelings, good ones. Doesn't matter. If the feelings are big, my eyes leak.'

'Which big feelings are these right now?' I needed to know.

Her gaze darted around the room, fast and almost frantic, at last coming to rest on a crude painting of a harlequin juggling dozens of balls. 'All of them,' she said. 'Every feeling you can think of.'

The Sidgwick Site had surprised me on Monday. It's near enough to the city centre that I'd expected at least Victorian

50

architecture, if not earlier, but this is where Cambridge has gathered its modern, statement buildings. Concrete and glass; curves and slants. These are departments, not colleges, squeezing in between Sidgwick Avenue and West Road: Law, English, History, Divinity, Criminology, Classics and Music. The West Road Concert Hall was where I was spending my afternoons for the week.

The holiday music course has been ongoing in Cambridge for decades. String orchestras and 'everything else' orchestras, from beginner through advanced, are the main show, playing cinema themes and classical's greatest hits, alongside general choirs and more specialised groups, like my *a cappella* girls.

Unlike at Jesus choir, young Imogen had joined her brothers in the summer orchestra. It was held at West Road even back then. She played violin with the beginner strings while their mum looked after Seb.

Im told me about it only after I was asked to coach the *a cappella* group. It hadn't come up before, I suppose because these memories don't include her parents or Seb. What she did describe isn't nearly as vivid as the choir memories, so I didn't have the same sense of eerie recognition as I'd had at Jesus. The concert hall and its environs were fresh to me. Out for a walk between a meeting and a practice, away from the stifling warm rooms overfull with adolescents, I felt briefly free, which must be why I did it. Giddy happiness is the only sensible explanation.

It was a childish action: I ran up a wall that slants over a bicycle-parking alcove. I couldn't have been the first. Not only is any slope naturally tempting, but on this one the concrete surface is patterned as a checkerboard in relief, creating unintentional footholds. I scampered up.

It was only at the top that it occurred to me: *I'm a grown man*. I sheepishly skidded down. I looked around; no one had bothered to notice me. *Of course I'm not the first*, I comforted myself. Freshers must do it all the time. Then my point was proved: a toddler in a harness clambered up, his mother hovering anxiously.

I felt a tether-snap in my mind, a sudden pull.

I was staring; the mother snatched up her child and hurried away.

I walked in the opposite direction, embarrassed, deeper into the Sidgwick Site. I crossed the placid Zen pond in front of the red-lettered all-caps CRIMINOLOGY building and into a back car park. I passed through it to a bland academic building where a statue of a Greek figure faced me from inside a glass vestibule. This was Classics.

Another pull, another weight. This time it wasn't an urge; it was a certainty. I knew what was at the top of those stairs.

Up I went, to where an outsized Ariadne lounged, her toes pointed towards windowed double doors. Through them, I glimpsed the gamut of ancient Greek and Roman sculpture. According to the signage, this was a museum of plaster copies of marble originals. I opened the doors.

The picture was clear in my mind: Hercules, huge, bearded, muscled, nude. But he wasn't there.

There were nudes, plenty. Serene women were covered in flowing drapery, perhaps out of accuracy or modesty, but I suspect that the choice was made mostly to show off the sculptors' skills. The men were all naked, their bodies lithe and strong, but not massive. Not quite life-sized, most of them; more two-thirds or half-sized. I walked among them: wrestlers and athletes and soldiers. A mum tried to shush her little son who was excitedly pointing and shouting, 'Penis!' I recognised them from the concert hall. Her older children must have been making music there.

I sat down in a chair at the end of the aisle. I breathed deep. Around me, centaurs brawled.

I must be thinking of a different collection, perhaps in London, or that museum in Berlin . . . Like everything here, the statue in the window downstairs is a copy. I'd probably seen the original, somewhere where they have the Hercules too. Perhaps not as large as I remember. Perhaps it was a child's memory, head tilted back to look up.

I stood. My break was almost done; it was nearly time for my singing group. I headed out the way I'd come, through a gauntlet of spears and snakes.

The giant statue was next to the door. I'd missed it as I entered just by walking forward instead of turning around. He was huge, truly huge. Even an adult would have to hinge their neck to look Hercules in the face. I tilted my head so far back that it felt like falling.

'Hi, Mum. Just leaving you another message. I need to talk to you about the wedding. Im really hopes you'll come. So do I. Maybe you can visit sooner, actually? I really need to ask you some questions. About my dad. I'm sorry, but . . . Well, I don't think I should have to apologise for that, should I? I'll try again later.'

My mother doesn't like to talk about my early childhood because that's when my father was with us. '*Emotional abuse*' is as far as she'll go with description,

53

and that restraint is fine with me. All I wanted to know was whether we had ever spent time in Cambridge. We certainly could have. That would explain a lot. Not everything, but enough.

Our hotel room door rattled from Imogen's key. 'I'm home!' she called, as if we were living in a house instead of a room. 'I got work,' she announced.

She already has work: she does Spanish translation freelance. Her adoptive parents were employed by the British Council in a sort of cultural ambassadorship, sent to live in various countries for multi-year spurts, hosting artists and actors and authors to dinners and parties on behalf of the country. Imogen lived in Lima for much of her teens. She also speaks good German and decent Arabic.

I closed my laptop and turned towards her from the desk.

Imogen sat on the bed and untied her sandals. She lay back, stretching, then rolled onto her side. Her face was at my elbow. 'Did you hear me before? I said that I got a job.'

'I heard you.' *So that's it, then. She's decided that we're moving here.* As with the DNA results, she didn't feel the need to spell it out. She just moves forward, always, assuming that I'll catch on.

'There's a shop that sells jewellery on King's Parade. They had an advert in the window for counter help. I'm going to be a shop girl!'

'You sure you aren't getting ahead of yourself?'

'I went for a walk after you went off to the concert hall. Cambridge isn't that big of a city. Once away from the college, I didn't recognise a thing, not anything.' That sounded right; Im's family had lived in a village and gone to the village school. All they'd done in the city centre was their music: choir, and occasionally orchestra.

'And?' I prompted.

'Nothing. It's just a city, a city I've never been to before. There's nothing to stop us moving here. You're happy, aren't you?'

'Of course. But . . . I wonder if you'll be bored with shop work, is all.' She has a Master's degree.

'Well, I need some way to meet new people,' she explained. 'In London, I had the government work. I need a reason to get clothes on in the morning.' She tugged her blouse and bra strap down off one shoulder. 'Do I need an excuse to get my clothes off now?'

Her tan traced the outline of where her bathing suit strap had clung. She is gorgeous gold and gorgeous paper white, take your pick. She undid buttons. I held up my hand.

'Not now. Sorry.'

She narrowed her eyes and lifted her chin. 'Fine. I meant I'm going to have a quick wash.'

She doesn't like it when I say no. She made a show of the rest of the undressing, her back to me. She popped off her bra and slid off her skirt. She gave me every chance to change my mind.

I wanted to. My body was responding already. I – *No, not now*, I told myself. I had to dispel some concerns. That's how I'd settled on saying it to myself. That phrasing assumes a positive outcome. I needed to be sure, and would become sure, and life would return to normal.

She shut the bathroom door more emphatically than necessary. Most of her personal things had gone in with her, but a few items were scattered across the dresser top, including her hair brush.

When we did the DNA test a year ago, we swabbed the insides of our mouths. But that wasn't the only option. I'd looked it up. We could have sent in toothbrushes, or hair.

Im's hair is thick, so brushing with any vigour pulls some out. I needed that skin tag at the root. I plucked three suitable hairs and slid them into an envelope. A pair of tweezers was also on the dresser. I plucked three hairs of my own and they went into another envelope. There was a mirror on the dresser too. I avoided it. I didn't want to see myself like that.

I put both envelopes into my work bag. We each have our own laptops, so I knew she wouldn't stumble on my recent search history of DNA test accuracy. What if the test we sent in a year ago was mixed up or performed incorrectly? What if the results were someone else's? This new test would be a double-check.

She also wouldn't see how my Googling had started with legitimate DNA comparison companies that send special kits and require consent signatures, then ended with the more dodgy ones that are willing to bend the rules and get faster results. I didn't need the results to stand up in court; I just needed to know.

When this test came back, we'd both be sure. That was all. I opened a housing website to search for Cambridge flats. If we wanted to be settled next month, we had to be quick.

Through the door, I heard the bath drain pop. Any moment, she would come into the room smelling of vanilla soap. She would expect me to be affectionate.

Imogen isn't clingy. She takes time for herself, in the bath, in the gym, working, reading. But when she gives she expects to be received. When she tells a joke, she expects a laugh. When she dresses up, she expects a compliment. When she offers sex . . .

It's not just sex, I reminded myself. Even before we were sleeping together, she was physically expressive with her whole body. She holds hands with friends and kisses as a greeting. She laughs from her belly and quivers when she's excited. She needed to be close now. Sex was how that came out.

I pressed the heels of my hands against my closed eyes. I saw in my mind that statue of Hercules towering over me. How did I know that it would be there? How did I know that Imogen and Seb had called the horse Marco? No one else knew. That had been their private nickname, which I can't remember having been told.

In a week, I assured myself.

In a week, I would know for sure that we're not related, that the original test wasn't wrong or misaddressed. I would also know that something else wasn't true, something I was trying very hard not to consider:

I would know that she didn't get a result that confirmed relationship, and sleep with me anyway. Or, worse, *because of* that relationship. She loves Seb. She stopped searching the Internet for him when she met me. Maybe there was a reason other than maturity and moving on.

She came out wrapped in a towel. 'Don't worry, I won't molest you,' she pouted, reaching for her hairbrush.

'I'm just not feeling well is all,' I said. *Excuse number three.*

Her face softened. 'Is it the job stressing you?' she asked. 'I'll just rub your back. It will help you fall asleep.'

I turned, pulling my shoulders out of her hands. 'I'm not ready for bed. We need to look up flats. No point either of us having jobs if we have nowhere to live.' I felt hypocritical, deflecting physical contact with what could be argued is a similarly intimate interaction, shopping for our first married home.

The difference to me was that one is about intimacy now, and one is a plan for intimacy later. I was happy to plan. I believed in our future. I was sure that, in a week, I'd receive a DNA result that would mock my fears. I'd be shown to be wrong, and then we could be fully happy.

'I love house hunting,' she said, grabbing up her own laptop. She was on the bed again; I was still at the desk. 'Number one, I need a bathtub. And no automatic lights!' That was a callback to our weekend away last winter, in a supposedly luxury apartment that had had motion-triggered lights, even in the bathroom with the Jacuzzi tub and bookshelf. Every ten minutes the room had gone black and she'd had to throw a roll of toilet paper at the detector on the opposite wall to trigger the lights on again. It became our favourite vacation story. When we bathed there together, we prepared by stacking a pyramid of loo rolls and a basket of scented soaps in arm's reach. The soaps required more skill, because they were small and didn't always work. I made rules. Imogen tallied points. We added more and more hot water and stayed in for over an hour. When we'd run out of things to throw, we'd giggled in the dark.

'Ooh, look,' Imogen said, tilting her screen towards

me. She pointed to the list of nearby villages in the sidebar. 'Highfields Caldecote.' That's where she'd lived when she was small.

'We need to live in Cambridge,' I said firmly, not acknowledging the reminiscence. 'We want to walk to work, remember?'

'I don't mean to live, I just . . .'

I shook my head. 'Not yet. Cambridge is enough to start with, don't you think?'

She nodded, but she clicked the link. She turned her screen slightly away, so that I couldn't see what she was typing. I could guess, though. Maybe her old home had been up for sale in the recent past. Maybe there were photographs.

I began to type 'houses flats Cambridge' and auto-complete suggested the recent search 'how accurate are DNA tests?' I angled my screen away in the other direction.

I felt light. I'd just sent the hair samples next-day-air, and now that they were out of my bag I found my arms swinging and my steps bouncing as I left the post office.

My music was done for the day. One of the girls had missed *a cappella*, which threw off the harmonies a bit, but we'd been able to make it work. I crossed the street and ducked into the mouth of a large, high-end mall full of summer shoppers, tourists, teenagers. *Where did Im say that she was going to work?* Someplace on the high street, across from King's College. Not here, inside the clearly labelled *Grand Arcade*, with its high, arced skylights and shiny floor slabs and very expensive shops. Im prefers the historic storefronts. I joined the swell of anonymity. My skip turned into a shuffle in the crowd. Guilt over the mistrust inherent in what I'd just done slowed me to a near-halt.

Maybe I can get Im to go back to London, to get started on subletting our flat. I'll say I need more time here to prepare for the job. Then, within a week, I'll know for sure that I was wrong. I'll dispose of the results, pretend I never suspected. Everything will slot back into place. We'll marry in the chapel, if that's what she wants. I'll suggest this now, and say that I'm meeting someone for a working meal, don't wait up. I couldn't face sitting across a table from her tonight. I couldn't make light conversation, not with what I'd accused her of by posting those hairs.

I bought a croissant as an excuse to stop and sit, at a cramped little cafe table sprinkled with other people's crumbs. I pulled out my phone. I'd turned it off before rehearsal, and forgotten to turn it on again. A dissonant electronic jangle announced calls missed, voicemails left, texts received.

The Bursar at St Catharine's (or 'Catz' as I should start calling it if I want to fit in), who's a friend of an old teacher of mine, wanted to meet up for a coffee. One of the flats that Im and I had emailed about last night was free, and did we want to come round for a look? My mother called. No message, but I recognised the number on the screen. Then the phone lit up with that same number again, and almost jumped in my hand as it rang.

'Mum!' I said, too loudly, trying to hear myself over the nearby conversations bouncing around the vast mall interior.

'Maxwell, you didn't answer before.'

'Yes, I know, Mum. I was working.' I could barely hear her. I stuck a finger in my other ear.

'You asked me about your father.'

I wished that I hadn't phrased my messages to her that way. I'd only meant that I needed to know about that time of my life, the time when we were all together, and whether we may have ever been to Cambridge or even lived here. I curled my shoulders protectively around the conversation. 'Yes. I only meant . . .'

'Why?' she asked.

I wondered if I was missing something. 'Why what?'

'Why do you want to know about him?' Not *what* do you want to know, but *why*.

I tried to take it all back, to stop what was sure to follow. 'I'm sorry. I shouldn't have . . .'

'He left us, Maxwell. What else is there?'

I tilted my head back. I should have known that this topic is a train, not a car: it runs on a track.

She continued, unstoppable: 'He left us because I loved you. He wanted my attention all to himself, and for the house to be like just two adults lived there instead of two parents and a baby. He didn't like waking up in the middle of the night; he didn't like the dishes undone, or the smell of nappies. He didn't like *us*, Maxwell. So he left.'

I'd heard all of that before. 'I know, Mum, I—'

'Is it Imogen who asked you to do this? To invite him to the wedding? Because that's not fair, Maxwell. He didn't do any of the raising, so he doesn't get to be "father of the groom".'

'This isn't about the—'

'I'm not saying I won't come. Of course I'll come. But

61

you'll hurt me if you have him there as well. That's all I'm saying.'

'He's not invited to the wedding. This isn't about the wedding.'

She breathed into the phone, a pulsing, whistling sound. Then: 'What do you want him for, then?'

'I just . . . Did he ever work in Cambridge?'

'No.'

Then it was me breathing down the line, until I found my voice: 'Oh. All right. Did we visit friends here, maybe?'

'I avoided travelling when you were a baby, Maxwell. You didn't do well on car trips. Don't you remember?'

She couldn't mean, *Don't you remember from when you were a baby?* No one remembers being a baby. She must have meant, *Don't you remember that I've always told you that you hated car rides when you were a baby?* The distinction was suddenly sharp to me.

She'd been frantic since my engagement to Imogen. *Why is that?* Weeks ago I'd asked her for my birth certificate, for our giving notice of marriage. I'd always left paperwork up to her, even after university. Given her bureaucratic job, it had made sense. She'd stammered and stonewalled. I won't need my birth certificate if I have my passport, but I'd felt like ticking all the boxes. *I'm an adult; I should have my own papers.*

It occurred to me at that moment in the mall that I'd never even seen my birth certificate, never. *Is that normal?* I'd always assumed it was. She's my mother, after all. And what would I do with it? Frame it on the wall? It's not 'hiding' it to keep it in a safe deposit box, just prudent.

'Are you going to get married there?' she asked. The

words each had the same heavy inflection, *thud-thud-thud-thud-thud-thud-thud*.

'In Cambridge? Yes,' I said. 'In a college chapel, actually.'

More of that ghostly, whistly breath. 'Is she pregnant?'

'What? No!'

'Good.'

I shook my head in frustration. 'All right, well, thanks for calling me back. We'll let you know the—'

'Maxwell, please. Please.' She coughed, and sighed. 'I feel guilty that I didn't give you a father. I feel guilty that, in some ways, I let you fill a space in my life that should have had a partner in it, not a child. I've depended on you, and I've been made happy by you, probably too much. I'm going to miss you. You're taking a step away from me that's bigger than university, bigger than living away or even living abroad. I'm supposed to be happy for you, and instead I'm grieving for me, selfish old witch that I am. Please tell Imogen that I'm sorry, and that I'll try to do better. Should I send flowers? What's the name of your hotel?'

I said it, and spelt it, and murmured consoling, reassuring words, then goodbyes.

There was a new message on the phone.

'Max' – this one was from Imogen – 'I have good news. Please call me. I – I just have really, really good news.'

I froze. At the table behind me, a toddler spilt her mother's orange juice. *Good news.* Im never leaves voicemail. She texts. She wanted me to hear her voice. She wanted to say something out loud.

No, it was just my mother's question, and the toddler behind me, and the pushchairs rolling past . . . They were the reasons my brain had gone there. Not because that's what she was talking about. *Look, there's a pregnant woman window shopping, sipping bottled water.* I'd made a random association. 'Good news' can mean lots of things. That's *not* what she was talking about.

I called her back. She was quick to answer, after just one ring.

'Max? Where've you been? I tried calling . . .'

'I . . . What's your news?'

'My news is that my fiancé finally picked up his phone.'

'Im . . .'

'It's just really hard waiting to talk to you. Your orchestra thing finished over an hour ago.' I heard a guitar behind her voice. *A busker? Is she on the street nearby?* There was a guitarist by the mall entrance . . .

'I'm calling now,' I said, wondering what she heard around me. An industrial coffee maker. A cash till. This could be any coffee shop. I considered lying if she asked. 'What is it, for God's sake?'

This wasn't how it should be. If she were pregnant – she shouldn't be; we use protection – but if she were, it shouldn't be told over the phone, to end an argument. I tried to soften my tone. 'I'm sorry. I really want to hear it,' I said through my teeth.

'I've found him,' she said, and I heard it twice: through the phone, and behind me. I turned around. She was smiling at me, standing firm in the crowd, forcing shoppers to eddy around her. She waved.

I closed my phone. I wasn't sure what she was talking about. She was suddenly right in front of me. Then, perched on my lap. This was how it was supposed to be, except that she wasn't pregnant. She said she'd 'found' someone.

'Who?' I said, but it was obvious.

'Seb,' she said, and she kissed my forehead. It was as if my bones had dissolved. It was as if all the light in the room had diverted to just her face, then into a pinpoint.

Good news, I thought. The same good news that she'd brought me after that original DNA test, but which I hadn't, then, understood. She'd never said the words, after all, and I hadn't asked. I'd read her face, and assumed that her happiness came from a result that meant that the two of us could be together, as a couple. But, to Imogen, me being Seb would have been the best news. She loves Seb more than anything.

I stood, dumping Imogen off. She caught herself but bumped the small table over. I shook my head hard. I blinked and rubbed my face. She brushed her skirt, her pink-and-white-striped summer skirt, and flicked her hair out of her face. She was fine. There was no need for the dirty looks aimed at me. She'd admitted it. She'd as much as admitted it. *Does she really think I'll accept it?*

I pushed shoulder-first between two women and set their shopping bags swinging. There was just one heaving corridor with single-room shops on both sides; no place to divert. I strode forward, weaving around clumps of people huddled over maps and gaping at window displays. A saleswoman urged me to try a sample moisturiser from her cart; I lifted my hand to mean 'no' and accidentally knocked the jar. Again, the people closest stopped and stared.

'Sorry,' I said, and picked it up. It had spilt. I didn't have anything to clean it up with. It smelt like the sea, and I thought of Imogen, wet in her red swimsuit, finding me.

Imogen was among the starers. She'd caught up, part of the ring that had formed around the mess.

Her mouth was open, as if honestly amazed, as if she'd expected me to be happy with her revelation. *Does she really imagine that we can go forward like this, knowing?* She must have lived with it for so long that it seemed normal to her now. She must have seen the envelopes before I mailed them. She must have guessed that I knew. *I knew.*

The saleswoman had got a rag and was hunched at my feet, wiping the floor. The people who were staring a minute ago were wandering off. Imogen stood, face crumpled, arms wrapped around herself. She was crying, and the mall's bright lights bounced crazily off her zigzagging tears.

I stepped forward. It was her turn to run away. She did, and slipped on the shiny stone, falling onto her elbow. She cried out.

I pulled her up. *I can't leave her now, not like this, even if I must leave her eventually.* She slid easily into my arms, her forehead and fringe against my cheek and mouth. I'm bigger than her, even if years ago I was the smaller one. Even if years ago she'd mothered me, I'd become the steadier one. She needed me.

'I worried you might be jealous,' she said. 'But I didn't think . . .'

Jealous? 'What do you . . .'

'The timing could have been better, I admit, but good news is good news, isn't it?'

We were in the way. I pulled her aside, out of the foot traffic, into an alcove where there were lifts and parking payment machines.

'What news?' I demanded. Deciding to admit something isn't *news*.

'That's what I've been trying to explain. Seb contacted me, on one of those adoption boards I'd posted to years ago. He hadn't known he was adopted until recently. His parents – his adopted parents – never told him. They never even told him his real name. He was young enough that they could do that, as if it were best for him to forget we'd ever existed.' She spit the words. 'As if it were best for him to think that he had no siblings still looking for him, wishing for him every day.' Tears again. In the shadows of the alcove, they were dark stripes.

'You got an email? From Seb?' I spoke slowly, and enunciated carefully. None of this made sense.

'Yes!' Imogen said, and her open-mouth smile sucked in some of the tears. 'Yes! His name is Patrick Bell, but he's really Sebastian,' she explained, hands clutched under her chin. Behind us, someone bought a Coke from a machine. Coins tinkled and the bottle thudded. 'I said I would show him the house where we grew up. Highfields Caldecote isn't far. He doesn't remember it. We were so happy there, and he doesn't remember it at all . . .'

I squeezed my eyes shut, and shook my head, slowly, back and forth.

'Max?' she said.

I couldn't look straight at her. I opened my eyes but turned my head. 'I promised to meet the Bursar at Catz,' I said, as if the invitation had meant today.

She bobbed her head in a nod, and tugged on the hair over her shoulder. 'I *was* going to ask you to drive me tonight, for us to meet him there together, but . . . If you can't be happy for me then maybe we shouldn't get married.'

'I'd be happy for you if I thought it were true.'

She gasped. 'You think I'm lying?'

'No, of course not.' *Of course not. A lie wouldn't make any sense. Unless she thinks I suspect something and wants to throw me off.* I shook off that far-too-elaborate thought. 'I think he's a scam artist or troll picking on vulnerable people.' I grabbed onto that. That put the baddie 'out there' instead of inside our relationship.

'"Vulnerable"? What exactly makes me *vulnerable*?'

I declined to go down that road. 'Can I see the email?'

'To see if I'm really telling the truth? No, thanks!' Quick, in a second, Imogen was gone; she jumped into the lift just as the doors closed. She would end up on some parking level rather than deal with me for another minute. *Fine.* It spared us both a scene.

I got out, past the wafting oversweetness of an American cookie stall, and the victorious theme-tunes playing on a loop in a videogame shop. Outside the mall, facing straight at me, were the double doors of a church.

The doors tempted me. I don't know which is the more relevant question: Why did I stop being serious about religion? Or, why did I ever start? Both, probably, can be answered by the cliché that the youth pastor of our neighbourhood's 'Friday Night Club' had been a friendly, willing father figure. Then I'd moved away for university, and the link had been broken.

The chaplain at Jesus had offered to counsel me and Im. Could he counsel me alone? *Will he keep what I say from Im, or is that just Catholics and confession?*

On the next corner, with the sausage and crêpes vendors, there was another church. They were everywhere. I crossed the road and cut through the alley beside Waterstones. There was King Street, where I'd parked the car for our first visit to Jesus College just four days ago. Left, then cross. At the entrance to the college, a long stone walkway led up to a shortish tower, as if the walk were the tower's stretching shadow.

Through the archway of the college entrance, the bronze horse posed. I tried to feel that recognition that it had sparked in me before, but my recent memories had eclipsed any older ones, if indeed there were any. The world is full of equestrian statues. My head must be full of them, too.

I might be losing my mind. My suspicions seem so logical, but I don't think anyone else would believe me. If that's so, doesn't it mean I'm crazy?

I stepped into the Porters' Lodge. 'Excuse me, I met with the chaplain the other day. Any chance that he's here now?' I gave my name and sat in a generic metal chair, like waiting for a doctor's appointment.

When the chaplain came, he seemed to want to talk right there. 'Have you and your fiancée made a decision? Do you have any further questions?'

'I – Yes, do you think we could talk in your office? Or the chapel?'

He tilted his head to one side but didn't put his curiosity into words. I followed him past the horse and through the cloister. In the chapel, he sat in one of the dozens of wooden chairs that were lined up in rows as if for a concert.

First, I apologised. 'You're not my pastor. I haven't had one for years. But I think I may need one and you're the only one I know here.'

He nodded.

'I think I may be crazy.' My voice sounded too loud in the echoey space. 'I'm thinking things – suspecting things – that I don't think are true. Except, I *do* think they're true. But I know that I shouldn't think that.'

'I think it would help for you to be more specific.'

'Would you have to tell Imogen what I tell you, if we're going to get married here?'

'No, but *you* should tell her, especially if you're getting married, anywhere.'

I leant forward, elbows on knees. I told him, about Im's parents' death and the subsequent adoptions; about the Spanish beach and how I look like Seb and my left hand. I told him about Marco and Hercules, and that I'd never seen the results of the DNA test, only the happiness on Imogen's face.

'You think – you think she lied to you about the test results?'

'Not lied. She never said *anything*. It was implied. We slept together that night for the first time so—' I looked sideways at the chaplain to gauge his reaction. He didn't seem perturbed. 'But now I wonder. I have these memories of my own, at least I think they're my own. I don't remember her telling me all of them. And my mother, she's not happy about the wedding. I suppose that's common enough, but listen to this. Listen:

'My mother's been unhappy ever since we told her that we're engaged,' I continued. 'That's standard enough, for a certain kind of parent. But that same conversation is the one in which Im and I told her about Cambridge, and about Imogen having been adopted from near here. What if my mother's reaction is to that revelation, not the engagement? What if . . . What if she knows?' I pulled at my hair. 'I don't have any baby photos. Mum says that it's because my father destroyed them in one of their last fights before he left. I've never seen my birth certificate. I've never asked to, but is that normal? Has everyone else seen their birth certificates? I don't know.'

The chaplain tapped his lips with a fingertip. 'So it's not only Imogen who you think has lied. You suspect your mother as well.'

I wagged a finger. 'No, no, not necessarily. I'm not saying for sure that Imogen lied. Maybe the DNA test was wrong, mixed up with someone else. Maybe she has no idea.'

'But you think that if she did know, that she would still want to marry you? That's what you think?'

Hearing the summation from someone else made me laugh. 'I said it was crazy.'

I looked away from his face and instead at the painted ceiling high above us. I imagined my suspicions and elaborate explanations floating upwards, like heat does.

'It *is* crazy, isn't it?' I asked. It was like talking to my old youth group leader again. I needed the chaplain to agree with me, to approve of me.

He gripped my shoulder in a man-to-man way that made me straighten my spine. 'Have you been in any serious relationships before Imogen?'

'Of course I have.' I wish I didn't sound so defensive about it.

'Did they break up amicably, or did one of you leave the other?'

That seemed far afield of the actual point of the conversation, but: *All right, I'll bite.* 'My last relationship broke up when she got a fellowship at a university in Germany. We weren't serious enough about one another to justify uprooting my life, and we both knew it. I also dated at university, but not so officially that stopping constituted a "breakup".' That summary sounded meagre. 'I also kissed a girl on the playground when I was five. Exactly how far back do you need this to go?'

'So it would be fair to say that the level of relationship you've attained with Imogen is new for you?'

'I've never been engaged before, no.'

'Has she?'

I don't know, I realised. She'd never mentioned being engaged before, but I hadn't asked. 'It doesn't matter,' I said, shaking off my uncertainty. '*We're* engaged, that's what matters.'

'Of course,' he agreed. 'I'm only clarifying that what you have with Imogen is special to you, and unique in your life experience so far. And, she being older, perhaps not so unique for her.'

'She's not that much older.' I'm tired of people teasing about that. Five years is hardly anything between adults; it's not as though we're teenagers.

'Nevertheless,' the chaplain said, as if one word were a whole sentence. 'Nevertheless' rang in my ears, and I finished it myself: *Nevertheless, she's had five more years of her twenties, and she didn't spend them celibate.*

'I know she's had serious relationships before me, with

men better-looking than me, men who make more money than me . . .'

'It sounds like you feel you don't deserve her,' he said, and it was such an obvious fact that it seemed idiotic to have bothered putting it into words.

'Of course I don't deserve her!' I said, panting.

The chaplain tilted his head to one side, mimicking my angle. 'You believe that you, just you as you are, aren't special enough to attract her; but she's been looking for her brother her whole life. Does this resonate with you?'

Yes! 'Yes, that's exactly true. Exactly.'

'So, could it be that you don't suspect that you're her brother, not really, but that, in a way, you *wish* you were?'

I sputtered in protest, but he held up a hand and completed the thought:

'If, according to you, you aren't good enough for her just as yourself, then imagining that you're the one that she's been searching for all these years is, in a way, a satisfying fantasy. Does that ring true?'

I breathed, blinked, nodded.

'If that's so, then your insecurity is what you need to resolve, not a web of lies from your loved ones. Isn't that good news?'

The chaplain's smile stretched across his face. I nodded and stretched my mouth wide too. 'That is good news, yeah,' I said. It sounded so simple. Despite the chaplain's young age, I wondered if this was what it's like to have a dad.

He smiled back at me. 'It's good to admire your partner, and to feel like the lucky one of the pair. Ideally, each of you should feel like the lucky one. But it's something to consider, that you feel so out of step with her . . .'

'No, I . . . We're fine. I just . . . I needed to think about things differently. You've helped; you really helped. Thank you so much,' I said, pumping the man's hand. 'You make me want to come back to church,' I admitted.

'Of course you're welcome, here or elsewhere,' he assured me. But he stood as he said it, and I knew it was my cue.

I rose too, pushing my wooden chair askew behind me. 'Well, I really can't tell you what a relief it's been to talk it out. I couldn't tell anyone we both knew and . . .'

'I'm honoured that you felt you could trust me, and I'm glad I could help.' He gestured towards the door.

'We *will* have the wedding here,' I decided.

'If that's what you feel ready for. You can set the date with the Conferences and Events Office, and email to schedule further counselling,' he said, and his eyes flicked to his watch. *Of course; he must have duties and appointments.* My face heated.

'Sorry,' I mumbled.

'I'm glad you felt you could talk to me,' he said, with what appeared to be genuine warmth.

I rallied. It would have been unkind to leave him with anything but a smile.

I held that smile until I was through the college gate, then let my face twist in guilt. The chaplain had explained my suspicions of Imogen away, which should be a relief, but in their absence I could see that I had treated Imogen horribly for no good reason at all.

I phoned her but she didn't pick up. I didn't know the city well enough to walk to our hotel directly, so took a roundabout route, past the few landmarks I knew. It took half an hour. I jogged the last little way; I needed to see her. Upstairs, I thrust the key into the lock and turned. 'Imogen?' I called, ready to apologise. She wasn't there. She could have been at any of a dozen places.

Most likely, she was on her way to where she'd told me she'd go: meeting the man who claimed to be her brother.

I opened my laptop. The keywords *adoption, discussion, sebastian* and today's date got me what I was after.

The Reunions website looked like it was created in the early days of the Internet and never updated. I turned my volume off to avoid the sentimental and tinkly background music, and squinted at the light blue type on a dark blue background.

Eight years ago, Imogen had posted:

Baby brother Sebastian,
We were separated fifteen years ago and I've never forgotten you. Now that you're eighteen I hope you'll come looking for us. We want to see you again! I want to tell you about Mum and Dad, and how much they loved all of us. You have a big sister and two brothers waiting for you.

We all went into care in July 1989, in Cambridgeshire. You were almost three years old. Curly blond hair, brown eyes. I had long brown hair and was eight years old. Dad was a surgeon at Hinchingbrooke Hospital and Mum looked after us. She was beautiful and wore bead necklaces because you liked to play with them. Robert and Ben were eleven then.

Before we were adopted:
Parents: Isobel and Joseph Llewellyn
Children: Robert, Ben, Imogen and Sebastian Llewellyn
Home: Meadow View, Highfields Caldecote
I hope you'll contact us soon!

The only responses were contemporaneous, and merely in the way of encouragement, until today:

Are you still reading here? I think I'm who you're looking for. PM me pls.

I didn't know her login to see her private messages, but this was enough to tell me that this was for real. Whether this 'Patrick Bell' who contacted her is genuine or a scam, she believed that she'd found Sebastian. She'd come to me with genuine good news. I'd treated her terribly.

The theories that had swirled in my head seemed bizarre to me now. Imogen had said that she was going to ask me for a lift. I, foolishly, stupidly, idiotically, had speculated that she'd dangled that possibility in the same breath as taking it back only to bolster a lie. Had she said tonight? I think she'd said tonight. Without me to drive, what would she do? Get dropped off by a taxi, left alone to meet a stranger? Or, worse, ask Patrick Bell to pick her up?

I opened Google Maps. The house name and town were sufficient to find her old home. The map pinpointed it within a non-specific stretch of green, but the satellite photo showed the house and its colourful neighbours, separated by lawns or field and reached only by a meandering dirt road. It's isolated. I wiped my damp forehead with my sleeve.

I couldn't be privy to the private messages and emails that Patrick Bell and Imogen had shared off the message board, but the man's proofs must have been convincing. Still, Imogen had left enough information around the web that anyone could put together a fairly reasonable version of Seb's life, especially as filtered through a small child's faulty memory. *I'm proof enough of that, aren't I? I let her descriptions seep so deeply into me that they surfaced as my own.*

Part of me hesitated.

Could that really be true, though? We haven't known each other for so long that I should have forgotten her telling me her brother's nickname for the college's bronze horse. *How can I have remembered the name itself but not the larger discussion that had included it?*

I shook it off. That wasn't urgent. The meeting with Patrick Bell could be.

I Googled around some more. Lots of Patrick Bells online, though none I could pinpoint as him. I tried his username from Reunions. It appeared nowhere else.

There are a lot of reasons why someone would create a burner account instead of using an existing profile. Some of those reasons are benign; others aren't.

I wished that she'd arranged to meet him in a public place, or that I'd insisted on going with her. I punched the mattress. Patrick Bell could be anyone. Even if he was Seb, that doesn't mean that he should be trusted. *He has to earn that.*

I locked our hotel room and headed down to the car.

Whoever Patrick Bell is, I decided, *Imogen and I will meet him together.* Imogen's childhood home was only half an hour away.

It's still bright out when I get there, summer bright, giving the illusion of late afternoon well into evening. I find the turning onto the dirt road, but the vista isn't what the satellite photo promised me.

The half-dozen houses that I'd seen from above aren't here. I check my position; I look in all directions. The billboard for *affordable and comfortable village life coming soon* gives me a clue: the original houses have been recently razed.

I picture Imogen's face, crumpled with disappointment, but maybe it's better like this. Maybe the small but uncountable changes since her childhood would have hurt worse than this enforced fresh start.

I pull over and get out. There are only two buildings left, one red and one white. I'm unsure of my place and can't tell which of the original ones they are. I'd expected to identify them all in relation to one another, not in absolute on an otherwise empty expanse. I don't think one of those is Meadow View; wouldn't it have been to the right of where I drove in? But I can't be sure. A siren-sound pulls my attention, and I feel suddenly worried, suddenly guilty. *Police? Ambulance?* My body tenses.

Has something happened to Imogen? Has she come to this changed place, this near-deserted place, and been threatened? Was she able to call for help herself, or has some witness called for her? Are they near? The siren sounds like it's coming from over there, the end of the road, where the last houses stand. There must be a road beyond, on which emergency vehicles are travelling, on their way. But the noise isn't getting louder.

I'm still dithering when I hear two gunshots and a shrill whistle-like sound that might have been a scream.

I duck beside the car, assessing. The shots weren't close. They weren't aimed at me.

Was the high-pitched sound Imogen? Was it a voice at all?

That fucking siren is still going round and round, up-down-up-down, high-low, high-low . . . I can't think. I'm sweating.

There, again. No more shots, but for sure a voice. Not a scream, but words shouted, by a woman. The only word I make out is *No*.

I run for the buildings.

CHAPTER TWO

DORA KEENE

I hate sweating. The concert hall is designed for acoustics, not air flow. Walls are what make sound bounce around; windows would just let it escape. So the band room is four wide walls, windows only at the very top. You need a stick with a hook to open them. No one had bothered to do it.

It was a relief to put my flute away and get out. The corridor was choking on instrument cases and discarded sweatshirts. I picked my way through on my toes. Alexandra caught up; I shook her hand off my shoulder. Then we both stared.

The open space in the lobby of the concert hall stretched wide. In it, kids and teenagers between rehearsals crowded against the walls and pillars, hunched over books and DS games. They were the normal ones. The ones we stared at were the girls lying on their backs. There were at least six on the floor. *No, seven.* Three adults catered to them, propping backpacks as pillows and offering to phone parents. None of them were Fiona.

'That's nothing,' Alexandra said. 'Two years ago, a dozen girls fainted.'

No, seventeen. That summer session, seventeen girls had fainted. I had been one of them.

It had been hard to explain to Mum and Dad when it happened that it wasn't the kind of faint you call a doctor for. I didn't lose consciousness. It was just a light-headed floaty feeling, from the unusual heat, from standing too long, from breathing too deeply, from seeing other girls around me go down and . . . Here in the present, I shook myself. That was two summers ago.

We walked a loopy path around the bodies. The girls on the floor blinked, lolled, swore they'd try harder and that their parents didn't need to be called.

'I'm looking for Fiona,' I told Alexandra. We needed her for the tight harmonies in our next group.

'She probably has one of her *headaches*,' Alexandra said, emphasising the word sarcastically. 'Let's get some water and go to the choir room.'

'Why do you say it like that? How do you know how her head feels?' Fiona got bad headaches with her period and was always begging paracetamol. I brought her a whole pack the day before. Fiona's mother acted like Fiona made up her headaches. She didn't believe in free time, either, so if it weren't for music week I wouldn't have seen Fiona until school starts. I checked the toilets; Alexandra followed. Girls at the mirrors, girls slamming stalls closed behind them. No Fiona in there.

'What if she's really ill?' I worried.

Mr Gant motioned me and Alexandra into the practice room. Some of the other girls called him Maxwell, but I didn't feel right about that. He was a teacher, after all. He was our singing tutor for the week.

He lifted his head and smiled. He's young. He looks more like someone's older brother, an age it wouldn't be weird to have a crush on, would it? I couldn't remember what I was going to say. He was patient, holding up a hand to make Alexandra stop and wait. He wanted to hear me.

I remembered. 'Mr Gant, Fiona isn't here.'

'I'm sure you can manage the harmonies without her,' he assured me.

I wasn't sure of that at all. *A cappella* is a lot harder than accompanied singing, and we were a small group. The seven of us sorted ourselves into two rows.

'She's probably not feeling well, Mr Gant. I had to give her some paracetamol this morning,' Alexandra said, leaning over my shoulder from behind.

Today? I wondered. The pills yesterday should have been plenty. How many were in there? Eight, maybe? The packs have got smaller since the laws to make it more difficult to commit suicide, but that was still a lot. Surely Fiona hadn't gone through all of them.

'How many did you give her?' I whispered to Alexandra.

Fiona never takes them in front of me, I realised. She always takes them to the loo, she said to wash them down with tap water from the palm of her hand. I'd never seen her actually do it.

'You don't think . . .' I started to say, but Mr Gant lifted his hands and we all breathed in.

Our dog isn't home. There's no yapping. That's how I know that Dad isn't here either.

85

I dump my music bag and flute case, and just need to get my bicycle. *If Fiona's at her house, then I can stop worrying. Maybe she really did just have a headache and go home early.*

I wanted to phone Fiona from the concert hall, but, if her mother picked up, I couldn't ask if Fiona was there. What if her mother thought Fiona was still at the concert hall? What if Fiona had really gone off somewhere? Things would get worse than they are if her mum found out.

It's late enough now that if her mum answers the door, I can just say that Fiona accidentally left her bracelet with me and that I'm bringing it back. It won't be as if I'm checking where Fiona is. I don't have to say anything about when Fiona left. She'll be there, I'm sure. She has to be. *And if she's not, I'll call Dad.* I correct myself: *I'll call Chloe.*

The bracelet had been a surprise. I'd found it when I reached for my bus pass. My fingertips slid against something hard, sharp-cornered, and unexpected.

It was a little red cardboard box with an enamelled bracelet on cotton inside. It was made of ceramic with vines and flowers painted on, and even a few daubs of gold underlining the prettiest petals. I recognised it. It used to belong to Fiona's grandmother, Rowena. Fiona's not allowed to wear jewellery, but we'd found Rowena's old things when we were little and used to play with them. Fiona sometimes hides a bracelet under a sleeve, or tucks earrings in a pocket to put on at school after her mother's left.

Finding that little gift had made me more worried than I already was about the pill collecting, but the farther I got from West Road, the stranger my worry seemed. It must have been seeing all the fainted girls that made me think that way. Fiona has a perfectly good reason for collecting pills. She's been having these headaches for a long time.

Well, she *said* she has.

I pedal faster, ignoring the sweating under my helmet. And remind myself: Fiona isn't the sort of person to do that. She's a perfectionist. She's more the type for an eating disorder, right? The worst that can happen is that I'll catch her being sick after a meal, right? *Right?*

It'll be my fault. Mrs Davies had been strict, but not crazy. Then I convinced Fiona to skip school for that day. Just one day! There hadn't been anything important going to happen, nothing that we couldn't make up, nothing that would affect our exams. We'd never risk our exams. My parents understood that. They told me off but let it go. Fiona's mum went crazy over it. The rules changed. Maybe Fiona couldn't take it.

I normally go round the long way to get to the cycle path, but Fiona is more important. I turn the direct way, into Codling Walk.

The dog barks at me. He's tied up outside the house with the dried-flower wreath on the door, on the corner. I lean down over my handlebars and get past fast. I don't want him to see me. Not the dog, Dad. Not that he'll be looking out the window. *He'll be looking at something else, right? That's why he's in there, right?* Then it's out of the mazey village streets and onto the cycle path.

At first, I'd liked having Dad home. Mum had sat me down like I was little to explain that *'Dad needs to take some time off work and he'll be able to spend more time with you.'* Mum said it like there would be football on TV and cooked dinners and maybe teaching me to drive. So I thought, *All right. Good, that's fine.* Mum's job has picked up after years of part-time. It's supposed to be good to have Dad there instead, like he and Mum are having a trade.

Sure he does laundry and the other sorts of things whoever is home has to do. But after that he takes the dog and just goes.

Once a call came for him at home that seemed important. I'd thought, *How far away can he be with the dog?* He had to be in the village. So I got on my bike, like now. The dog barked at me, like now. The girl who used to live in that house, the one with the wreath on the door? She used to babysit me. She's off at university now, in Edinburgh. Her mum lives alone. I've seen her jogging around the village. She wears a ponytail for that. Her hair bounces. Mum always sighs and says that she should do that. Mum doesn't know. I haven't told her where Dad goes with the dog.

The cycle path turns to parallel Broad Street, and then Cambourne Road. Two roundabouts, over the A428, and then it dumps me on St Neot's Road to ride with traffic.

Lower Cambourne is relatively new. It has wide roads and lots of parking and cycleways designed in. Fiona lives in Highfields Caldecote. The main village, Caldecote, is old enough to be in the Domesday Book, but the area around it is being built up. That's what happens when you have fields. The area's going to become an 'affordable planned community'.

Fiona's family is holding out. They've been offered buckets of money, which Fiona's mum wants to take, but Grandma Ro owns the property. I had to listen to them argue about it that last time I was over there. That was months ago. Fiona's mum doesn't like me to come round any more, not since that day we skipped school.

I turn off the main road. The fields are different now. Instead of green and yellow, they're churned up and only brown. A noisy construction vehicle prowls. The fluorescent vest on its driver flashes sunlight in my eyes.

The absence of the neighbouring houses is shocking. They'd each been painted a contrasting bright colour, every colour except green, because grass is green, and not blue either, because sky is blue. There had been a purple one and a pink one, a yellow one and a peach one, all gone now. Only Fiona's family's white one, with the red-painted barn, are left.

A billboard shows the houses to come: tall, terraced, matchy-matchy pastel coloured. The old houses had been distinct from one another. Not just separate, but different. Without the yellow house and the pink house, the sign pointing to Fiona's 'White House' makes little sense.

The edge of Fiona's family's property is obvious. Their grass is fenced in, the prepared ground of new development coming right up to it. The main house, the white one, is down a long drive. The barn, which Fiona's Grandma Ro calls the 'Red House', is closer to the property line. Blackberries are ripening along one of its long walls.

I prop my bike against the front of the White House and dump my helmet into the panniers. I push the doorbell. It buzzes inside but there are no answering footsteps. I push it again. Even if Fiona isn't home her mother should be. Maybe something really is wrong. Maybe she and her mum are both at the hospital. Maybe there's been an emergency and her mum picked her up from the concert hall. I realise what could cause that.

I clatter down the front steps and run to the Red House. Grandma Ro has lived there at least as long as I've known Fiona. Things have got pretty bad for her. She tried to climb the loft ladder and sprained her ankle falling off; Fiona's mum took the ladder down. Ro was cleaning and mixed ammonia and bleach. Again, Fiona's mum caught her and took all the cleaning things away. Maybe she tried to climb something else. Maybe something fell on her.

The barn had been converted years ago: floored, insulated, windowed. But I can't see through the dirty glass, not past the piles of magazines up against the window on the inside. I knock on the barn's original sliding door, the kind you use to let animals in and out. My fist doesn't make a loud enough noise against the construction buzz nearby. I have to drag it open, pulling sideways.

I stand just inside the doorway. 'Grandma Ro?' I call cautiously. I don't want to shock Rowena or make her afraid. 'It's me, Fiona's friend.' I don't say my name. The last time I was allowed over, Ro didn't recognise me. Fiona had said simply, 'Ro, it's Dora. You know Dora.'

But Ro had gibbered and panicked. 'Dora?' she'd repeated, in a slurred way that made it sound foreign. She'd pushed us out of the barn. 'Get out!' she'd said. 'You have to get out of the house!' Ro's hands had grabbed at me. It wasn't a way she had ever been before. I'd been scared and Fiona got embarrassed and cried. I told her that it was all right. My grandparents aren't like that yet but I know it could happen.

'Sometimes she thinks I'm Mum when she was my age,' Fiona had confided. 'When Ro's like that she only remembers things from a long time ago. It's better in the mornings.' The wailing inside the Red House had continued. Fiona's mother had heard it too; the construction vehicles weren't at work yet then, even though the houses around them were all sold already. Fiona's mum had pushed past us and slid the door back and gone in to calm Rowena down. Ro was just repeating the name and sobbing. She'd pleaded, 'She's got to get away from the house!'

I shake the memory off.

'Grandma Ro? I mean, Rowena?' I try. If Ro's in her forgetful phase, she probably doesn't know that she's a grandmother.

I can barely enter. If the door had been meant to push in instead of slide, it would have been impossible to open. 'Fiona?' I add, slipping into the dimness and accumulated heat inside. The blocked window didn't let in much light and my eyes had to adjust. Fiona and I used to spend time in here when we were little. It had been different then.

Well, I had been different then. Maybe I just imagine that the once seemingly vast space is now smaller. But entering confirms my first impression: the space has in fact tightened, choking on its own contents.

The Red House had been full of Ro's things then too, but not as bad as this. Fiona and I had pawed through boxes and suitcases, and played on a braided rug while Ro made us hot milk on a camp stove, or napped. Even though it was all one ginormous room, areas had been delineated. Now the borders between spaces have grown into teetering walls made of boxes. The remnants of the jury-rigged systems of conversion from a mere barn remain, but now seem sad instead of clever: a hose extension leading to a squat bathtub, a dodgy electrical connection to the house.

We had always used the toilet in the White House, and I'm not sure what Ro did. I'd never asked.

I had originally assumed that Rowena had moved into the barn later in life, the way that lots of grandparents do, after she'd retired from working at the hospital. But as Fiona and I had explored the barn's contents, it had become clear that Rowena had been there for a long time, even before Fiona was born.

I don't know what's in all the boxes, but they're stacked up past my height. Some of them are plastic and have tops and their towers are straight. Others are stacks of open-top cardboard, and they sink into one another and list. I follow the one possible path deeper in. The little kitchen is there only in part: the sink, yes, but the stove is gone, the kettle too. Maybe a fire hazard? Or just too dangerous for Ro to operate alone? I remember Fiona saying that the small refrigerator had stopped working last year, and that she'd had to bring Ro every meal, not just the cooked ones, after that.

The stuff back here is out in the open, not boxed. Toilet paper rolls, jarred instant coffee, sealed bags of cereal, raisins, nuts. It's stocked as if for a siege. Overhead, the loft is crammed with old-looking equipment, precarious and too heavy. I wonder why any of it has been kept. Maybe Ro has refused to let it go, and Fiona's mum at least got it out of the way. I wipe sweat off my face.

The heavy velvet curtain that separates the bed area is pulled to. There are no windows back there, so it must be all dark inside. Or, maybe there's a lamp. I try to remember how Fiona and I had lit the place when we were younger, but I don't know if we ever did. We only played in here in the daytime, with the door wide open, on the rug in its mouth.

'Rowena? It's me,' I say, letting Ro think that I'm whoever Ro wants me to be. If she doesn't always remember Fiona, she certainly won't know who I am. The dusty air dries my throat. I reach for the curtain.

A squeal and a thud behind me. I hold still. A muted clank. I drop the heavy curtain.

I rewind the path quickly, too quickly, bumping and scraping. A box stack wobbles and I shove it back, which slides its bottom out from under. The contents get under my feet. I scrabble in place, kicking magazines up behind me, and something else. Pill wrappings, little popped packets. There are lots of them, peeking out from under the jumble, spilt out of a tin box I recognise.

I listen. No more construction engine in the field. It's stopped. *Builders are usually big men, aren't they?* Fiona had told me that Rowena was afraid of one of the men, that he had a shotgun. I shiver despite the heat. *What had I heard?*

I get my feet off the spilt pages and push out a held breath. *Calm down.* I carefully make my way down the rest of the thin, winding aisle back to the door. It's closed.

Had I closed it? No, I'd wanted the light.

I grab the iron handle and tug sideways. It resists. I brace my feet and bend my knees. I pull so hard that my feet slide forward, but the door doesn't budge. I have to catch myself from falling on my back. There's a heavy clacking of metal against metal on the other side. I shake the door hard. Padlocked.

I pound with the flat of my hand. 'Mrs Davies?' I call

through the cracks between boards. I tiptoe to get my eye up to a knothole. *No one.* My bike is still there, up against the White House. My bag, everything, is in the panniers. *My phone.*

'Fiona?' I try. 'I'm in here!' I call, as if it were an accident. *It must be an accident, right? Maybe they lock Rowena in, for her own safety?*

I turn. 'Rowena?' I call, back towards the curtain. Ro could be asleep. Ro could be hiding. I retrace my steps.

Maybe it was Grandma Ro who locked me in. Maybe there's another path to the door from her bed, and my coming close drove her to escape. Fiona and her mum will come home and try to check on her and find the barn locked and find me. That's what will happen.

The curtain. Fiona and I used to use the bed alcove as a theatre. The heavy fabric had been difficult for us to sweep aside in the kind of grand gesture we'd been after, and we ended up wrestling it much of the time. It should feel lighter now that I'm older, but it still resists. It sticks at the top. The rings aren't sliding on the rod.

'No,' I say out loud. I'm not talking to the curtain; I'm telling off my stupid imagination. I pull hard.

Rowena had made the curtain when she moved into the barn fifty years ago. No, not the barn, she'd corrected herself as she sewed. The Red House.

The sewing machine had plunged the needle, dragging the thick thread through the heavy material. She used this same needle to make coats and upholstery fabric. She used the same machine but a finer needle to make clothes. This is what she'd originally cleared the barn for, for her sewing. Pumping the foot pedal, the answering whirr of the machine would calm her.

Her mother-in-law, Petra, always refused to enter the 'dirty barn'. That had been most calming of all.

At first, Rowena had retreated here only when each day's housekeeping had been completed. Petra ruled the White House, but did none of the work of it. She demanded petty errands anytime Rowena sat down.

'Where are you going?' Petra always wanted to know, whenever Ro readied to leave the house.

'I'm working,' was how Rowena answered. Work was always to be admired. Petra couldn't fault that.

Ro used those early afternoon hours to scrub the barn clean and fix up old wooden furniture that neighbours were getting rid of. They were redecorating in a modernist style and wanted their old, dark, thick-legged and claw-footed furniture out. Rowena stroked the wood with polish and gloated over her good luck. She was sure that they would come to regret their new, fashionable orange vinyl and translucent plastic. Ro worked in the barn until she had to make a hot meal for her husband, Alun, and a separate meal for Petra, who preferred broth and sandwiches to slabs of meat.

Rowena first slept in the barn one night after a fight. Petra had accused her of poisoning the food. The old witch overturned her tray and called for her son. The sandwiches fell open, exposing damp lettuce and ragged cheese that had been cut from a block with a dull knife. Coffee stained the unvarnished wood floor. The women had both shouted at one another, then both at Alun, demanding that he arbitrate.

'Please,' he'd begged Ro, *having pulled her into another room. 'Just apologise. Then she'll stop.'*

'I won't apologise! You know it's not true and I won't say that it is!'

Rowena had just reupholstered an old chaise in the barn, so she slept on it that night, to demonstrate clearly to him where her line was. She woke the next day, peacefully, without his snoring, to streaks of morning light in lashes across the floor.

She returned to the White House only to carry her clothes across the garden, her well-mended full skirts and sweater sets, and hung them from a bar. She pillaged a mattress from a spare room in the White House and hauled it atop a platform under the loft in the newly-christened Red House. She moved out, and moved in.

She still took care of the White House, appearing cheerfully and early each morning for her duties, and again in the evening for dinner. When Alun wanted sex, he had to detain her after she washed up the dishes, Petra glaring at them as they went up the stairs. Ro never said no. She always left the room right afterwards, washed in the bath and then crossed the garden back to the Red House, where he was not allowed.

As she spent more and more time in her domain, she began to delineate areas within the open space. Another neighbour was refurnishing after a fire and gave up her velvet curtains that smelt of smoke. Rowena bagged them with charcoal, then hung them in the sunlight and beat them. She sewed them together to make a single grand drape. She fixed a rod under the loft to hold it. She made an elaborate tieback for when she wanted to gather it to one side in a sweeping curve.

Petra died of heart disease, and Alun assumed that Rowena would return to the White House, to take her place as its mistress. But she didn't come. She began training for work in the afternoons. She continued to clean in the mornings and cook at night and not say no, but she slept in the Red House, and wouldn't allow him in.

Alun was unhappy. After dinner one evening, while she washed the dishes, he walked across the garden. The kitchen is at the back of the White House and Rowena didn't see him go. He slid open the door to the Red House.

He picked up a teacup and threw it. It chipped, but didn't break. He threw it again so that it shattered.

He lifted a chair and beat it on the table until a leg snapped off and the back detached on one side. He overturned the table and tried to break a leg off that as well but it was too strong, and only lost a carved cherub from a corner.

Her pillows were flung about and stomped on by his muddy boots. He climbed onto the cream-coloured chaise to scrape footprints along its length. Lastly, he pulled on the curtain, stretching and tearing it, practically hanging from it to get the rod to detach at one end from the underside of the loft. The rings slid off the downed end and he dragged the velvet wide over the floor.

Rowena stood in the open doorway, hand over mouth. She ran at him, but he grabbed her wrists and twisted her down to the ground onto the spread curtain. He raped her there and left her in the mess.

Ro moved back into the White House. Thirty-five weeks later, she gave birth to a premature daughter. Once the girl was weaned and sleeping through the night, Ro righted

everything in the Red House and cleaned and rehung the
curtain. She added one new thing.

That's why the Red House door has a hasp on both sides
for a lock.

The curtain gives in. I shove it aside.

The bed is heaped with pillows. Rowena's face is nestled between two stiff ruffles, and the quilt edge is pulled up to her chin.

'Grandma Ro?' I say. I want to jostle Ro's shoulder, but her whole body is under layers of thick blankets.

But it's summer.

'Rowena!' I snap, hoping my voice will bring Ro to.

Rowena doesn't move. Not at all, not the blankets on her chest, nor the ruffle by her mouth. A dangling cord hits my face. First I bat it away, but it's not a spider's web. I then fumble for it, in hope of turning on a light.

Outside, a sharp, echoing bang pierces the construction rumble. *Gunshot.*

MAXWELL GANT

That fucking siren. I can't think. I'm sweating.

There, again. No more shots, but for sure a voice, a woman's: 'No!'

I run for the buildings. In the summer light I'm visible from all angles on the exposed path. There's no breeze, just my motion churning through the still air. A stitch seizes up my side; I'm out of practise and out of breath. The path curves and brings me up to the front of the buildings: a white house and, to its side, a red barn. The door of the barn is open. The siren sound is coming from in there, just that horrible sound, over and over until—

A smash and a clatter, a grunt and a crack, rattle the barn. I rush the doorway, tripping over a shotgun on the ground. I catch myself and stagger-hop into a maze. Box towers balance precariously on both sides of me, and the strip of space between them pulls me around the corner in the only direction it's possible to move. It's like walking into sudden twilight. I squint, to try to see her. 'Imogen?' I call over the siren. I can't find any button or lever to stop it.

Around the next turning, the box-walls lower and spread out into what appears to be a sort of pantry area. Opposite, a curtain hangs from a loft. In front of that curtain, a man's legs stretch out from under . . . something. I lean forward. It's a small refrigerator, tilted off the man's back. I look up.

I squint. *Legs, metal legs,* is all my brain processes. I twist before the thing hits, giving it the back of my head instead of my face. It pushes me hard down, straddles me, then rolls off me to one side. It's some kind of a gym apparatus. I rub my shoulder. The stretch of reaching across my chest triggers pain in my back that makes me gasp.

A scraping sound above alerts me. I spring back. A box is advancing towards the loft edge, slowly, slowly. Whatever's inside the box must be heavy for it to resist so hard.

In an instant, I monkey up the stacked crates that make something like a stairway up. I push the box back, against the force squealing behind it. I'm groaning with the effort, and the siren sings round and round, louder here, louder than it was at the door, and the box scrapes along the wooden loft floor. I keep pushing, even when the box stops, until the squeals turn into words: 'Stop! Stop!' Behind the box, a flash of nut-brown hair.

'Imogen!' I shoulder the box aside, and she pops out from behind the old equipment and appliances, blinking, crying, dirty. I pull her out by the arm, by the shirt, though I don't mean to, and it rips. It's only a small tear, on her sleeve, that makes a triangle up her arm as if it were unzipping. In the dim light her skin is barely different from the dull-coloured shirt. The lack of contrast makes the rip seem less violent. 'Imogen?' I say, squinting into the dark. Something isn't right.

The woman, the not-quite-Imogen, springs to push me, and I topple back towards the edge. I roar and return the push, pinning her down by her shoulders, on top of her. Her ribcage pulsates and twists under my thighs. I hover my weight so as not to crush her, but I don't let her go.

'Mr Gant?' she says, suddenly still. Everything is still, except the noise.

The siren hurts, it physically hurts. I can't think. I must be hearing things.

'Mr Gant, get off me! Please,' she begs. A girl, not a woman. A young voice, an alto. Dora, from the concert hall. 'Please.'

The siren expires. Its absence fills up the barn, fills it like water. I feel like I'm floating in it, floating in nothingness. I hear my own heartbeat; I imagine hers. I hear panting below.

Three beeps; a phone. 'I'm calling the police,' a male voice announces.

I get off of her. Dora sits up and clutches her torn sleeve. It's only a sleeve. I haven't done anything wrong. I've only defended myself.

I lean over the edge and see the new man more clearly. There are two of them, in green. Paramedics.

'There's a man on the ground,' I tell them. 'He needs help.'

The men approach but stop short of the loft. The one with the phone shines a torch on me. I cover my eyes. 'Let her come down,' the man says. Dora scampers down the makeshift ladder of boxes shored up by a large wardrobe.

She barely rattles it. She's young, and light. And fast. *She's scared of me*, I think, wincing. Once her feet hit the floor, one of the paramedics uses a broom handle to prod the top of the stack over so that I can't follow. It falls into the next tower, which wobbles but, thankfully, holds. *Idiot.* What if it had all dominoed to block the way out?

The torch remains trained on me. That man watches me while his partner attends to the man under the mini-fridge. 'Don't move,' torch-man warns me, and the fridge is rolled off the man below with a crash that rattles the barn. I can hardly see anything, just the brightness, but I hear Dora.

'He had a gun,' she says. 'He locked me in. I hid up there. And when he got too close, I pushed it.' Pronouns are fragile things. *It*, the fridge. *He*, the man down there . . . or me.

'Not me,' I say from my perch. My hands are up, though they haven't asked for that, because I watch too much American television. 'Him,' I say. 'Him down there.'

'Shut up!' says the man with the torch. Its beam wavers. He's nervous. *Thank God this isn't . . . Florida, right? Where, on TV at least, even the CSIs carry guns.*

'Are you hurt? What did he do to you?' the calm, kneeling paramedic asks, apparently, Dora. *Why isn't he performing CPR?*

'What's wrong with him?' Dora asks. Panic, she's panicking.

'You just tell me what happened to you. Did he hurt you?'

Again with the *he*. 'I did not hurt her,' I say.

'Shut up!' Again, the man with the torch. And, immediately following, a siren, a real siren, one that you can tell is moving, approaching. Police. *Thank God.* Anything to defuse the situation. With police added to the paramedics, surely I won't seem a threat any more, not one against many. They'll let me come down and explain myself.

Dora says, 'He had a gun. The first man, *him*.' She must be pointing at the man on the ground. She must have finally twigged my awkward position. '*He* tried to help me,' she adds, kindly, presumably pointing up. I had entered to help her, but in defending myself her sleeve had got torn. I'd pushed her. I'd pushed her to save myself from pitching backwards, but I did push her . . .

The man with the torch asks, 'Who is he? You know him?'

'He's my teacher,' she answers simply.

I close my eyes. *Oh, shit. Oh, shit, shit, shit.* She's what, fifteen years old? In the evening, in an isolated barn, with her teacher.

'I did not know that she was here,' I say. 'I heard screams. I came to help.' It sounds ridiculous, even to me. There's nothing here, nothing but one barn and a house, and it's not a through-road. I had no way to know that Dora lives out here. But, looking around, what else would I be here for? There are no other houses.

I'm not the only one thinking along those lines. 'You live here?' the paramedic asks her. The new siren seems to fade briefly, but that would be from the wide curve necessary to access this road. They're coming.

'No,' Dora says, and my hopes rise. 'No, my friend Fiona does.' My stomach clenches. The police have rounded the bend.

'Bloody hell!' exclaims the man without the torch.

Dora sobs. 'That's Ro,' she says. 'Grandma Ro. She died.'

Phone sounds again. He requests more police. The sirens are deafening, and I can see the lights now, spinning and flickering. I feel woozy.

'You pulled on this?' shouts the man. 'You called for help?'

Dora says, 'I thought it was a light!' She has to shout too. She's still crying. 'Then it made that noise.' Some kind of emergency pull-cord, for . . . an apparently dead old woman. I lower my arms to steady myself.

'Don't move!' says torch-paramedic, in a tone that reveals that he watches American television too.

Two officers jog in and flank him. 'Please let me come down,' I ask, meekly.

They allow it and I lower myself over the edge to hang from my hands. I could drop, but the other man is right below, still spread out. He can't be alive. They would have removed him on a stretcher. He would be on his way to hospital by now.

The officers catch me by the middle and plonk me, standing, into a corner. Not a corner made by walls, but of *stuff*. At least the torch is off me.

The man on the floor is still. When I came in, the mini-fridge had been on the man's back; now it's beside him, partly pinning one hand. His head is just under a low table. He likely hit its edge as he fell. It's too dark to see blood from here, or to see the rise and fall of shallow breath, but the lack of action from the paramedics is all too apparent.

I don't resist the handcuffs. *If that's what they need to keep calm, so be it.*

'He didn't do anything!' Dora wails. 'It was me! I did it,' she says. 'I killed him.' She repeats it, seemingly mesmerised by the realisation: 'I killed him.'

They repeat for her the caution that they have just recited to me.

'He was coming for me,' she says. 'He was angry that I tripped the alarm. He had a gun. Mr Gant tried to help.'

I would have given anything for a pronoun at that moment. 'Mr Gant' screams teacher more loudly than a whiteboard and a desk. Police eyes hit me with new disgust.

'Call my father!' Dora commands. 'Morris Keene. Call him. Call Chloe.' She's sobbing again.

'Who?' asks one of the police, the one who'd cuffed me. *God, they look like teenagers.* More sirens round the bend.

Dora pulls herself together, announcing herself imperiously. 'My name is Dora Keene. Call Major Investigations. Detective Inspector Chloe Frohmann of Major Investigations. She'll help me.'

If you're the type to become a policeman, chances are that you don't appreciate being told what to do, at least not by someone you've just cautioned. To my surprise, the man makes a show of the call, and, after some transfers, says 'Detective Inspector Frohmann, I think you should get out here. We have two bodies, and a teenager who feels in a position to order you from off the menu. Dora Keene.'

The conversation doesn't continue beyond the giving of the address, so apparently those were magic words.

More flashing lights. Dora and I are escorted out. The door hangs, as if off-track, but it's more than that: the whole latching apparatus is hanging. A broken chain dangles, its still-closed padlock hanging on like a charm.

If he's the one who locked her in, why did he have to shoot the lock to get in himself? I wonder.

What if the dead man isn't the one who imprisoned Dora? I eye the broken chain.

I think he was using the gun to get her out.

MORRIS KEENE

I see her, Dora, on the steps of Fiona's white house. She's not in the ambulance, not in one of the police cars, though an officer stands nearby. Her knees are drawn up, and she's hugging them. I run right over. I want to scoop her up but stop short. She looks different: older, haunted, matured by trauma. Then she sucks snot back up her nose and wipes her eyes, ageing backwards towards being my baby again.

I crouch next to her on the step. 'Are you hurt?' I ask.

She shakes her head.

'Good, good,' I say, trying to keep it together.

Jesse licks Dora's fingers. Dora pushes at her, so I shoo the dog off.

Chloe had told me that Dora had been in the barn, with one of her music tutors, called Maxwell Gant. Also that someone might be dead. *Not Dora.* That's the only important thing. Dora's not dead.

Chloe had given us a few minutes while she checked in

with the officers on scene. Now it's time. She ambles over, huge now, her belly sticking out ahead of her. She heaves herself down on Dora's other side. Her posture is friendly, but I know this is official. I keep my mouth shut.

'Are you hurt?' Chloe asks.

Dora shakes her head.

'Did he touch you?'

Who? I want to scream, but I squeeze my lips together.

'No. I didn't let him,' Dora says. She tells how a man locked her in, and how she accidentally tripped an alarm. She tells how he came to get her and she hid, how she climbed into a loft and tipped an old fridge off the edge.

'And . . . ?' Chloe prompts.

'It hit him.'

Chloe nods. She looks over towards the barn door, where a stretcher is being brought out. It's hard to see past the men tending it, but it appears that much of the body is covered. Maybe all of it. I raise my eyebrows, but Chloe ignores the obvious question on my face.

'Did you know him?' she asks Dora, forcing Dora's eyes away from the procession to the ambulance.

Dora shakes her head. 'He had a fluorescent yellow vest on. He's the man who was driving the bulldozer.' She points. The vehicle is alone in the dirt. The neighbouring houses are . . . gone, just gone.

'Just one man? Working by himself?' Chloe clarifies.

'I think so. It was just him.'

'What about your teacher? He was there, too,' Chloe corrects.

I tense. Chloe shoots a glance at me that says, clearly, to not say anything, not move, not react.

'He's the *a cappella* tutor from orchestra week,' Dora says. 'He tried to help me.'

I try to picture the tutors and conductors from past summers, but *a cappella* is new this year. We've been letting Dora take the bus so we haven't been around the concert hall. It's a familiar place, the same as it's been since I was a kid, playing the same summer music week decades ago. It's a safe place. It's always felt like a safe place.

'Good. That's helpful to know,' Chloe says to Dora. 'Did you come here together?'

I hold in my breath.

Dora says no.

Chloe keeps at it. 'Did he follow you here? Does he treat you differently from the other girls?'

'No!' Dora says to everything. 'Mr Gant helped me. You shouldn't act like he did something wrong.'

'This is your friend's house. Was he here with her?' Fiona goes to music week too. She plays harp. Dora plays flute. I don't know if Fiona sings.

'I – I don't know.'

'Do you know if they ever saw each other outside of school?'

'It isn't school. It's music.'

'That's fine. Do you know if they ever saw each other outside of rehearsal?' Chloe has this calm voice, as if she's not upset, just interested. As if Dora doesn't know what she's after.

'Mr Gant is engaged,' Dora explains. 'He has a fiancée.'

'Really? How do you know that? Does he often talk about his personal life?'

'No!' Dora shouts, and Chloe and I both flinch. 'No,

he's a good teacher. He's a good person. He helped me. Why are you trying to make me say something that isn't true?' Dora's voice sounds like a howl. I hate letting Chloe do this to her.

'How did you get this rip?' Chloe says, pointing at her sleeve.

Dora shakes her head.

'Was it when you were climbing up to the loft?' Chloe suggests. I'm trying to picture it. I've never been in there. Dora's been playing here for years, and neither Gwen nor I have ever been in that barn.

Dora blinks fast and rubs her eyes. 'I didn't recognise Mr Gant at first. I thought he was someone helping the bad man. So I tried to hurt him and he stopped me from hurting him.'

'Stopped you how?' I interject.

Chloe's glare tells me plainly: *You're not police any more. You're not supposed to be talking.* I pinch my lips shut.

'I tried to push him off the loft and he pushed back. He—'

Dora's pause feels minutes long.

'He stopped me from pushing him and then we recognised each other. That's all,' she finishes.

'And that's how your shirt got ripped?' Chloe asks.

'That's how my *sleeve* got ripped,' Dora says.

Sleeve sounds less intimate than *shirt*. She's protecting him.

'What did he—' I begin, but Chloe intercepts me.

'You did a really good job,' Chloe tells her. That's how I talk to the dog. That's how Chloe's going to talk to her baby. Dora won't like that.

'He shouldn't have handcuffs on,' Dora says, indignant and bristling. 'He didn't hurt anyone.'

I follow her gaze. There's a man with cuffs on standing with a uniformed officer. He looks humiliated, upset, and angry. *And young. And attractive.* I look at Dora's face, looking at him.

'Please?' she says to Chloe.

'Stay here,' Chloe says. She pushes herself to standing. She talks to the officer with the man and the cuffs come off. Then that officer puts him in the back of a police car. Dora's still watching him. The man turns his head quickly when their eyes catch. The car isn't driven anywhere. They just keep him in it.

A text comes in on my phone. Gwen, at last. 'Your mother's on her way,' I tell Dora.

That does Dora in. She cries, the noisy, hunching-up-your-shoulders kind of crying. I lay my hand on her back. The side I'm sitting on, that's my bad hand. It just splays there on her.

'Why were you here?' I ask, when the heavy sobs turn into light panting.

She snuggles into me, squeezing her eyes tight. 'I was worried about Fiona. She left early.' Suddenly, she looks up. 'Fiona left before we had our practice with Mr Gant, so he couldn't have gone home with her! You have to tell that to Chloe. She left way before he did. We had practice without her.'

I nod and pat her arm. 'I will. I'll tell her.'

'I don't know where she is. Maybe she and her mum had an emergency? But they wouldn't leave Rowena, would they? She can't look after herself . . . Couldn't, I mean. She died, Dad. Fiona's grandmother died.'

Dora's shaking. I pull my arm up around her shoulder. My fingers can't curl at the end to complete the hug, but the bend at the wrist is enough to pull her towards my chest.

Behind us, the front door slaps open. Fiona's there, escorted by an officer. She looks dishevelled and disoriented, as if she's just woken up, though who could sleep through all of this? One earbud is still stuck in, as a kind of answer to that question, and the other one dangles. Dora jumps up and hugs her. 'I was worried about you!' she says. 'You weren't home. Were you? Where were you?' Fiona's just staring at her. They both gradually calm down, breathing in sync.

Fiona says that she left early on the bus because she felt sick and she's been sleeping. She says she had music on.

'Are your parents home?' I ask. Then I correct myself: 'Is your mother home?' Fiona doesn't live with her father.

'Mum's not home,' she says.

Dora tilts her head quizzically. I'm about to ask where Fiona's mum is when the dog starts barking. I shout, 'Jesse!' She doesn't stop, though. The yaps are sharp and persistent. I go after her. Dora follows us around the barn.

Jesse's there. She's got her nose in the blackberry bushes. She stops barking when I pick up her lead. She lies next to the bush and won't budge, even when I pull and say 'Up!' I pull on Jesse again. She won't come. I recognise her posture from a training years ago: she's found something. *Don't mince words; she's found a body.* That's what she'd been trained to do.

Chloe tells me to get Dora home, *now*. She phones for a larger forensic team and for lights. They're going to have to work into the night.

I force Jesse up and bundle her in my arms. I dump her in the back of Chloe's car. Dora follows, and flings herself into the back with Jesse, squeezing her while Jesse whines.

I wait in the front. A tap on the window startles me. I don't know the man, but his ginger hair fits Chloe's description of the 'new boy'. His hands gesture and signal incoherently, so I open the door.

'I've been told you take you home, sir.' He has Chloe's keys.

I slide over. He takes charge.

IMOGEN WRIGHT-LLEWELLYN

I try to recognise Cambridge but, unlike the college, the city centre stirs no memories. *A lot of it must be new,* I remind myself, and, honestly, it's so crowded who can see anything? The pavement is busy with shoppers and families and tourists; I slip between a shopping trolley and a pushchair, and duck out of the way of someone's photograph. *And, after all, I was only eight when I left.*

I cover my mouth and blink, hit with one of those sudden pangs that's become common since I've come back. 'Left' is such a benign word to describe what happened. I was eight when my parents died and my brothers and I were given to three different families.

I stop at the crosswalk, jostled by bored teenagers, waiting for the red man on the pedestrian light to turn green.

Maxwell's grateful to me for facing Cambridge. He's thanked me a thousand times. I am doing it for him, partly, but I need it for me, too. It's time.

I step out into the road.

Even if Maxwell didn't have the job offer, it's important that we do this before getting married. It's important for me that I do this. That Patrick Bell's contacted me this week, of all weeks, well, it could be a coincidence, or it could be that returning here has triggered something, something in the universe that—

A purr of acceleration then a squeak of tyres against the road. The subsequent lack of impact feels shocking. I'm pinned by surprise. Counting by heartbeats it's only a few seconds, but the time stretches and thins, like the skin of an expanding balloon. Then, *pop*, the driver hoots the horn at me, two sharp blasts, and I dash the rest of the way across the road.

Breathe, Imogen. I turn around. From the side I can see that it's not the same car, obviously not. *Just because it's the same colour doesn't make it the same thing*, I chide myself. I know that the paranoia springs from guilt. I should be able to tell Maxwell anything. *I can*, I remind myself. I choose not to, for his sake. That's a good thing, not a weakness.

The restaurant is all alone on the edge of the green. On the map, this place is called Parker's Piece and is crossed by two pathways making the shape of a big X, as if for treasure. That's why I'd noticed it. That, and its proximity to a large P for parking, and the city centre bus station. I don't know if Patrick Bell will come by car, or if he'll come at all, but I needed to remove reasons to refuse.

A waitress looks up at me as I enter. None of the tables are occupied; it's that restaurant lull well past lunch and not quite late enough for dinner. My ears adjust to the sudden quiet inside, the way that eyes become accustomed to dark, and faint pop music coming from the kitchen gradually becomes intelligible.

I'm seated. I nestle my phone on the folded linen napkin by my bright white plate.

Maxwell is right. I can't trust someone from just a few emails. So I told Patrick Bell that I can't get to Highfields Caldecote this evening. Instead, I'll be waiting here at Mai Thai. I'll buy dinner, I wrote, hoping that that sounded light and cheerful. Not suspicious. Not clingy. It's not strange for a woman to prefer to meet in a public place; he shouldn't be surprised, or offended. *He won't cancel. Will he? I don't think he'll back out. Not if he really is . . .*

'I'll have the vegetable satay, please. And a coffee,' I say. I can stretch that out, make it last. I'll order an entrée later. It's early; it's not like I'm making anyone else wait for the table. 'No, wait!' I wave my hand as the waitress reaches to take away the place setting across from me. 'I'm waiting for someone,' I explain.

Out across the grass, there's a decorative lamppost in the centre of the green, and volleyball and Frisbee players packing up. Tanning girls will have left hours ago. I was supposed to meet Patrick Bell in Highfields Caldecote in fifteen minutes. *Has he got my email? What if he hasn't and waits for me there? He won't know the house. Maybe I wouldn't either. It's been a long time. What if they've repainted? New windows, additions, people do all sorts of things . . .*

'Yes, thank you,' I say. The waitress places a dish in front of me, and the heat and smell waft up into my face. I wrap my hands around the coffee cup, searing my palms. *I deserve that.*

The phone rings. Coffee rolls over the lip of the cup. On the screen: *Max*.

No.

I can't face him until I know whether Patrick Bell is really who he claims to be. I press the button to refuse the call.

What if Maxwell's right? What if Patrick is just some scammer? He doesn't even have to be a scammer. What if this is just a joke?

Finding Robert and Ben when I turned eighteen had been simple, and in the end we'd even recognised one another. They had been eleven when adopted, and kept together because they're twins; I had been eight. We'd all grown taller since then, and Ben had grown a beard, but we'd been still visibly ourselves. Sebastian would be different. He'd been only three, still pouch-cheeked and baby-cute, when we were separated. Even if this Patrick Bell is our lost brother, he isn't 'Sebastian', not any more, and hasn't been for most of his life.

For all that I've fantasised about this meeting, it has never been literal in my mind. He's never been an unrecognisable grown man in my imagination; instead he runs into my arms and I scoop him up into a snuggle, his curly hair tickling my nose. I've always, from the day he was born, felt like a mother to him.

There's so much that I want to tell him. Mum had let me come with her to hear his heartbeat for the first time. It had been magical, that swishing sound that heartbeats make in utero, so different from the thump that comes through stethoscopes. I had tried to describe it to my brothers afterwards, but my attempts sounded like the *shew, shew* sound you make to pretend lasers are firing out of a plastic blaster. Mum and I had caught eyes, the boys tussling between us. Only we, mother and daughter, had understood.

Only when I was older did I realise what Mum had been through. She'd been trying for a fourth baby for years, for my whole childhood, really. The cryptic marks on the wall calendar, the times Mum and Dad scheduled 'special dates' and we all went to bed early; the times Mum cried in the bathroom . . . Now I understand. I feel it myself. It feels urgent, aiming to have a first at the age my mother had had her last. I wonder if Maxwell and I will have a difficult time. I wonder if I'll cry in the bathroom once a month when we start trying.

Maybe I should call him back. I lift up the phone.

The waitress' face leans in front of mine. 'Miss? Is this your date?'

I freeze. I feel suddenly haggard, and panicked, and worry that my eyes are wild.

A man steps out from behind the waitress, wearing a casual suit and looking nervous. His hair isn't curly, but it's cut too short to tell, really. He's not as tall as Dad was, but what about Mum's side of the family? My heart is thudding. *How will I know? How can I tell? What if he's lying to me? What if he's not lying?*

'Sophie?' he asks.

'No, I – Patrick?' I stammer.

He laughs and ducks his head. 'You're waiting for a blind date, too?'

I wriggle my ring finger automatically. 'Engaged,' I say. 'But, I am waiting for someone. Sorry, I thought you were . . .'

'You didn't look happy to see me,' he says. 'I mean, him.' He's smiling, and affable. I wonder, briefly, if he *is* Patrick, testing me.

No, ridiculous. I shake my head. 'Would you like to join me?' I ask, 'while we both wait?' The need to chatter, to distract from the memories and theories and panic, has made me bold.

He seems surprised, stunned even. 'Really? I—' He sits across from me and flaps the napkin into his lap. 'I just assumed, I assumed that you really were Sophie and trying to get out of it.' He's good-looking but clearly nervous.

'You won't get anywhere putting yourself down like that,' I tell him. 'Maybe seeing us together will make her jealous. That could work in your favour.'

He's staring down at his empty plate. 'Any woman would be jealous of you. Your fiancé's a lucky man.' Just his eyes tilt upwards to my face, gauging my reaction through thick lashes.

'Not available,' I reiterate, wagging my ring finger again.

'Sorry,' he says, and lifts a menu up to cover his red face. I ask for a glass of water. I feel too warm.

'Are you all right?' the man asks me. He's touching my hand. *Patrick? Not Patrick.*

'What's your name?' I ask in return.

Sebastian, I hear, and shake my head, hard.

'Simon,' he repeats, and I laugh, because of course he isn't Sebastian. I'm hearing what I expect to hear, not what is.

Unless he's lying, I think. *Maybe he did say Sebastian the first time.*

'Simon, look, I think you should wait for your date at

another table.' I don't explain. I learnt long ago to not give men a reason; they'll just try to argue it away.

'Of course. Sorry,' he says, and gets up in such a way that he tilts in a little bow towards me.

'You're very sweet, Simon. Sophie will be glad to meet you,' I assure him. All those S names. No wonder I'd heard 'Sebastian.'

He sits alone with his back to me and Sophie doesn't come, not as long as I'm there. No one comes to my table either, or emails to decline. The waitress asks everyone who comes in, even in couples or groups, if they're meeting someone. She's motherly. She doesn't want us to be alone.

What if Sebastian does come? I twist my hands in my lap, anxious, like when Maxwell and I had Skyped with his mother to announce our engagement. It had been my idea to add video. I'd worn a string of lapis beads bought from a museum's gift shop, and a conservatively buttoned blouse. I'd wanted to impress, desperately. It had been a shock to see that Maxwell's mother had put in the same effort, like looking into a mirror, but one that reflects intentions, not results. She'd appeared to have tried applying make-up after years of not bothering. She'd worn her hair down, in a way that had probably looked nice when she was young, but didn't fit with her now-loose cheeks and her thick eyelids. I'd realised in that instant that we were both equally fragile, hopeful, and jealous.

Thinking of Sebastian now, I remind myself, *He's probably as nervous to meet me as I am to meet him.*

Sebastian had been born at night, in our parents' bed. My own hospital birth had involved conflict with the attending doctor, which Mum told like recounting a battle, and the forced administration of drugs, which Mum told like a horror film. With Seb, Mum had got the birth she wanted.

I remember coming down to breakfast. Sun had shone through the kitchen windows. Mum was at the dining table, in her dressing gown with her hair loose. Dad was scrambling eggs. Toast popped up – that springy sound so metallic that it almost rings – and Mum lifted her head. She smiled at me, and the baby cried. That's the first I'd noticed him, snuggled in Mum's lap with his head lolling on the inside of her elbow. Mum slid her dressing gown open and he found her breast and suckled. Mum was naked underneath, not even a nightgown, and I hesitated to get the boys. Dad nudged me, and put a plate of toast and eggs under my nose. He led me to the table and pulled the side of Mum's robe over her other breast. He went upstairs to tell the boys and get them up for school. Later, I got to feed Seb from a bottle, I remember that clearly, but the first day Mum had fed him from her own body. I pretended to feed my dolls like that for years. Once, I even tried to feed Seb, but Mum shook her head and closed my shirt. Ten years later, the first time a boy licked my breasts, I saw bright light and almost passed out.

The phone rings again. The screen says 'Max' again. I snatch it up this time, anxious and emotional, and as if to prove to the restaurant, now full, that I haven't been stood up: *Here he is, calling.*

'Max!' I say, loudly. The waitress seems visibly relieved.

'Imogen,' he says. 'Thank God.'

'What's going on? Where are you?'

He says he's calling from a police station. 'Can you come? Where are *you*? I need you to explain to the police that you grew up here, that you grew up in Highfields Caldecote.'

'What are you talking about?' Heads are turning. Simon has swivelled his body around. I'm too loud. I lower my voice: 'Why do they want to know that?'

'Did you meet him? I should have gone with you. I was worried about you. I should have offered to drive. I need you to explain to them why I was there.'

'You were in Highfields Caldecote? What happened? Why are you with the police?'

I wish I hadn't said that out loud. Conversation has stopped at the tables near me.

'I helped a girl who was in danger and she turned out to be one of the teenagers from my music group. I'm all right, and so is she, but now the police want to know . . .'

I could finish the sentence just fine: They want to know that he hadn't been inappropriate with her. They want to know that he had a truly coincidental reason to be wherever they'd found him.

I wait for the buzz of conversation to resume, for people to chew and swallow and get back to making their own noise, but they don't. They wait for me.

I can't leave him hanging any longer. I have to say something. I choose one word: '*Again?*'

It turns out that the Cambridge police station is just across the green. An officer from there drives me to the station in Cambourne, where Maxwell is. I gaze out the car window, waiting for the journey towards my childhood home to become familiar. It never does.

MORRIS KEENE

I stand in Dora's doorway.

She's in bed, now, finally. I wasn't sure if she'd go up when we got home, but she obeyed the suggestion without question. She looks safe in there. She looks safe.

We'd moved into this house when she was six and had bought the bed new then. We'd got it in pieces and screwed it together tight. The linens have changed over these nine years, from candy to stripes to the plain blue and purple they are now. It's too hot tonight for the duvet, which is rolled up at her feet. She's under a sheet, pulled up to her chest. The bed looks smaller now, too small for this full-sized person still trying to fit in it. She pushes her hair off her shoulder in a smooth, mature gesture. I barely recognise her behind her weary and wounded expression.

'You want a cup of water? Hot chocolate?' I offer.

She shakes her head.

I cross the room and check the locks on her two

windows, trying to look like that's not what I'm doing. I've already checked the rest of the house, while she changed. I pull down the blinds, as if curtains aren't enough.

Maybe they aren't.

I pull out her desk chair and sit on it. 'You should sleep if you can.'

She shrugs.

'Music, maybe?' I suggest.

'No.'

'I used to read to you, remember that?' I look on her shelves, but none of the books are the ones I'm thinking of. The last book I'd read to her was *Swallows and Amazons*, years ago.

I reach for a paperback that's face down on her desk.

'Alexandra gave it for my birthday. It's about vampires,' she says, dully.

I start from the beginning, reading in that sing-song way left over from picture books, wholly at odds with the story's teenage angst and earnestness. I plough through up until the young, fumbling lust between the two protagonists becomes embarrassing.

'Shit, I can't read this out loud,' I say, laughing, then catch myself. 'Don't tell your mother that I swore in front of you,' I add lightly.

'You shouldn't lie to Mum,' she says, looking hard at me.

'I don't lie to your mother,' I say, meaning that I don't lie about anything important. She turns her head away. I'm not sure what she's referring to.

The door downstairs rattles from a key. I jump to standing, protective, but I know who it must be.

'Dora?' Gwen calls up the stairs.

She's in the room a second later, kneeling next to the bed. She's got her hands on Dora's cheeks, looking hard into her face. 'I'm so sorry,' she says, as if it's a bad thing that she was at work, and hugs Dora, pulling her close.

I leave them to it, and step into the hallway to call Chloe. She's not answering; I have to leave messages. I'm pacing back and forth, and my voice is clenched tight. I pause in Dora's doorway, noticing how much they look alike, she and Gwen. They both look tired, and worried, and scared.

'I think he's dead, Mum,' Dora says.

I've already explained the broad strokes to Gwen over the phone. 'Good,' she says.

'I didn't mean to do it, not that. I just meant to stop him, to—'

'Ssshhhhhhhh.' She jerks Dora back and forth, like rocking except that Dora's not a baby any more.

The dog barks outside. I put her out the back when we were dropped home. It's an idle bark, a chatty one, not like the urgent bark behind the barn. I need to know: *What did Jesse find under the blackberry bushes?*

Gwen sits back and tells Dora that she won't go back to work tomorrow and that we'll all stay home together.

'No, I want to sing tomorrow,' Dora insists. 'It's the performance.'

'You don't need to, sweet. They'll understand,' Gwen says, stroking Dora's arms now.

'I want to.'

'No,' I say, supporting Gwen. 'You're not seeing that tutor again.'

'Well, what am I supposed to do? Stay home with you

and watch TV and pretend that none of this ever happened? It did happen and it sucks and it's horrible and . . .' She's crying again. Gwen glares at me over Dora's shoulder. I was agreeing with Gwen; I'm not sure what I'm supposed to have done wrong.

'It doesn't matter if Mr Gant is there,' Dora insists. 'He *should* be there. He didn't do anything bad. He helped me.' Dora pleads her case: 'I worked hard. I want to see my friends.' Her eyes go big. 'Where's Fiona going to stay? They won't leave her alone at home, will they? Ask Chloe.'

'Chloe isn't answering.' I rub my face. 'I'm sure she's looking after Fiona.'

Dora comes to the door and tugs my sleeve. 'We should check. Fiona can sleep here.'

Gwen and I exchange looks. I've missed this: that way we used to communicate every day, right over Dora's head, just using our eyes. It's been a while.

I get my keys and say I'll drive over to check; my car has automatic transmission and I can control it fine despite my damaged hand. Gwen guides Dora back to bed. 'If he brings her back I'll look after her,' Gwen promises.

'I really do want to sing tomorrow,' Dora repeats, to be sure that Gwen gets the message, but Dora's exhausted. Instead of making Gwen promise that she can go, Dora lets herself fall asleep.

Gwen won't let it go. 'Why didn't you notice when she didn't come home? Did you try to phone her? Why didn't you call me sooner?' The three lights over our kitchen table make three distinct oases in the otherwise dark downstairs. Her head seems to hover.

'I called Dora's phone but she didn't answer. I called you as soon as I knew that something was actually wrong,' I say, in my self-consciously 'reasonable' voice even though I know that it pushes Gwen's frustration up a notch.

'I would say that not coming home when expected is something "*actually wrong*".'

'She's fifteen! She doesn't have to come straight home!'

'I was the stay-at-home parent for fifteen years and I promise you that she does. She has to come straight home or call and say that she's not. That's how it works. It's not because we don't trust her; it's because we don't trust the entire rest of the world, and with apparently good reason!'

I pound the table with my hand that can make a fist. 'You're right. You're right! I'm not fit for this job. Not fit for my actual job, either. Not fit, full stop.'

'This isn't about you.' Gwen's voice is wobbling.

'No, it's not. So let's stop discussing what I should have done and how nothing bad would have happened if you'd been here.'

'I'm not saying that it wouldn't have happened! I'm saying that I would have been here and not two hours away! Do you know what that feels like?'

I do. I did the working for most of Dora's life.

'Stop it!' Dora calls from upstairs.

We freeze. Gwen's covered her eyes; she might be crying. I reach out and she turns her head away.

'I'm sorry,' I say. I pull her other hand, the one that's dangling. I squeeze it.

We go upstairs together.

'Sorry, sweetheart,' Gwen whispers, and kisses Dora's

cheek. 'I'm upset about what happened to you and I shouldn't take that out on your father.'

Dora says, 'No, you were right.' She gives me another hard look.

'I'm sorry.' I've already said that, but it's important for Dora to hear it. Gwen lets me hug her around the shoulders. She closes her eyes and leans on me. 'And I'm sorry we woke you up,' I say to Dora, then correct myself to a whisper, because Fiona's on the rug, in a sleeping bag, her eyes shut tight.

Fiona's mother is in Ireland and there's no flight until morning, so Spencer was relieved to have a safe port of call for the girl. Chloe confirmed with her that she knows our family and accompanied her to pack up a toothbrush and tomorrow's clothes. Two of the uniformed officers knew me, and told me about the empty pill packets found in the barn. So much for hoping that at least one of the deaths was from natural causes.

For all the time that Fiona and Dora have spent together over the years, Fiona's never stayed the night at ours before. I don't know if that's by chance or convenience, or if her mother had forbidden it even before the school-skipping.

Bringing her back here, the summer sun had been setting at last. Lights had been erected around the red barn to enable the forensics team to work into the night to secure the scene. Some of those lights were aimed at the patch of blackberry bramble behind the barn that had caught Jesse's attention.

As I'd swung the car around onto the long dirt road out, I'd seen the White House in my mirror, partly lit up inside. The corner bedroom, where Fiona had gone to gather her sleepover things, had at first appeared to have a cheerfully striped curtain. As my perspective changed, I'd realised that the window was barred.

'Are you all right?' I'd asked Fiona, glancing nervously at her, slumped against the car door.

'No,' she'd said simply, and nothing else for the rest of the ride.

DORA KEENE

When Mum and Dad go to their bedroom at last, 'Fiona?' I say. She's still pretending to sleep. She's good at pretending.

When I'd first got to the concert hall this morning, Fiona had paused by the name-tag table. We were always each supposed to make one, so that the tutors could call us by name. There were lots of pens, all different colours. Fiona didn't choose one. She just stood there, being jostled. At arrival, everyone's carrying, and bumping, their instruments. She's lucky. Her harp is so big that it gets to stay for the week, instead of her dragging it back and forth.

I'd picked an orange pen for her at random and put it in her hand.

'I have a crazy idea,' she'd said.

'What?' I'd asked absently, distracted, then reached across for a bright blue pen and printed my name in clear, capital letters. I peeled the backing off and pressed the sticker onto my shirt.

'Do you want to go to Milton Keynes again? Today?'

I'd laughed, assuming she was joking. Fiona had caught hell over that one day we skipped school. Her life had already been strict, but, after, it became near-jail. It's not like we'd snuck out at night; we'd cut school one day, one out of every other tightly organised day of our lives, and didn't even go to London. We took the bus to the mall. We browsed, and drank coffee. It didn't hurt anyone. *Well, in the end it hurt Fiona.*

'No, I mean it,' she'd said in front of the name tag table, pink from excitement. 'We can just . . .'

She hadn't written anything on her sticker. That's when I realised she meant it.

'We shouldn't have done it the first time. Your mother—'

'Sorry, I knew it was stupid.'

She looked really sad.

'Maybe we can go next week?' I suggested. 'Before school starts back?' We both knew that her mother would never let us.

'Yeah. I'll ask her. I only . . . Thanks for that. I think that was one of the best days of my life.'

I didn't know what to say. 'Yeah, it was fun,' I'd agreed. It had been fun, but not worth it, surely? Then the lobby chaos around us had started emptying out into the rehearsal rooms. It was almost time to start. 'Can you watch my bag?' I'd said, needing the toilet.

When I came back, and scooped up my backpack, I'd headed to the band room. Fiona and I play in different groups for the first session, so it's not strange that Fiona turned the other way. I hadn't thought anything about it then. I hadn't realised what she was trying to get away from. Had she already done it by then? Had she been about to do it? Is it because her mother was away?

In my room, I sit up and nudge her with my foot. I kick her and hiss, 'Fiona!'

She rolls over, eyes open. She props up on one elbow.

'I know what you did,' I say.

Grandma Ro hadn't been happy. I know Fiona would never hurt her, would never do it against Ro's will, and you couldn't make someone take that many pills anyway. They have to want to, even if you grind them up; who would drink something that tastes like that? Ro must have asked Fiona to do it. It had been a kind of love, I get that. But she shouldn't have involved anyone else. Most of those pills had come from me.

Pharmacies have sold paracetamol in tiny packets for years now, to discourage suicides. You have to make an effort to collect enough, not just give in to a whim with the bottle in the bathroom. There had been packaging for several dozen pills in the barn, enough to do the job. She had to have been lying to me for weeks, claiming monthly headaches. Her mother doesn't believe in PMS and doesn't keep paracetamol in the house. Ever since we cut school, Fiona hadn't been allowed to cycle home on her own any more, and it's not like she had money of her own even if she could get to shops.

Fiona's face is blank. It's like she doesn't even feel guilty. Maybe she really doesn't; maybe Grandma Ro was in pain or something. Maybe she had cancer.

'You used me!' I accuse, as loudly as I dare, but I'm running out of energy. Fiona looks like she's punishing herself already. She looks . . . stopped, like her switch is off.

'I'm sorry,' she says.

I think about how long it would have taken, one pill at a time, handing them over, then maybe tilting a cup of water to Ro's lips. Ro, who Fiona loves. Fiona loves her better than she loves her own mother. Maybe Fiona assumed that she would be in jail by now. Maybe she'll go to jail tomorrow.

I slide off the bed and throw my arms around her. Fiona makes this humming noise, which turns into hiccuping and tears. I'm crying too. We just cry into each other's hair and hold tight.

Dad knocks on the doorframe. He's wearing a dressing gown now, and shoves his hands into the pockets. 'You all right?' he asks.

I nod. Fiona nods too, our heads in sync.

'Did that builder ever hurt you? Did he even talk to you?' Dad asks Fiona. He's lost his job but you wouldn't know it from the way he talks.

Fiona shakes her head and crosses her arms over her chest.

'Good,' says Dad. 'If you want,' he says to both of us, 'go ahead and watch TV downstairs, or I could make you something to eat, or . . .'

'No,' says Fiona. 'I need to sleep.' Her head is bobbing slowly. She looks terrible.

'We have to sing tomorrow,' I remind him. I want it, that feeling of being inside a note that fractures into a chord so beautiful that you wouldn't mind breaking into pieces yourself.

'Me, too!' Fiona blurts, sounding surprised at herself. It's like she forgot it was ahead. 'We need to sing tomorrow,' she repeats.

136

Dad looks like he's about to fight, but instead he just says, 'We'll talk about it in the morning.'

'Sorry I missed practice today,' Fiona says, as if it were a normal day, reaching out for my hand. The bracelet she'd left in my bag hangs from my wrist now. We used to dress up in Rowena's jewellery when we were younger. Now I understand why Fiona had wanted me to have it. Now that Grandma Ro is gone, I have this little memory I can wear.

'It's all right. I know you weren't feeling well,' I answer, which is how I promise, right in front of Dad, that I'll keep Fiona's secrets.

IMOGEN WRIGHT-LLEWELLYN

Cambourne didn't exist when I was growing up; this area used to be part of the ubiquitous farmland that framed my village life. Now it's become relentless iterations of coordinated housing, which contrast with the singular police station. The building is hyper-modern. What isn't green copper is glass. I'm led through a hotel-like atrium to an office with a floor-to-ceiling window. It must normally give way to a view, but the summer night has gone dark at last. I can only see myself.

The person I'm to speak with is distractingly pregnant, and dressed in ordinary business clothes rather than a uniform. Her only jewellery is a plain wedding band. I feel like my engagement ring is gaudy in comparison.

'Ms Wright-Llewellyn,' the woman greets me formally, introducing herself as Detective Inspector Chloe Frohmann.

I'm glad that I'd dressed conservatively to meet Patrick. It feels exposed enough being subjected to questions; I wouldn't want to bare my shoulders or cleavage or thighs to the suspicious, tired glances of the men I'd passed on the way into this private room, or to this Detective Inspector, who seems like she wouldn't approve.

'Have a seat,' she continues, gesturing to the other side of the table. 'It was good of you to come.' She isn't even looking at me. She's sorting through pages of notes, reordering them, then tapping them together on the table to align them. Our London address is on one, and the name of our Cambridge hotel. Maxwell's name is in the middle of a long paragraph on another. I wait.

The Inspector sets the papers aside and leans forward, far forward to reach the table over her belly.

'Where's Maxwell?' I ask, interrupting whatever she'd been about to say. I need to see him. I need him to undo what the accusation has stirred in my imagination.

'We'd like to hear your version without him. Do you know where he went this evening?'

'Yes. That is, he told me where he went. Highfields Caldecote. He was looking for me.' *Surely,* I realise, *that must be true. If he wanted to do something illicit, he wouldn't do it in the very place he was expecting me to be.*

'But you weren't there.'

'No. No, I – I'd told him that that's where I would be, but I changed my mind.'

'Without telling him.'

'Yes, well. We'd had a fight. An *argument*,' I correct. I wouldn't want her to think that we'd had a physical altercation. 'I changed my plans to meet my friend in Cambridge instead.'

'Name of this friend?'

'Patrick Bell.' The Inspector writes it on one of those

pieces of paper, along with some key words from my brief explanation.

'Why were you planning to go to Highfields Caldecote?' Maxwell must have said. She's testing me. 'I grew up there. I was a child there,' I correct myself.

'Years?'

'1981 to 1989,' I answer without hesitation. Those years are burnt into my brain.

'As the Wright-Llewellyns?'

'Just Llewellyn. The Wrights are my adoptive family.' We'd discussed carefully which name to put first. Together we eventually settled on Wright, so that I'd be alphabetically sorted near my adopted siblings. 'My parents were Joseph and Isobel. Isobel with an "o".'

'Address?'

'Meadow View. That's what I remember. It was painted peach, at least it was back then.'

The Detective Inspector leans back in her chair, her belly making a hill over the table. It's mesmerising, and has a kind of energy around it. I remember my mother's bump, and how protective she'd been of it and the baby inside.

'Did you know Rowena Davies?' the Inspector asks, startling me out of my reverie.

I shake my head. 'I'm sorry, who?'

'In the white house with the red barn. Back then she would have been . . . forty-five, maybe? She worked at Hinchingbrooke Hospital.' I ignore the coincidence of this Rowena Davies' place of employment. The police have reason to ask me about Maxwell. My father's job at that same hospital isn't their business. 'She had a daughter,

Morgan, who would have been a teenager then. Maybe she babysat for you?'

'No.' The times that Mum and Dad went out, we had looked after ourselves. Besides, 'What does this have to do with anything? I thought one of Maxwell's students lived there.'

'Indeed. Morgan Davies' daughter Fiona. Has Maxwell had any previous relationships with students or teenagers?'

'He hasn't had any relationship with a student or teenager since he was no longer one himself,' I say precisely. The Inspector's sloppy question had been purposeful in its implication that there is a current relationship.

'Is he attracted to underage women, for example on the Internet?'

'Of course not.'

'You check his computer?'

I narrow my eyes. 'If I say I have, you'll ask me why I was suspicious. If I say I haven't, you'll ask me how I know.'

'Of course. Reasonable, if you ask me.'

'Look at me. I'm five years older than he is. He near worships me. I hardly think that's the behaviour of a predator of teenagers.'

The Inspector looks me up and down, as if taking inventory, then has to shift her whole weight over to lean forward and write something down.

'Must be uncomfortable,' I add spitefully, about her temporary girth.

She acts like that wasn't a direct hit, but she winced when I said it. She shuffles papers again, not meeting my eyes, then drops a bomb of her own: 'Any accusations?'

I suck in a breath. *She knows.*

Then, *No, she's fishing.* And what does it matter if she does know? He hasn't done anything wrong.

I admit it: 'Three years ago, a girl in one of the choirs he directed sent an inappropriate photo of herself to his phone. He immediately reported this to the headmistress, who called in the girl's parents. At first the girl claimed that they had a relationship, which she later confessed was an elaborate fantasy to cover her embarrassment. Meanwhile, her parents had whipped the families of the other girls into such a frenzy that the one girl's denials were hardly heard. Rightly, there were no formal repercussions, but he was encouraged to "move on", which he did.'

'You were together then, were you?'

How much detail does she have? 'No, but that's what I know.' I don't phrase it as *That's what he told me.* Even inside my head that sounds weak.

'And now he's' – paper shuffling again – 'taking a job working with a girls' choir?' Our eyes meet.

'Yes,' I say through my teeth. 'And if it were a boys' choir, you'd make something out of that, too.'

'Well, that's all, really. Thank you very much.' The Inspector stands, which in her case requires a heave.

'Where's Maxwell? I want to see him.'

She holds the door open for me. 'You can wait out here.'

Back to the atrium. I settle myself in a rounded plastic chair.

I scroll through email on my phone. Nothing new from Patrick Bell. Maybe the whole thing was a joke. Or maybe he went to Highfields Caldecote and was frightened off by the police activity. That doesn't mean he's necessarily a scammer who's set me up. Maybe he had drugs in his car or unpaid parking tickets. He could still be Sebastian.

I try to imagine him as a grown man. What if his adopted family hadn't been good to him? What if, by chance, he'd been given to people who were unkind, or uneducated, or extremists of some kind? Would he be jealous of my luck, and Robert's and Ben's? I don't only need to wonder if Patrick Bell is truly Seb or not. He could be Seb for real, and still be angry, or after money, or just not safe to be around.

Can we talk on the phone? I email him. In our original back-and-forth, we'd leapt to the plan of meeting as soon as we realised that we were geographically able. He'd said he's in Norfolk, a few hours' drive. He probably had gone to Caldecote. He probably didn't have email on his phone, and found my message only after returning home, disappointed, and frustrated. Or perhaps he's not home yet, wondering why I didn't show, still looking for me. *Why hasn't he called?* I'd given him my number straight off.

He hadn't offered me his phone number in return. I remember thinking that that was strange, but maybe he doesn't have a mobile. *Not everyone does,* I remind myself.

'You all right?' Maxwell says, suddenly standing over me. His voice is hesitant, apologetic, hopeful. He's been escorted out by the same Detective Inspector who'd interviewed me.

I click off my phone. 'Max!' I jump to embrace him, but the Inspector's presence makes me hold back. I reach out for his hands instead. We lean and touch foreheads.

She, the Inspector, says: 'I'll take you back to your car now.'

I glare at her. I just want to be alone with Maxwell. I want to get into his car and drive and drive with him, without getting anywhere for hours, just talking. I've already explained everything away in my own mind, and just need him to colour it in. *You went there for me. You were sorry. You didn't know the girl would be there. Finding her there instead of me was an accident, just an accident, surely . . .*

I want to ask him about the girl, but I can't do that in front of the Inspector. I ask instead, 'Why didn't you drive your own car here? Did it break down?' I whisper, though that doesn't make sense either, because it would do no good to then take us back to it now. 'Were you hurt?' I add, picturing an ambulance and a hospital, though he doesn't appear damaged.

'I was near-arrested,' he says.

'Why? What exactly did they catch you doing?' My voice has upped. The Inspector walks ahead of us, leading the way through the car park, but I'm sure she's listening.

'I'll tell you when we get there,' he hisses.

An arrest – even 'near' arrest – has changed the situation. I'm no longer willing to wait. 'Why not tell me now? *She* knows everything already,' I point out, tossing my head towards the Inspector. I'm not sure why I feel surprised by Maxwell's revelation of the extremity of the situation. He'd called me from a police station, after all. But I'd pictured it like it had been at the school: just a formality, a mediated discussion, not an arrest. *Near-arrest,* I correct, wondering what, exactly, that means.

'A man was killed,' the Inspector says, clicking a button on her key ring, making her car lights flash.

'Who?' I bark. *Is that what happened to Patrick Bell?* Had Maxwell caught up with him? Had Maxwell done something to him?

'I had nothing to do with it,' Maxwell says, to both of us. He doesn't look like he's been in a fight. Dishevelled, but not like he's taken any punches. I don't think he's ever punched anyone.

We belt ourselves into the back seat. It's an ordinary car, so it feels more like riding in a taxi than being escorted by police. 'Who was killed?' I demand of the Inspector in the driver's seat.

'We're not yet releasing that information.'

'Was it Patrick? Patrick Bell?'

The Inspector pauses the car at the mouth of the exit. She tugs up the parking brake and turns to face Maxwell. 'You said they weren't there.'

'They weren't!' he defends himself.

To me, she says, 'I thought you changed your plans to meet your friend in Cambridge instead.'

'I did change the plans. He hasn't replied. He didn't show up. He probably didn't get my message.'

The Inspector releases the brake and drives forward, shooting questions back at me over her shoulder. 'So you're saying that he could have been there? He might have been there, looking for you?'

My breathing gets faster. I tamp down the panic stirring in my stomach. 'Is it him? Tell me!' I insist.

'Is Patrick Bell a builder?'

'No. No, he said he works with computers.' I don't know what that means, I realise. Does he program them, or repair them, or sell them? 'I don't think he's a builder.'

'What does he look like?'

'I don't know!' I wail.

I'd ridden in a police car once before, with Robert and Ben, the night that Mum and Dad had died. Seb had fallen down the stairs and Mum and Dad were taking him to the hospital. They didn't make it that far. It took the police hours to wonder if there was more to the family than the miracle toddler in the back seat who had survived the crash. They came and woke us up to take us to a foster home. They turned on the lights in my room and I had screamed.

The Inspector turns off onto a narrow road and parks. I can't see much on either side of us in the dark, just a cluster of bright lights and activity far ahead. Big lamps splash light onto a red wall, throwing the people near it into silhouette. *Someone died.* A man. A builder. Probably not Patrick Bell.

I rattle the car door to get out but it doesn't give. The Inspector gets out and opens it for me. She must have the back seat doors set to child locks. I remember trying to get out of the police car that night twenty-three years ago. *If the doors hadn't been locked back then I would have fallen out onto the motorway . . .*

'Where are we?' I ask, getting out of the car, turning in a circle. Maxwell's car is here, foregrounding wide, empty fields.

Max slips his arm around my shoulders. 'The houses have come down, Im. It's gone.'

I blink fast but, to my surprise, don't have to fight off any bigger reaction. My old house is gone now, but the home had evaporated decades ago.

The Inspector counts instructions off on her fingers as she tells us: 'I would like you to stay in the county, please. I'll let you know when you're free to return to London. I want you' – she turns to Maxwell – 'to claim illness tomorrow. You don't deal with those girls in any way. You understand that?'.

Maxwell nods.

Then it's my turn, and the Inspector taps her third finger: 'If Patrick Bell contacts you, arrange to meet him. Then call me.'

'Why?' I'd been afraid that he was the dead man. *If he isn't, then . . .?*

'If he was here, he may be a witness,' the Inspector says, and she returns to the driver's seat. She starts up the car and heads for the activity around those two houses in the distance.

The air is warm and still. I smell the churned-up earth. The land around us isn't just houseless, it isn't even fields any more, now I can see that. Even the grass is gone.

'I'm sorry, Imogen. You shouldn't have to see it like this.' Maxwell draws me against his chest. I ride his breathing for a little while.

'Who was she?'

He knows who I mean. 'Dora Keene. Sings alto.'

I shove him back. 'I don't care what her fucking vocal range is!'

Maxwell can shout just as loudly. 'That's all I know about her! Nothing else! She's nothing to me but a voice. What do you want me to say about her?'

'What do you think I want? I want you to explain to me how this happened. This is the second accusation I've had to put up with.'

'That *you*'ve put up with? You? These things haven't happened to you. They've happened to *me*. What the hell, Imogen? We didn't even know each other for the first one.'

'Exactly. So how do I know what really happened?'

'Nothing. Nothing happened because I don't touch my students. I don't touch teenagers. And I haven't touched anyone but you since the day we met.'

My body wilts. I'm wrung out. I don't know what's finally broken me: the accusation against Maxwell; Patrick Bell, who might be scamming me or might now be lost to me; Cambridge, and memories, and my childhood home razed. I cover my face and cry into my hands. He touches me gingerly, gently. 'What's wrong with you?' I demand.

'*Wrong* with me?' he asks, incredulous. Almost angry.

I only need to push a little harder to get the reaction I need. 'If you like grown women and not teenagers, then maybe you need to start acting like it.'

Maxwell slams the flat of his hand onto the hood of his car. 'I thought she was you,' he chokes out. 'I came here for you. I heard a scream. I ran into the red barn and she almost fucking killed me. But I thought it was you, so I climbed up into that loft. I climbed up after *you*. That's why I was there.'

'So you're making this my fault? If you'd agreed to come with me tonight to start with, we would have been together. You wouldn't be able to claim to have mistaken a fifteen-year-old for your nearly ancient fiancée!'

'I didn't have a clear view. She was skulking up in that loft. Size and hair and general female-ness were all I had. And so what if she wasn't you? She was frightened and defending herself. Would you prefer it if I walked away from that?'

'I'd prefer that we trust one another enough to face things together. I'd prefer that we not fight in shopping malls, and that you give me some credit for reasonable judgement, and that I not run away, pouting like a child. I'd prefer to start today over and that we both face it differently!'

Both our chests heave from shouting.

Maxwell touches his fingertips to my cheek. When I don't flinch, he pushes his whole hand round the back of my neck, and pulls me to him.

Our eyes adjust to the dark.

'You said the girl was called Dora Keene?' I ask.

'Yes.'

'The Inspector asked me about a Davies family, not Keene.'

'Fiona Davies. Another alto. It's her house.'

'*Another* girl?' All my breath whooshes out of me. I take a step back.

'I know, Im. I know. That's how I felt, too. But I can't force you to believe me. That's up to you.'

I don't want to have to make that decision.

'Do you need me to quit teaching? Is that what you need?' he asks, apparently rhetorically, because he doesn't leave me room to answer. 'I can't make a proper living as just a musician. I'd like to, but I really can't. Shall we live like *La Bohème*, in some attic, while I compose? We can do that, without any teenagers around, but I don't think that's what you want.'

'It's not what I want.'

'It's not what I want, either. I want you, Im. And I want

150

Cambridge. I want to marry you in the chapel and work at St Catharine's. I want it, but I can't make you give it to me.' He lifts then drops his shoulders.

He really doesn't know. He doesn't notice the crushes and the looks he gets. He's a musician, and all that that implies: sensitive, expressive, nimble fingers. He has that light-heartedness that youngest and only children have, used to being indulged, forgiven, and adored. *He's happy,* I remember. I saw it in him in Spain, on that beach. He was happy, if shy, and in awe of me. I'd been glad then that I'd worn the red bathing suit, that it was wet, that my recent boyfriend had broken up with me two weeks before. I feel age pushing me in the back. I have to make progress. I won't be beautiful forever.

We get into Maxwell's car to drive back the hotel.

He explains more fully what had happened: that Dora had been locked in, had triggered an alarm, had defended herself. 'He had a shotgun,' Maxwell says.

I shudder. 'The builder?'

'He used it to blast open the locked barn door.'

I wrinkle my forehead and ask the obvious: 'If the dead man's the one who locked it, why would he have had to shoot it to get it open?'

Maxwell nods. 'Dora assumed he was after her. But I don't think he was, Imogen. I think he was trying to help her. The Inspector isn't stupid. She's thinking the same thing. If he didn't lock her in, who did? Who else was there? *Me.*'

'Or Patrick Bell,' I realise.

'I didn't want to be the one to say it. But, yes, Patrick Bell. She looks like you, Imogen. Dora Keene, the girl locked in the barn, she looks like you: same build, same hair. I'm sorry, Im. I know you were hoping that he was your brother.'

'He still could be.' Now I'm crying again. The loss of the house is nothing compared to this. 'He could be my brother, and do bad things. Maybe falling down the stairs that night did something to his brain . . .'

'He's probably just a scammer, Im. Some creep. The police will get him. Sebastian's still out there, as good as you remember him.'

I sob frantically, my shoulders bouncing in little shrugs.

MORRIS KEENE

The girls come downstairs together, dressed. They don't speak, just sit, on the same side of the kitchen table.

Gwen makes hot chocolate, and I cook eggs and toast. We're in constant motion: scooping, stirring, serving. Our smiles are tight, and Dora smiles back, and sips, and bites into what's put in front of her. Fiona is quiet, not interested in her food. Gwen nudges orange juice at her.

The outside sounds have started up. Today is recycling pickup day, but our boxes are still full at the foot of the kitchen island. The bin lorry rumbles outside, coming towards us.

'Mum, do you want me to do the rubbish?' Dora asks, rising.

Gwen makes a barking sound that I realise is a single laugh.

'Honey, we can skip a week,' I say. 'It doesn't matter.'

Dora's eyebrows knit together. The lorry's grumble is nearer. She gets out from behind the table and heaves up the blue box of empty tins and bottles.

I reach out. 'Sweetheart, you don't have to . . .'

She waddles to the door, legs wide because the box is heavy. She lifts up one knee to rebalance things. Tears are running down her face; she can't wipe them because she needs both hands. I sprint ahead and open the door for her. I don't try to take the box away. She'd only wrestle me. *Rightly so,* I realise.

When I'd hurt my hand, Gwen had tried to help by brainstorming different kinds of work I could switch to. I didn't want to look at the pages she'd printed out off the computer, about police desk jobs or training new cops or going back to university. We'd argued about my 'inflexibility', that was Gwen's word. She just wanted to help, she said, and I wouldn't let her.

Dora had taken Gwen's side. *Why can't you just try?* she'd begged me, during one embarrassing dinner. She and Gwen hadn't understood my resistance. They'd thought that they were both in the same place as me, and that we all needed to figure out what we 'want to be when we grow up', Gwen because Dora's not a child for her to look after any more, and Dora because she has to choose her A-level subjects. They wanted to know why I didn't just pick something new and do it, like they were.

I think Dora, at least, understands now.

Dora needs to take out the recycling. It's bad enough that she's changed; she can't bear the world around her changing too. It's good that the rubbish pickup still comes every week, that there are things outside her that she can depend on. She's not strong enough right now to hold herself together, but if everything around her stays like it was, then that can force her into shape from the outside. It can hold her up. That's what I need too. Jumping into a new job, a new world, would only make me frighteningly formless. It would make me so new that I wouldn't be myself any more.

Dora doesn't make it in time. The lorry is just pulling away. She could run ahead and dump our bottles and cans into someone else's bin, but that's not the point.

She puts the box down on the pavement and hugs herself. She has her dressing gown on over her clothes and it's flapping in the breeze. I stand behind her, and wrap my arms over hers.

The lorry is leaving the street now. Beyond it, coming towards it, someone pounds on a car horn. The beeping car squeezes past before the lorry's finished the turn and I'm amazed that the car's wing mirror doesn't crack off. It speeds down our little street and comes to a stop in front of us. I tense. The sun is reflecting off the windows and I can't see who's inside.

Legs slide out first, in pointy-toed shoes and shiny tights. The rest of Mrs Davies pops out all at once, fast, like she'd been compressed in there. She pushes past us, brushing Dora with a crackling static charge. Our door is open, and the woman charges in. Gwen hops to one side just in time.

A minute later, the woman drags Fiona out, pulling on her arm, not even her hand. Fiona's shoulder looks wrong, like it's being twisted.

'Stop it!' Dora says, stepping out in front of them on the path.

Mrs Davies is wild-eyed. Her hand moves fast and connects hard with Dora's face. This isn't just a smack of fingers against cheek that makes a sound and a sting; this is the palm of Mrs Davies hand against Dora's jaw, pushing her head halfway around.

155

I lunge forward, but a small, furry body hurtles faster than me. Jesse has got out of the back.

Mrs Davies shrieks and backs away. Jesse gets her mouth around her skirt and pulls, growling. Gwen is yelling too, and I get Jesse's collar. She lets go at my sharp command. We're all panting. Dora's rubbing her neck.

'Sorry,' Fiona says, and walks to the kerb. She stops at the car and waits, shoulders hunched. Her mother follows, and they get in together, both doors slamming at once, like snapping jaws.

I'm the one who gave in and said that Dora could perform. Chloe had finally called me back and assured me that Maxwell Gant won't be there; they'll have someone else to conduct and a pianist accompanying them instead. I was relieved to be able to let Dora go. I played music when I was young; I understand.

At the concert hall, Dora plunges into the crowd. She doesn't look back. Gwen and I stake out a spot on one of the vinyl sofas.

It's been three decades since I played Shostakovich and Berlioz in this place, and the blue lobby and orange auditorium are as they were then. There are more kids playing, now. It's busier, seems to skew younger, but has the same energy. When you do it right, making music is a whole-body activity: breath, spine . . . Everything gets to be part of the work.

I wipe my forehead. It's a hot day and all of the bodies crammed in here make it worse. The instruments attached to the children and teens give them strange, humped, exaggerated silhouettes as they mill about the lobby.

Fiona appears in the doorway. She's pale, and flashes

quick glances all over the room. Suddenly, she turns back to look over her shoulder, then pushes herself forward into the mob.

Gwen nudges me. She wants us to move away from the entrance. No sense setting ourselves up for confrontation, assuming that Fiona's mother isn't far behind.

All of them from the formerly *a cappella* group sit together in the front of the auditorium. Just before their turn, they exit and line up in the wings.

The girls file on, curling into a half-circle around the replacement conductor. She cues the piano and they start low, all on the same note.

I close my eyes for a moment when they split into harmony. I'd almost forgotten what this feels like.

I hear it before I see it, just by half a second. A voice drops out. Then, Fiona crumples, straight down, accordioned at the knees and at her waist. The girls all trail off but the piano pounds on for another line, before the accompanist, too, stops. The last chord hangs in the air, unresolved.

The house lights snap on. I can't see Dora clearly, behind the other girls. Gwen and I are near the back, up high. Gwen has already headed into the aisle. I stand up but stay here, trying to see what's going on from this better vantage point.

The girls are shoulder to shoulder. It's hot. Stage lights make it worse. Crowds make it worse. This building has been full of people all day, every one of them generating the heat of effort. Dora touches her forehead. I want to reach out and steady her but I'm too far away.

The director is calming the audience, asking them to return to their seats or to stay in them. A parent-helper wearing an usher sash brings the girls cups of water. Fiona's mother is shaking her shoulders. Her body bounces but she doesn't open her eyes. Someone dabs water onto her face. Her mother keeps shaking her. Someone else is trying to make her stop.

Dora covers her mouth and looks around wildly. Realisation hits me at the same moment. *Why would Fiona's grandmother need pills? Could someone that delicate even swallow that many?* There are easier ways to help someone who wants to die.

Dora wails.

Most people are sitting as told so I'm able to get down the aisle fast, with the phone to my ear.

'Get off the stage!' the parent-helper who brought the drinks yells at me, trying to clear everyone away. If she gets her way, Fiona and her mother will be left alone, on display like the last scene of an opera.

Gwen has Dora by the arms and faces her like a mirror, breathing deeply until Dora mimics her and calms down.

I get there. 'She's taken pills,' Dora tells me. 'You have to call a doctor.'

'I'm on with 999.' I turn back to the call.

Dora's kneeling with Fiona now. She won't let Gwen pull her upright.

The ambulance is on its way. I lean down to Dora. 'What about you? Did you take anything?'

'No!' she insists. Her look of spontaneous offence and genuine horror assuages my worst fear.

That parent-helper is still trying to clear the stage but no one is listening. Fiona isn't moving except to breathe. She's still breathing.

CHAPTER THREE

CHLOE FROHMANN

Detective Sergeant Spencer makes the mistake of darting his eyes from my paper cup of black-dark coffee to my inflated middle.

'If you find our case half as interesting as my caffeine intake, you may make a half-decent copper,' I comment blandly.

He blushes. He's a ginger, with paper-white skin, and his embarrassed cheeks near glow. 'Sorry,' he stammers. 'It's just, my mum had a baby last year, and she cut out coffee. Tea, even. I thought everyone did that. Well, every pregnant woman. I thought you all did that . . .' He must have noticed the mental arithmetic going on behind my eyes. 'My step-mum, I mean. She's not my real mum. She's my age.'

Our age. I'm not that much older. Spencer pushes his shoulders back and stretches his spine to add an inch to his height, but he can only look young. It's that damn hair. That, and his constant apologising. *Could be worse. He could be arrogant and then not apologise. At least this makes a change.*

It's morning at our desks after a long night in Highfields Caldecote, dealing with fresh witnesses and old bodies. Then, after too short a respite between cool bedsheets, I'd had to meet Morgan Davies landing at Stansted Airport, returning from Shannon. It's a short journey but Morgan had had to wait till morning for a flight.

I'd stoically absorbed her barrage of insults and demands while communicating the details of Rowena's death, trespassers in her barn, and her daughter's present location at a friend's home which, surprisingly, turned out to be what got the biggest reaction. I'd had to quickly prioritise my questions.

There was no time for tact. I pulled up a photo on my phone screen and put it under Morgan's eyes.

She sucked in a breath.

'Do you recognise this man?'

'That builder! He shoots rabbits.' She shudders. 'He used our toilet once. I didn't want him to, but he said that the Portaloo was broken and that the water was already off in the other houses. I thought he might commit vandalism of some sort if I didn't let him. He's – he appears to be – is he dead?'

'Yes. Do you know his name, Mrs Davies?'

Morgan pushed my arm to shove the image away. She turned to go and pulled her rolling suitcase over my foot.

I followed. 'Do you know his name?'

She stopped under a sign for the parking shuttle. 'Of course not! Why would I? We didn't natter through the bathroom door! Why are you asking me? If you think that

162

one of us had something to do with . . . with however he met his end . . . over some bloody rabbits!'

'No, Mrs Davies, but he was in your barn last night.'

She paled. 'With my mother?'

'He appears to have entered after she had already died. He responded to the alarm. Dora Keene was looking for Fiona and pulled it thinking it was a light.' In a panic over being locked in, but I didn't say that yet, nor how he had died. That would come. These were but the early pebbles of the avalanche, and they hit Morgan Davies hard just as they were.

'That girl is not permitted on our property. That man is not permitted on our property.' Tears balanced on her lower lashes then splashed down onto her cheeks. 'You can't leave children alone for a moment. I say this as a fellow mother. They can't be trusted. You need to know that.' She lifted her hand; I knew what was coming. She rubbed her palm against my belly, fingers spread. The baby kicked, which she took as a reward. I preferred to interpret it as the little one acting out on my behalf. I would love a chance to kick the belly-touchers.

Instead, I said, 'We'll need to talk more later, before you return to your home. The property is a crime scene.'

'That's absurd!'

'We need to talk. Please, Mrs Davies. I understand your urgency to get to your daughter. Just don't bring her home until we've had that chance.'

'It's not my home! It's hers. It's my mother's. I've only ever been a guest, a tolerated squatter. You don't know what it was like. She wouldn't even share the house with me. She lived in that barn for as long as I have memories. My father

163

died when I was fourteen and she left me to live in the White House alone. I did stupid things, disgusting things, but what else will a teenager do, unparented? When I left at eighteen I vowed I would never come back. Sometimes I wish I never had.'

The parking shuttle pulled up and she heaved her suitcase on board. She had refused my offer of a lift, needing to get her own car back.

I put one foot up into the shuttle doorway to make it wait. 'So your family has lived in the house for a long time? Forty years? More?'

'Why?'

'When were you eighteen, and when did you come back?'

'This is ridiculous!'

'I hate to guess, but all right: 1975?'

Morgan's vanity overrode her indignation. '1982,' she corrected, through gritted teeth. 'I returned four years later.'

I wondered if something other than a teenager's natural urge to move out might have driven her. Had Morgan Davies run away from something freshly buried under the blackberry bushes?

'There's more to discuss, Mrs Davies,' like what was found under the blackberry bushes. But the shuttle doors creaked in anticipation, I retracted my foot, and she was taken away.

Those buried remains are what I focus on now.

The pathologist has made preliminary observations. The remains are of a woman and child. The smaller skeleton is nestled such that the pathologist assumed at first sight that it was in utero but further examination in situ showed that it was separate from the woman, on top of her not inside her. They're both still in the ground, the dirt on and around them being swept away by little forensic brooms and then sifted. He's there, supervising the exhumation himself.

He's sent photos to my phone. I steel myself to not react. I force my face to fall into a careful neutral, and freeze it there.

The adult skeleton's arms are crossed over its chest, formally placed, not holding the baby. *So not buried alive, thank God*, I think, briefly, stupidly. It's not that deep a grave. Of course they were dead going into it; otherwise they would have clawed up and out. I shake the image off, literally shimmying my shoulders.

Spencer's head is next to my cheek, to share the view of the phone's small screen. He bites down on a cupcake and chews. A blue sprinkle clings to his upper lip. 'You want one?' he offers. There's a tin of them open on his desk.

'Somebody's birthday?' I ask, glad of the distraction.

'I like to bake. Go back one . . .' His finger darts out, like a frog tongue catching a fly, and slides across the screen to return to the previous photo.

I tilt my head. 'What do you see?'

He taps the screen, enlarging the image. 'That orange colour, there. Is that the edge of a blanket? Or clothes? A collar?'

'I expect Jensen will fill us in.'

'There was a blanket or bedspread that colour in the barn. Maybe part of a set.'

'What, on the bed?'

'No, in the back. I drew a map.' He pulls a paper out of his back pocket and unfolds it. It's the layout of the barn, with labels. He pokes at the phrase 'linens & clothing'. There are also 'food', 'appliances', 'furniture', and 'papers & books'.

'You mapped her hoarding?'

The surprise in my voice appears to offend him. 'I thought it could be helpful.' He plucks a second cupcake and consumes it in two bites.

'I'll put a gold star next to your name in my lesson book.'

I don't mean it badly, but he pushes the map back into his pocket, and wipes a streak of icing off his cheek. I pretend not to notice his hurt feelings and get on with it. Handholding doesn't help in the long run.

'There's more to this situation,' I say. 'Morgan Davies claims that her mother has lived in the barn for decades. Depending on how long the remains have been there, she could have known about them. She could have . . . Do you think the redevelopment may have triggered all this? Rowena Davies thought that the bodies might be found, so she killed herself?'

'Still waiting on what was in her system.' His breath smells like pure sugar. 'But the empty pill packets suggest . . .'

'Maybe she was just ready to die.'

'Maybe one of the girls had something to do with it,' Spencer says casually, but it's obvious that he's testing my loyalty.

I have to be careful. We'll need to talk to Keene, to get information about Dora and Fiona and their friendship together. At the same time, we're not supposed to give any information to him, at least not more than will be obvious from the questions themselves. I can't yet trust Spencer to understand that my history with Keene can be an asset here. I give him the answer he needs.

'Sure. Maybe one of the girls,' I admit. 'Maybe the old woman asked for help. It would be natural to ask her granddaughter.'

'Her granddaughter's not the one who was in the barn. What if that builder caught the other girl in the act?'

I decline to answer. 'Look, this is what we've got.' I rip pages from a spiral notebook and write a name on each.

Rowena Davies. 'She's dead. Probably suicide, maybe helped.' Next to that I lay another page: *Dora Keene.* 'Locked in the barn. Maybe by the dead builder? But he used the gun to break in, so . . .' Next to her, I place his page: *Dead man. Builder.* 'No ID in his pockets and his fingerprints aren't in the system. The car belongs to the development company. Shotgun unregistered.' I hate guns. 'We're still waiting to hear from the developer who bought the land, for him to ID his employee. Dora killed him in what she thought was self-defence.'

Spencer laughs, in a truncated burst. 'She says.'

My head snaps up. 'What's in it for her?'

'She was discovered alone in a friend's barn with a teacher. She was discovered alone in a barn with a dead body. Take your pick.'

I hate how reasonable his suspicions are. *I know Dora, I know her like . . .* Before I became pregnant, I would have said 'like my own child'. But I don't, not as close as that. And who says that even parents know anything about what their children are really up to, anyway?

I tear another page and write on it: *Patrick Bell.*

'Claims to be a long-lost, grown-up former resident of the area. Supposed to have been there last night. Looking to meet up with his sister, Imogen. A sister who happens to resemble Dora Keene.' I write *Imogen Wright-Llewellyn* and *Maxwell Gant* on two more sheets. On a seventh I write *Mother and child*, dead under the blackberry bushes.

'Aw, mother and child, like on a Christmas card,' Spencer jokes, and the image of a horrific skeleton Madonna flashes in my mind, skull tilted towards her skeleton babe, inside a border of mistletoe.

I shake it off. 'Imogen Wright-Llewellyn and Patrick Bell claim to have lived nearby. They were likely just children when the bodies were buried, if they overlapped with them at all, but they may know something . . .'

Spencer doesn't seem to be listening. He's rearranging the papers. I hold back the urge to slap his hands. It feels like he's fiddling around in my head.

'Right. Dead, dead, dead, dead,' he says, stacking three sheets. That's Rowena, the builder, and the macabre Christmas card, as I'll now be forced to think of them.

He continues: 'Present at the scene of the current crime or crimes.' That's Maxwell and Dora.

'Fiona too,' I add. I rip out another sheet, write her name and add it to the second pile.

Lastly, 'Ancillary,' he says, adding the sheets for Imogen and Patrick Bell.

I can't help but tease him. 'Big word.'

'Fuck off. Ancillary,' he repeats. He plunges a finger between *Patrick* and *Bell*, pinning the paper down. 'If he even exists. You think?'

I shake my head, not a negative shake but a who-the-hell-knows. I add a question mark to his name.

'We could have as many as four crimes here,' I say, reshuffling the papers. 'Rowena, the builder, and the two skeletons.' I put those three sheets in a row. I put *Dora*, *Maxwell* and *Fiona* in a column descending from between the first two. 'They both died last night. Any of these three could have been involved.' I move the *Mother and child* up to the top, above *Rowena*. 'Maybe Rowena knew they were about to found. Maybe she killed herself or had a heart attack. So this one' – I tap *Mother and child* – 'caused this one' – I tap *Rowena* – 'and the builder was an accident. *Ancillary*,' I joke.

Spencer smirks. 'Which makes the only actual murder the one that's too old to solve.'

'Maybe it wasn't murder. Rowena used to be a midwife, at Hinchingbrooke. What if she practised midwifery at home?'

'The baby skeleton is really small. Premature, maybe? A birth gone bad?'

'Maybe not murder. Maybe an accident, covered up. Maybe she buried a mistake.' *Maybe no killers, just cowards.*

'So who locked the barn?' Spencer says.

I lean back. 'Dora was in there, with Rowena.' I separate those pages and put them on top of Spencer's cupcake tin. 'Fiona, Maxwell, and the builder were there.' I arrange them around it.

'Maybe Patrick Bell.'

'Maybe Patrick Bell,' I agree, adding him. The cupcakes are now surrounded. I add the page with Imogen's name on it with Dora; someone may have mistaken one for the other. 'It was locked from the outside. So no one was locking themselves in *with* her. There's no room for a sexual motive.'

'Maybe he was already in there.' Spencer adds Maxwell to the cupcake tin.

'It's a strange place for a tryst. You wouldn't meet for sex with Grandma asleep in there.' *But where* would *Dora go?* I wonder. Now that her father's not working, there may not be the chance for privacy that one would expect around this age. She's fifteen already. *Jesus, I feel old.*

'Maybe Fiona was jealous and tricked Dora. Offered the barn to her, told her Rowena was away, or sleeping in the house. They show up, find dead grandma, freak out, they're locked in, they panic and set off the alarm. The builder comes to the rescue, but they don't know who he is. Boom, he's dead. All this time Fiona's in the house. She didn't come out when the alarm went off. That's odd, right?'

If that's how it happened, I could probably get Dora to confess to her part. I'm just not sure it would be ethical to do so, either from the side of being a friend abusing Dora's trust, or of being an officer required to provide evidence that can stand up to challenge in court. 'Shit, she and Fiona have been together all night.' Maybe getting their stories straight.

'What if Imogen was the jealous one?' Spencer suggests. 'Maxwell's her fiancé. She follows him leaving the concert hall with a student, locks them in the barn out of anger. Figures she's taught him a lesson in humiliation, and makes up this story about a long-lost brother so that we think Maxwell was following her instead of the other way around. Protecting him from a charge of sex with a minor, and now he owes her.'

'That's a little convoluted. Would your first thought be making up a fake brother? Why not just say she was going to see her old house by herself?' This is working; Spencer may yet be a decent partner. Not that we've found the answer yet, but it's as if we might work well enough together to find it eventually. 'Imogen was in Cambridge city centre when Maxwell Gant called her from the station in Cambourne, but she'd had the time to get there from Caldecote if she was trying to establish an alibi.'

Spencer leans forward. 'Do we know she actually lived in Highfields Caldecote? The whole thing could be something she made up. Maybe she's a compulsive liar. It's not as if she's attached to anyone else we've interviewed besides her fiancé. Maybe he's in on it. Or maybe she lies to him, too.'

I lean in too, one hand on the small of my back to keep my balance. 'Maybe it isn't a coincidence that she showed up just when these bodies were ripe to be discovered. Even if the dog hadn't done it last night, the developer was sniffing around. Do you think that could have something to do with her presence here? We need to know Morgan Davies' stance on selling the land. Were they holding out or giving in? Who was resisting and who was pushing?'

I tear out another piece of paper, to write my version of a shopping list:

1. *Track down the developer. Identify the dead builder. Find out the status of the Davies' land.*

2. Confirm or disprove Patrick Bell's existence. Check for those online discussions Imogen W-L claims he was responding to.
3. Confirm Imogen's past. Did she live in Highfields Caldecote as a child?
4. Find out if Dora or Fiona were having a relationship with Maxwell Gant. Talk to their friends. Look into his past.
5. Find out how Rowena died. Pathologist.
6. Find out when the mother and child died. Pathologist.

'You made the list, you take your choice,' offers Spencer, contrasting the gallantry with a tiny belch.

'I'll look into Imogen and Patrick Bell. I'll either find something interesting or we'll knock them out of the equation. You run the developer to ground and get him to name our dead man. If he doesn't answer his phone, find him in his office or at another property. We'll both go after the Davies family. Something's not right there.'

'You skipped one,' Spencer points out. He touches number four on the list. Dora.

I dodge it. 'We can't do everything at once.'

He raises his eyebrows at me but doesn't put his opinion into words. I turn away from him towards my computer.

I wish I could wriggle out of this suit jacket. It's ridiculous to wear in this heat, and it doesn't even close around my maternity blouse, but I feel exposed and lumpy without it. I search the county property database for the ownership of the properties in Highfields Caldecote. Decades past won't be in there, but I need the property names and recent

172

histories to accurately request the older records.

Spencer's listening to the developer's phone ring unanswered. 'What if . . .' he muses out loud. 'What if he *is* the developer? Lance Keats. If it's his own land, that would explain him working alone sometimes, as they described. That would explain him not answering his phone . . .'

'No, too young,' I say, shaking my head. 'You don't have enough money to buy land at that age.' But I try an image search. No photos of developer Lance Keats.

'Some by that name on Facebook, but not from around here,' Spencer reports from behind his computer.

'Aha! LinkedIn. No photo,' I say. 'No personal information. Same phone number we've been trying.' I absently tap a pencil on a closed book.

'The County Council. Planning permission. They'll have met him,' Spencer says, rising.

'Call me when you find out.'

His earnest thumbs-up makes me crack a smile. I bounce the rubber end of my pencil off my stretched lips.

My request for the current titles to the homes in Highfields Caldecote has spit a list onto the screen. All of them in that little area belong to March Property Group. I submit a query for the chain of ownership of Meadow View back to the eighties, to confirm Imogen's claim, but the main interest is the recent sale of the White House, which appears to include the Red House as an outbuilding. I phone the solicitor who handled the transaction. He, of course, is not permitted to divulge much, but tells me what he can from the public record:

The former owner of the property, Rowena Davies, had been represented by her daughter with power-of-attorney,

Morgan Davies. It was Mrs Davies' signature that gave up the land. It seems to point towards Morgan's innocence. *Or her cunning*, I consider. *If Morgan Davies did know anything about the skeletons, she could have been setting up her mother to take the fall.*

I track down Morgan Davies' peers. It would make sense for a friend 'in trouble' with a pregnancy to turn to Morgan's mother for discreet assistance. It takes half of the day to say for certain that there are no local missing persons who fit that scenario. We'll have to cast a much wider net. Wider nets, I rue, often have bigger holes.

When my phone rings, I snatch it up, hoping that Spencer has got farther than I have. The hysterical female voice on the other end is hard to understand. I finally make out that it's Maxwell Gant's fiancée, and resort to a verbal slap: 'Ms Wright-Llewellyn, control yourself! Where are you?'

Imogen sniffles on the other end of the phone. 'I'm in Highfields Caldecote. I took a bus.'

Damn. I hope that the officer at the scene has the sense to keep her away from it. I put on my gentle, persuasive voice: 'I'm sure you understand that the area around the barn is a crime scene as well as private property. Perhaps I can send an officer to—'

'You don't understand! I think I've been followed.' This is a whisper, full of breath that makes a staticky buzz through the phone.

She's not crazy, I have to remind myself. Just twenty minutes ago, I found the recent discussion posts from someone claiming to be Imogen's brother, and received confirmation that she – they – really had lived where she claimed.

'Where exactly are you?' I ask, opting for a crisp efficiency that I hope will prompt direct answers.

'I was in the village, trying to remember things. I thought I recognised the way home so I started walking. There wasn't a pavement, so I had to be in the road. I was careful. But this car came around the bend too fast! I – I ended up full-length in the stinging nettles on the side. He didn't stop, but I know the car. I've seen it before.'

'Where? And where are you now?' I ask, unimpressed but obligated.

Imogen says in a different voice, not aimed at the phone, 'What are you—' A click, and the call terminates.

I freeze, tilted forward. 'Imogen?' I say, and say again.

I call the number back. Straight to voicemail.

My phone rings. It's Morris, calling on his way to Addenbrooke's Hospital. Fiona's taken pills.

Fiona? I smack my hand on the desk. *Damn, damn, damn . . .*

I phone Spencer on my way downstairs. 'I'm off to Addenbrooke's. Get to Highfields Caldecote. Imogen Wright-Llewellyn may be in danger.' *Or she may be playing games.* I can't take the chance of ignoring what may be a legitimate concern, but I can't help wondering at the wake of drama that Imogen seems to drag behind her. 'Alert the officer at the property. Pathologist, too, if he's still there.'

I picture us as mirrors of one another across the county, phone to ear and hand on car door.

'I'm on my way,' Spencer confirms. 'What's happening at the hospital?'

'Fiona Davies has collapsed. They think pills.' *Damn again.*

'Good news here. *Erik* Keats is our man. The son. His father owns the property. Makes sense that he worked overtime at it. The dad's in France on holiday; that's why no one's answering the phone.'

'Family besides the dad?'

'Still working on that. No wife or official children. I was about to visit his address in Hardwick. The electoral roll says he lived alone.'

'We'll do that together, later. For now, we have fires to put out.'

In the afternoon heat, the involuntary image in my mind is less of the 'to do' lists and overcrowded schedules that the expression implies, and, instead, of dry, crackling flashes.

IMOGEN WRIGHT-LLEWELLYN

What's gone hurts badly enough, but even what's left doesn't look right. The white house and red barn are marred by police chaos. Large lights flanking the barn make it look like a film set. A tarpaulin juts out, sheltering a tool case and a heap of cut-down brambles underneath it. I step closer.

An exposed skeleton below it lies face-up, skull tilted back. Small sweeping tools have left their patterns in the stubborn, clinging dirt like brush marks in an oil painting. A smaller bunch of bones, which had at first seemed to be a strange, knotty tangle, resolves into a curled figure, and I suck in a breath. I knew that a man had died, but not about this.

I stare. The remains are old, but how old? Had they been under the ground when I walked on it as a little girl? The hand with which I'm holding my phone falters. A uniformed police officer rounds the corner of the red barn and heads straight for me.

'What are you—' I protest.

He snatches the phone and clicks it off. 'No photographs.'

'I wasn't—'

'This is a crime scene.'

'I'm sorry!'

'You'll have to leave.' He takes me by the elbow and urges me away.

I look back over my shoulder. The red barn wall looms over the bodies. *No, the bodies are gone. What's left is just bones.* I shiver, and the sun in my eyes makes me sneeze. The motions combine into a jolting shimmy. 'May I have my phone back?'

'If I see it come out, I'll confiscate it.' He hands it back, and I slide it into my jeans pocket. I feel vulnerable for a moment, alone and off-kilter, with this authoritative man. I'm not sure that he actually is police; how would I really know? Anyone could get police-looking clothes if they wanted to. I want to leave but I'm afraid to turn my back on him. I wonder if he came here in a green car.

An older man comes around the house. He's wearing a white plastic jumpsuit over his clothes, and carrying a boxlike bag. He kneels by the bones, against the pulled-up berry bushes heaped beside. He appears to be the pathologist, or at least a forensic person. So the uniformed man surely is police, which is a good thing, even if he's staring at me, suspicious.

'I'm going,' I say, backing up the way I came. I lift one leg, then the other, over the cursory fence marking the border between lawn and dark earth, lumpy from caterpillar tracks. I stumble, catch myself, then turn and run to the clot of dirt on which my house used to stand.

Not just 'my' house. Our house. That's the point; that's what made it special. We all lived in it together.

I turn and look back. I try to remember the white house and its red barn. I'd seen on small signs coming in that they are actually called that: the *White House* and the *Red House*. Our house had been called *Meadow View*, properly, but had it been referred to as the 'Peach House' by neighbours? *Orange House?* Maybe. Probably. You would do, if your houses were all different colours, wouldn't you?

None of the neighbours had had children my age, not that I can recall. I'd played on all of the grass, without thought to property lines, but it had been by myself or, later, with Sebastian.

An image darts, blurry, between one clear memory and another. I *had* played by the back of the barn. I remember the berries, and the red painted wall. *Had the bodies been under me then?* What if I'd chipped at the hard ground with a plastic spade? What if it had rained and I'd scooped and patted mud cakes there? I remember a hem against that colour red, and bare feet, and short, pink toenails.

A woman, yes? An adult woman. I would think 'young woman' now, but back then any grown-up had been by definition old. The woman had had long hair, worn loose. It had been damp from washing and she'd had a comb in her hand. I had never been allowed to leave the house with wet hair. I'd hated my mother's hair dryer so instead washed my hair at night and slept on it. This woman, with her heavy, damp waves, had been lovely, freckled, and burnt pink on the shoulders. She'd worn a loose summer dress tied just under her breasts. She'd walked me over to the steps of the White House and asked me to help her comb her long hair, which I'd then undertaken with solemn care. I had never been able to grow my own hair that long.

Was that the woman who died last night? I wonder. But, no, it wouldn't have been. Last night's death had been an old woman, grandmother to a teenager. This memory-woman would have to be from the next generation down. The old woman's daughter, it must have been. She had seemed, to young me, to be about twenty. The police had said that there was a granddaughter now, a girl who was in Maxwell's singing group. Fifteen, then? Sixteen? That could fit that her mother would have been around twenty when I was little. She had been carefree, loose-haired, barefoot. She'd worn a chain round her neck, dragged into a sharp V by the painted head of a lion nestled between her breasts. That'd fit twenty. She'd been listening to the radio, I suddenly remember. 'Walking on Sunshine'. Loud. She had turned it up. She'd had a basketball in her lap, and I'd grabbed it and tried to dribble with it, dropping it and chasing it down, down, down the grass slope. When I'd finally caught it and turned around the woman had gone.

I look around. There is no slope. The land here is flat.

Has the developer levelled it? I consider, but I know he hasn't. This is the land I knew. I can't think why I pictured a tilt. Am I even in the right place?

I stand. I put my hand up as a salute-like visor and squint. Without the buildings, the land is anonymous. I could be anywhere. The only landmarks are the red and white houses now guarded by the gruff policeman and by the science-person packing up his bag and getting into a car. Not a green car.

The policeman is taking a call. He looks in my direction, at least he faces this way, and I hold still.

He goes behind the house, the white one. Is he looking for something? Is he improving his phone signal?

An urge pushes me back to the property line, the edge between the land being developed and the land that's still lived on. I scramble over the fence that emphasises the border between the dirt and the grass. No slope. I turn to face the dirt – no slope there, either. But there, yes, our house had definitely been over there. I'm sure.

I turn towards the White House. Yes, I'd sat on those steps, with the long-haired woman. But where had I started? I allow myself to drift forward. I'd been playing over . . . *there*. Near the bodies? I stop myself and shudder. I'd started there, then wandered over to the barn door. The woman had taken my hand, tugging gently. I wrap my arms around myself.

Footsteps. I bolt forward, wanting to dodge the policeman. I put the barn between us, ample cover for me to get off the property.

I hesitate. The mouth of the barn hangs open. *No, not mouth, the door*, I correct myself. Just because there are windows for eyes doesn't make it a mouth. It's been slid to the side to allow thick electrical cords to pass through. Outside, they're attached to lights aimed at the burial, the huge bright lights that we'd seen from Maxwell's car last night. I gingerly step over these electric snakes.

Maxwell had said that he and the girl had been up in a loft, that it was small and crowded, which had made things 'look bad' to the paramedics. Having slept in a loft for a year at uni, and not always alone, I want to see this loft for

181

myself. *Ridiculous, the girl's just a teenager,* I berate myself. But I slip my arm inside, just to peek.

Purposeful footsteps come around the building. My body slides in the rest of the way.

The Red House is large but surprisingly crowded, full of thick, hot air and countless *things*. Even as my eyes adjust, the piles and stacks remain in silhouette as the sun shines through sideways. It all seems skewed by the slanted light, as if the towers might fall. My heartbeat speeds. I should run away. The door is behind me, still open, the jaw of it still slack, but I push forward.

The path through the clutter turns sharply. Suddenly, the bed on which the old woman had died, the loft over it – everything that Maxwell had confessed, that the Inspector had described – comes to life in my mind, acting on this real stage. There, the fallen refrigerator. There, a cleared space, where paramedics will have worked on the body. Up above, Maxwell and that young girl in a tangle of sorts.

I stare. Nothing enticing or even forbidden about it. Just messy, crowded, horrid. No one would want to have sex up there, or in here at all. I go cold from guilt. I should never have doubted him.

He's gone to St Catharine's. He hasn't told me his decision about the job, just that that's where he needed to go. I know there's a chance that the offer will be taken away, given the events of last night, though that would hardly be fair. *Really? If even I had qualms, however small, how can I insist that the parents of schoolgirls blithely and completely trust in him?*

I back away, but my hip hits a sharp corner. The tower

that I've bumped into tips, then arcs, and ultimately falls, splatting across the exit path.

I clamber over the spilt boxes but another column follows suit, into yet another. The light has suddenly dimmed, and I turn my head frantically side to side to suss out why: the window that had let in the most light has been blocked by what appears to be an unusually long bolt of fabric, or maybe a rolled-up carpet, that's fallen across it and partly unfurled. I don't see how I can have knocked that over, even in a chain reaction. I push through the mess I created, but the path that should be just beyond isn't clear any more, and I can't see the light from the door. *Unless I'm facing the wrong* way. I turn in a slow circle. I cough, and assume that it's a reaction to my panicky, shallow breaths, but then I catch an acrid smell and the prickling of nearby heat.

I plunge forward, towards that carpet roll, and mount it, trying to shimmy up. The window is big enough for me, if I can open it, or break it, but it's got no hinge or slide, and is leaded into too-small quarter-sections. Still, I hit at the thick, wavy panes, looking to break a hole to breathe through, and to shout through. I don't even make a crack.

No one knows I'm in here. The policeman must have seen or smelt the smoke. He may have gone to his car to get help, or to meet the fire engines that he's surely called, to guide them in. Is anyone else even around? I pound again, and try to shout, but the attempt dissolves into coughing. It's better to get low, I know, but the window is up here. There's no escaping through the ground. *Is there?* I briefly consider perhaps digging my way out, or lifting the whole building up off the foundation onto my shoulders. This ridiculous image gives me an idea, though. I climb higher, and reach for the beams holding up the roof. I pull myself up into the criss-cross of rafters.

Through the rising smoke I detect scattered pinpricks of light along the line where the roof connects with the stone walls. These are holes where animals have once gnawed, clawed and insinuated themselves.

I slip my fingers into a fissure, wriggling them to widen it. Mortar crumbles. 'Help!' I call, in what seems far too feeble a voice.

Suddenly, the beam on which most of my weight is pressed shifts sideways, nearly dropping me. I hang on, shoving it harder out of line. Where it meets the wall, a loose stone next to it is tilted by the beam's leverage. A gap appears. *Light.*

FIONA DAVIES

Mum always waits until we're in the car to tell me things she knows I don't want to hear. She likes me trapped. That's what she did three days ago.

'Where are we going?' I asked. This wasn't the usual way home from rehearsals at the concert hall. Mum was driving us deeper into Cambridge. 'Almost there,' she answered in a sing-song voice. I recognised Hills Road, making a bridge by the leisure park. We rode over it and Mum triggered her indicator for a right turn.

I sat up straighter. 'Where are we going?'

There wasn't a road to the right. It was an entrance. Mum just smiled.

While we waited for the light, I looked up out the window, at the stacks of luxury apartments. Mum is always careful to use that term with her clients, instead of calling them 'flats'. She's put people in this building before.

These apartments are new, well, newish. Very modern, very posh. There's a swimming pool in there. A gym. And, just a little further down the road, Hills Road Sixth Form College, where I was going to go with Dora in a year.

'Mum, who lives here?' I asked, my voice a squeak. Tears sprouted in my eyes.

'We're going to live here,' Mum said firmly. She turned hard into the driveway.

I folded my arms across my chest. *No.*

'We're going to look at the show home.' Mum parked and pulled up the hand brake, hard. She turned to face me. 'It's close to Hills Road,' she said, as if the location practically next to the school weren't obvious. 'You can bring your friends over after classes.'

'What about Grandma Ro?'

Mum sighed. 'She can't look after herself. You know that. She's getting beyond our abilities to help her, not while we have work and school. That's the reality.'

I shook my head.

Mum swallowed hard and forced a smile. 'We'll paint your new bedroom any colour you like . . .'

'What colour will Ro's room be? She won't get to pick a colour, will she? Not in a care home. It'll be dingy and . . . *generic.* They'll just wait for her to die so someone else can be slotted in. She doesn't want to go, you know. She's told me what you've said. She hates the brochures. She doesn't want to go!' I was shaking.

'She doesn't know what bloody year it is or even who we are all the time! *She doesn't get to make the decisions any more!*' The shouting bounced around inside the small car. I covered my ears.

'I don't want to go either! It's two against one! You can't make us sell!'

186

'I can sell, Fiona. I have power of attorney.'

'We'll fight it. Ro's not crazy. You can't say that she is.'

Mum turned the key and backed out of the wide space. 'We'll come back another day, when you've adjusted to the idea.'

She swung the car into traffic and aimed towards home. I looked out the window, giving her the back of my head.

'I'll be able to meet you at the school gate,' she said. She's always loved the story about how I'd cried and clung to her on my first day of school. Mum had then stayed in sight of the classroom window every morning for weeks, so that I could look up and see her whenever I needed to. The teacher had eventually asked her to stop, and she did, but she told me that she was still there, just invisible. I used to see the leaves rustle outside and had known she was there.

'The lift is big enough to fit your harp in. You don't have to worry about that,' Mum went on as she drove, as if I were a client who just needs to be persuaded.

My harp is why I have a downstairs bedroom. If I slept upstairs, I would have had to keep it in the living room, and play it in public. Well, in front of Mum.

When we finally got home, my fingers ached for it but it wasn't there. It's too large to carry back and forth to the concert hall, so I had to do without it at home for the week. My room felt unanchored without it, as if the rug might float up and away.

I got ready for bed.

Mum stuck her head in, inviting me to eat something. I wasn't hungry.

'The new apartment is for you, sweetheart,' she said.

'You don't need to feel guilty over being happy. Rowena will be happy for you, too.' She closed the door.

I hadn't realised till then how much I'd been counting on escaping in a year's time: a new school and a long commute, too long for Mum to drive me every day. I would have taken the bus, at least sometimes. I would have been almost free.

Mum wasn't the only one cornering me. Grandma Ro had asked for my help. *If I can't stop Mum putting her in a care home, Ro is going to make me . . .* I made myself stop thinking about it.

The sunset light made stripes across my rug, through the bars. That had been the compromise: for the privilege of a downstairs bedroom, I had to put up with security-gated windows. It's too easy for someone to break in, Mum had said. I'd asked for a key. Mum had said no. That's how I'd figured out that Mum wasn't only worried about what people from outside might do.

The next day we were in the car again, going back to the concert hall. We were going fast and I couldn't stop it, any of it.

'Do you understand?' Mum repeated, in that tight voice.

I answered quickly, 'Yes, Mum. I'll look after things. Have a good trip.' I made sure to say the whole thing, not just 'yes'. Mum is suspicious of agreement without specifics. She might have thought I wasn't really listening.

'It's not a trip,' Mum pouted. 'It's work.'

'Have a good work,' I said automatically, correcting myself. But Mum didn't like that, either.

'Are you being sarcastic?' She'd turned her head to talk to me and almost didn't see the red light.

'Mum!'

She hit the brakes hard, stomping her foot down. We both lurched forward then back. Mum tossed a glance at the rear-view mirror. No one was behind us, so she acted like it hadn't happened. 'You know the rules,' she said.

'Yes, I know the rules,' I agreed.

Dora has apologised a hundred times for getting me into trouble, but I'm not angry about it. The rules now aren't that different from the rules before. Different, but not that different. Dora thinks it was normal before and crazy now, but it was never normal. It was never like it is for other families.

Mum has had to leave me alone to look after Grandma Ro before, but not since the school-skipping with Dora. Mum is a relocation specialist, which she mostly does while I'm in school. She helps foreign professionals get settled quickly into rented houses and flats, and gets them leased cars and mobile phones and cleaners, whatever they need. It's usually local work and usually on her own timetable, except that she now had to go to a team-building event overnight – at least one night. Mum didn't tell me how many it really was, so that I couldn't plan to throw a party or have a sleepover. If I knew exactly which nights she would be away, Mum said, I might take advantage. One of my cousins is Bible-crazy and says that everyone has to be ready all the time because nobody knows when Jesus is coming back. Mum doesn't like her but I think maybe that's where she got the idea.

That's also why Mum didn't tell me until we were in the car. She didn't want me to have a chance to set something up with friends, or pack something, or do anything differently from normal. That's the point: she needed me to do everything as normal, as if she were home.

The phone was the exception. I used to be allowed to make calls or answer them, so long as I was in the kitchen where Mum could listen. Since skipping school, I've not been allowed to use the phone at all. For this trip, though, Mum explained, she would call at random times when I was expected to be home. I was to listen to the answering machine and, if it was Mum, pick up. If I didn't, I would be in trouble. If I picked up before the machine confirmed that it was Mum on the other end, I would be in trouble. If Mum called and the line was busy, I would be in trouble. This meant that I couldn't stay too long in the barn with Grandma Ro. Mum didn't like me in there. Mum said Ro wasn't a healthy influence. She was still angry about Ro living in the Red House, instead of in the proper house with us. I think she kept Ro alive as a punishment. Ever since the developers came, Ro had been trying to die.

Mum was concentrating on the road. I turned my head towards the window. I liked the blurring as we drove fast.

Traffic was light because of summer, until we got to West Road. It was as if the concert hall were a whirlpool that had sucked all of the cars in Cambridge into the streets around it. Mum stopped along the kerb, where the bus stop is. She could only wait a minute.

'I didn't want to have to do this, but you brought it on yourself. I put a camera in the house. I won't tell you where; it doesn't matter. If you're really being good, it won't matter where the camera is, will it?'

'No, Mum, it won't matter. I'll be good.' My harp was already inside. I had nothing to hold onto but the straps of my lunch bag. Mum chose it because it's small enough that I can't hide anything extra in it.

'You'll have to take the bus until I get back. I hope I can trust you with that.'

I felt a flutter in my stomach. The bus is freedom. But I'd forgotten; tomorrow wouldn't be freedom at all.

It was happening too fast. I had been preparing for weeks, just in case, but it still felt like I'd been grabbed from behind and forced up against a wall.

It just seemed to have come up suddenly, is all. I blinked fast. If I didn't take the chance Mum had just given me, it wouldn't come up again in time. I'd promised Ro.

A bus beeped at us. We were in the way. I got out onto the pavement and Mum jerked the car into the road.

It had felt exciting to sneak out of the concert hall. I didn't need Dora for that. I'd thought that I did, but I didn't. Once outside, I considered trying to find the bus to Milton Keynes by myself, but I didn't know where to catch it from Cambridge, and it had just been a crazy idea anyway. I'd thought I could run away from my responsibilities, and, maybe if Dora had come with me, I would have tried for a few hours. On my own, though, there wasn't anyone to pretend for. I couldn't pretend just for myself.

It had to be today. Mum would be away for at least overnight, probably two. That's what the pills needed: eight to twenty-four hours without interference before the antidote wouldn't work any more. After that, there wouldn't be anything anyone could do.

I locked the door when I got home.

I wondered where Mum had put the camera. I scanned

the front rooms, but nothing jumped out at me as new.

She wouldn't really put in a camera, would she?

If the camera was in the room, Mum wouldn't have liked seeing me look for it, so I went into the kitchen for a glass of water. We have only glass glasses, not plastic, and I worried that my shaking hand would drop it.

The camera could be in here.

I didn't think that there would be a real-time feed. *Mum wouldn't have time to watch it, would she?* She was supposed to be working. If she were watching, she'd be angry that I was home at all, never mind what I was doing. I was supposed to be at the concert hall still. 'I'm not feeling well, Mum,' I said out loud, just in case. I walked back into the lounge and said it again.

But if Mum thought that I was still out, she wouldn't bother checking any camera until later. It was having people over that she was worried about, or me not coming home. She wouldn't start looking until this afternoon.

If there even really is a camera.

I rubbed my forehead. *Stop it.* It didn't matter. A day and a bit, that's all I had to act normal for. Ro needed me.

Ro had tried to kill herself once before, long before I was born, but just went into a coma instead. Then, when all Mum's talk about selling and care homes freaked Ro out, Mum made sure that she couldn't do it again. It was like in airports after 9/11: nothing sharp, nothing flammable allowed in the Red House any more. A personal alarm was installed. The ladder to the loft was taken away. I was usually the one to make Ro's breakfast in the house and bring it to her ready to eat, instead of letting her toast her own bread or spread her own marmalade. No electrics. No knives. Not even a kettle any more, no appliances because of electrical fire hazards. It would have solved Mum's problems if Ro died but she wouldn't let her.

I poured a mug of milk and put it on a tray. I put biscuits onto a small plate. Ro wouldn't want them, but I had to give a visual reason why I was heading out there.

I carried the tray outside. That man was in the fields again. Sometimes there were lots of men; sometimes only him. That was an *only him* day. I put down the tray, and pulled the barn door to slide it sideways using both hands.

It wasn't always like this, so densely packed. There used to be a big oval rug and chairs in the barn, and Dora and I had played there. Sometimes we'd modelled Rowena's old jewellery and sixties clothes, which we'd discovered in the back of the loft, giggling at the surprising strangeness of the styles but never, at least I didn't, mocking them. Rowena had woken early from a nap once and caught us at it. She'd gibbered and berated us; I'd never seen her like that before. She didn't need daily care then, so I'd been able to avoid her for almost a week, too embarrassed to face her. When I'd at last come back, the rug had been rolled up, and the clothes and jewellery box packed away somewhere deeper, more hidden, that I'd only found again recently. Dora and I hadn't played in the barn again after that, though we still visited Ro, as the stacks grew taller and the space tighter. That's the week that, until today, I used to think of as my growing-up.

'Ro?' I said, leaving the tray at the door. 'It's me, Fiona.' This time of day, Ro usually knew that I was her granddaughter. It was only in the evenings that she forgot things. It had all got worse since the developer came, the forgetting and panic. *How can Mum force her to leave her home, her safe place?*

I unstacked boxes to get at a middle one. I lifted out three folded skirts. That was where the now-empty jewellery box had a new purpose, lined with a soft handkerchief so that it didn't rattle. *Twenty-nine pills.* Six more in my pocket from Alexandra today. I popped them all out of their blister packs and counted them out. *Thirty-five.* More than enough. I'd been careful of that. Ro hadn't taken enough the last time, more than twenty-five years ago. She'd warned me. I'd learnt from that mistake.

'Ro?' I said again, to let her know that I was still there. I tucked the pill wrappings back in and restacked the boxes.

All the pills were in my zip pocket now, loose. I pulled my hand out. I didn't want my sweat to start degrading them. I took a water bottle from the stockpile in the kitchen area and put it into my other pocket. It sloshed as I turned corners.

I pulled the heavy curtain aside and it fell against me as I ducked under. The tasselling on the edge tickled my cheek. I put on a smile. Ro had a light on and it was a little oasis of brightness in there. I had stirred up dust in the air and it sparkled. 'Hi, Grandma Ro!' I said. I sat on the bed and held Ro's hand.

Ro had been crying. I noticed a brochure from a care home on the floor. Mum had brought her her breakfast today. She'd probably put that with it, tucked under the edge of the plate like you would a newspaper if this were a luxury hotel. I pushed it away with the toe of my shoe.

'Don't worry, Ro, I'm here to keep my promise.' I was crying too. Ro squeezed my hand.

I told her, 'It's going to be little bit different, okay? I couldn't get enough pills,' I lied.

Ro looked scared. She started to protest.

'No, it's okay,' I told her. 'There's another way. I know I didn't want to before, but . . . I will. For you. Okay?'

I stood up. The care home brochure was under my feet, where it belonged. The pills were in one side of my jacket and were much lighter than the water on the other side.

Ro didn't know why I had waited so long. She didn't know why I had picked today, but she was ready. She tilted her head forward, tried to curl forward with her shoulders too, but she wasn't strong. I helped her, and slid a pillow out from behind her back.

Rowena fell back, eyes closed. She smiled. Her hands were loose at her sides, palms up.

I lay the pillow on her face and pressed. I'd thought standing would work, but the bed was wide and Ro was in the middle of it. I climbed on and straddled her, pushing hard, equally on both sides of her head. I didn't feel any movement between my legs, any up-and-down of breathing, but I kept pressing. I'd promised Ro it wouldn't be like last time. I'd promised her she wouldn't wake up.

I shifted all my weight forward, so that I didn't even have to push any more. I was just propped there, balanced like a yoga position. I made myself breathe slowly through my nose.

Suddenly, *Is the camera in here?* I wondered. I had assumed that Mum meant that it was in the house, but she might have implied that just to lull me. It might have been in something she'd left with breakfast, or propped behind the clock or on a high place. Mum might know that I let my guard down when in here, like Ro had always done.

'I love you, Grandma Ro,' I said, leaning back. The pillow sprang from its stretched form back into a fluffy rounded rectangle. I pulled it off Ro's face. It was light, like the pills. Her smile had slackened and her eyes were closed but not squeezed. I tried to find a pulse in her neck, but I wasn't sure I was feeling in the right place, especially with Ro's loose skin. I wanted to put a mirror to her mouth but didn't have one on me. I hovered my palm over her nose and mouth. I didn't feel any exhalation puffs.

I climbed off. If the camera was in there, I had to act fast. I smoothed the covers and tucked the pillow that had done it under the bed. I picked up the care home brochure and didn't know what to do with it. I shoved it in my jeans pocket for the rubbish in the house.

I turned off the light. There was some light from the window, but it came filtered through a dingy sheer. I couldn't see the dust motes any more. There was no sparkle.

I got on to the other side of Ro's heavy curtain and pulled it to. I wasn't done, and had to get on with it. There was a chair in Ro's kitchen area that used to go with a table, until the table got buried in the pantry stockpile. I sat down.

I twisted the cap off the water. I'd always been good at pills. I don't even need water most of the time, but with this many I'd thought I might.

I sipped after each one, to help it slide down.

After, I brought the tray back to the White House. I went back to my room and tried to sleep.

I knew from my research that feeling sedated isn't what would happen, but I still had that image in my mind that the pills would knock me out. I wished I could have added sleeping pills, or allergy pills, but there really wasn't any way to get any, not without making people wonder and worry. *Especially Dora.* We had been friends forever, some years more than others. Dora would have noticed if my requests had become too complicated. Dora would have cared.

The doorbell buzzed. My whole body spasmed, but I forced myself to keep still. My window didn't look out the front, so I couldn't peek at who it was. If that person walked around the house, though, they could peek in and see me.

I slid down between my bed and the wall. The doorbell buzzed again. That meant that whoever-it-was was still at the front. I crawled out of my bedroom up to a dining room window and lifted one curtain corner. I couldn't see the porch itself, but Dora's bicycle was leaning up against it.

I welled up. *Dora. She came.* That's what a friend does. Briefly, I considered letting her in, telling her everything, and asking her to stay until it's over. We could giggle and gossip together, watch TV, make popcorn on the stove, play music. Dancing would tire me, wouldn't it? Dancing might make the drugs move through my system quicker, maybe? Then I would fall asleep, happy.

Steps clattered down the porch stairs. Dora was clearly annoyed. She seemed to be in a hurry. If she knew, she would never stay and let me do it. She would make phone calls and cry and try to make me sick up the pills.

I wanted to run after her, not to tell her but to make some excuse that I was nervous staying alone in the house and maybe Dora could sleep over? If the pills started working and I got weird or tired, I could just say that it was a headache again. I'd already laid the foundation for that. Dora might even have extra pills. I could go into the barn in the evening and in the morning, pretending to bring Ro meals. I could answer the phone when Mum called. None of them would know. None of them would stop me, and I wouldn't have to be alone. I could write a note in secret and put it in Dora's backpack for later, so that no one would blame Dora and so that she would understand.

I got up and unlocked the front door, two locks: the key lock and the bolt. I flung open the door, ready to chase Dora down the drive.

Dora's bicycle was still there.

My mouth went dry. *Is that a symptom?* I wondered, hoping that something might be working at last.

A flash of movement by the barn. That grinding squeak: the door being pulled open.

I knew what would happen next: Dora would find Ro. Dora would phone for help. Police and an ambulance would come. They would call Mum.

I felt suddenly queasy and faint, and didn't know if it was from the pills finally doing what they're supposed to, or from worry. What if I passed out in front of the paramedics? They would take me to hospital. They would test for things. They would probably pump my stomach.

Ro had warned me: waking up when she didn't intend to had been the worst feeling in the world. She'd told me that, to make me understand that it had to work this time. She'd clutched my wrists and squeezed, hard, begging. Ro had meant it only for herself, but I had understood it as a more general truth. Ro had looked terrified, and I had believed her.

I hauled the sliding barn door shut. I clicked the padlock. I ran back up to the house.

That's what I tell the police detective. It's not Dora's dad questioning me. I'm glad for that.

They brought me to the hospital from the concert hall, which is fine. It was too late to pump my stomach or use charcoal, so they've given me an IV of an antidote. It's too late for that too, but that's the last thing left. It only works for sure if it's given within eight hours of overdose, or helps at all within twenty-four hours at the most. I took the pills thirty-one hours ago. I've made it. It'll take about a week to finish, but no one can stop the process now.

My liver and maybe kidneys will eventually shut down. I'm starting to feel sleepy at last, which is part of this later stage. I looked it all up, before I even started asking for the pills. 'Confusion' is something else that's ahead, which is why I have to tell all this now, before that happens.

Mum didn't want to let me talk to the police, but I insisted. I said I would pull the IV out of my arm. I said I'd scream and make the doctors sedate me. I knew Mum wouldn't want to make me unconscious any faster than is going to happen on its own.

She gave in.

The Detective Inspector is recording me on a video camera. That reminds me: 'If you don't believe me,' I say, 'you can look at Mum's cameras.'

Mum, who's standing in the corner covering her face, shakes her head.

'Cameras?' the Inspector prompts. She's mostly small but hugely pregnant, and has a tone of voice that makes you think you have to do what she says.

Mum sighs. 'There aren't any cameras.' She spreads her hands out, empty.

'At the house,' I explain. I don't think there were any cameras in the barn. If they were in the barn, Mum would have got back sooner.

Mum's mouth is open and she's shaking her head back and forth. 'I told you that so you would behave. I told you that so you would live to the same standard as when I'm at home. I'm a single mother trying to raise a teenager and hold on to a job. There are no cameras.'

'There *are* cameras,' I tell the Inspector. 'She told me there were.'

'That's fine, Fiona. Thank you,' the Inspector says, in a different voice, not the police voice. I look at her to make sure it's her talking, that it's she who believes me.

'Did you write that down?' I ask. The policewoman doesn't even have a pen. I don't know why I ever believed she was police.

'We're recording you,' the woman reminds me, again in that gentle voice. Of course I forget that she's police when she uses that voice.

'I told you there are cameras,' I say to Mum.

'Thank you, Fiona,' says the Inspector. She gestures to the nurse who's standing near Mum.

'No!' I say. 'No, I'm not done!'

The nurse smoothes my sheets and says she has some more medicine for me.

'No! I need to talk to Dora.'

'I can give her a message, sweetie,' someone says. I think it's the Inspector, but I'm confused that she called me 'sweetie'.

'I told Mum that I needed to talk to Dora, too,' I say. 'She's coming. Mum said she is.'

'I can get her,' says that voice, too gentle to be police.

Another voice says, 'No. Not that girl.'

'She didn't know!' I insist. I'm trying to yell it, to make it cut through whatever back-and-forth they're having without me. 'Dora didn't do anything! I lied to her. I lied to her and I've got to tell her I'm sorry.'

Someone says: 'I'll tell her you said that.' The words float up to the ceiling.

I want to tell her myself, but for some reason that's not coming out of my mouth.

Dora looks beautiful.

'Thank you for giving me time,' is the first thing I say. I whisper it, so that it's just for Dora. 'I told the police that you never knew.'

'I didn't know,' Dora says, enunciating loudly. 'I didn't—'

A hand lands on her shoulder and stops her talking.

The lights are off everywhere, except for a light that Dora's brought with her, so it must be night inside the hospital. They must turn all the lights off so that I can sleep.

'I'm sorry I lied to you before,' I say. 'I didn't think you would have given me the pills if I told you. I didn't know. I should have trusted you.'

'I wouldn't have given them to you,' Dora agrees.

I look for the bracelet, but Dora is hugging her arms

around herself, clasping her wrists. I try to reach out, to pry Dora's fingers loose and peek under them, but my arm feels too heavy. It had been a sudden improvisation, tucking the bracelet into her bag at the concert hall. It had been *sorry*, *thank you*, and *goodbye* all in one.

Dora looks up. Both her parents are standing behind her. The light has swollen to include them.

'I'm sorry I scared you,' I say, but it's not enough. There are too many different things that that could mean, so I clarify. 'I'm sorry I locked you in. When you came to the house, I thought you would just go away, but then you went to the Red House and I knew you'd find Ro and . . . I needed more time. You would have called the police. I didn't know for sure when my symptoms would start to show. It hadn't been eight hours yet. I needed at least eight hours, at least . . .'

'You locked me in?' Dora says.

It's suddenly very bright, and crowded. Mum is here, and the pregnant Inspector, and nurses. I cover my eyes. 'I'm sorry I scared you.'

Dora's face looks all wrong, her eyes squished and her mouth twisted. She's angry. I've got to make it up to her.

'You'll get that builder out of trouble, right?' I say to the Inspector. The police will have to. It wasn't that man's fault. 'They told me that you thought it was him who locked the door,' I tell Dora. 'But they'll let him out of jail now. I promise.'

I fall back onto the pillow, but it doesn't catch me. My head just keeps falling down, down, down, and the rest of me follows in a spiral.

Dora didn't believe me at first that I'd never been to

Milton Keynes before. I knew about the shopping mall, of course, but Mum doesn't like crowded places. Dora knew a bus that went straight there and we caught it one day instead of going to school. The mall was huge and crazy, spread out flat over acres, instead of built upwards like something in London or America would have been. We barely bought anything, but we tried on clothes and split an expensive latte. When we had to rush back, I cried a little, just a stupid gasp and some eye-rubbing. Dora thought that I was scared of what Mum would say, even though she didn't know how bad it would be. But that wasn't it. I wasn't scared. I was happy. I loved that day. That's why Dora doesn't have to be sorry.

My favourite part had even happened before we got all the way there. 'Look!' I'd said, pointing out of the bus window at the warehouses along the road. They were painted gradations of blue on up until they precisely matched the shade of the sky at the top. 'How did they do that?' I'd wondered. 'How did they know that the sky would be exactly that blue?' They'd looked like they were evaporating away.

MORRIS KEENE

'What did she mean, she locked me in?' Dora asks.

She's looking down. Her ankles are crossed and tucked under her chair. Her shoulders are curled. She's trying to get smaller, and looks like she's disappearing right in front of me.

We're still in the hospital, in a waiting area. Dora just wants to be near Fiona. There's been talk about the chances of getting a matching liver for Fiona, or even just part of one. Rowena's been dead too long. Fiona's mother is the wrong blood type. Dora's a match but too young. She'd tried convincing the doctors, but they said no, rightly so. Any surgery can go wrong. We have to protect her from herself.

Gwen puts her arms around Dora's shoulders to rock her. Dora lets herself be nudged back and forth, back and forth, her neck hurting from it, because the motion comforts Gwen who says, 'Fiona wasn't in her right mind, sweetheart. Don't think about it.'

'If she locked me in, what was that man doing?'

'Don't think about it.'

Dora stiffens, resists the tidal movement of the embrace, and wriggles out of it. 'Stop it!' she says, loud enough that nurses' heads swivel towards us and purposeful footsteps pause. She holds still until the world resumes its normal spin, then repeats it in a whisper, 'Stop it, stop it, stop it.' Gwen touches her hand and Dora pulls her hand away. Gwen reaches again and Dora pushes against her chest.

Dora's face twists up and spurts tears like a squeezed sponge. 'I'm thinking about it whether you want me to or not! I'm thinking about it and I can't stop. If he didn't lock me in, he wasn't going to hurt me. If he wasn't going to hurt me, then I did it for nothing. I'm the bad one. *I* hurt *him*. Is he okay? Is he here? I have to tell him I'm sorry . . .'

She knows he's not. He didn't come out of the barn alive.

'Fiona said . . .' she tries.

I shake my head. 'Dora.'

I pull her up to standing, and she lets me. I don't rock, just squeeze in a kind of pulsing way. Dora cries, every breath pushing her shoulders up because I'm holding her too tight.

'Did I really think that that man was going to kill me?' she asks herself out loud.

'Shhh. Of course you did.'

'I wasn't sure he would kill me. I thought that maybe he'd . . .'

'That's enough,' I say, hard, with a full stop in my voice. I mean two things: Whatever she thought, that was enough to justify what she did, and what's she's saying out loud has to stop right there. 'It was self-defence. Even if he wasn't going to hurt you, it was self-defence *to you*.'

She covers her eyes. Whatever he intended in that barn, he has a terrible power over her now: in her mind, what she did is only 'good' if he was going to hurt her. Whether what she did is good or bad is out of her hands, depending only on him.

I push her hands off her face and hold her cheeks with my palms and make her look right at me, bending to get eye-to-eye. 'What you thought at the time is what counts. That's the only thing that counts . . .' I straighten, and look beyond her. Dora turns. We see Chloe. 'Listen, Dora, you need to not say anything else right now . . .'

Chloe's walking in that brisk way I used to walk when I had the same job. She's holding a phone to her ear and looking straight ahead. She passes, down the long, long hallway. The walking has a pounding rhythm that echoes off the hard walls: *ta-tum, ta-tum, ta-tum, ta-tum . . .*

I grab Dora's upper arm and pull. 'We're leaving.'

'What?' she says, pulling back.

'Dora, we need to leave. Now.' It's not the I'm-angry-at-you voice; it's the get-out-of-the-road-a-car's-coming voice.

The car is too fast, however, and in the form of Fiona's mother, spilling out into the corridor, apparently propelled by rage.

'You!' she says, aiming the word at Dora. Dora flinches as if the word's hit her in the back.

'I'm sorry,' Dora says as she turns, and I wish I could stop her. Apologising just gives Mrs Davies another rock to throw.

'She admits it!' Mrs Davies flings up her hands and

turns to take in all of the surprised, slack-mouthed looks around us.

Dora swallows. 'I didn't do anything,' she says. She adds, carefully, 'on purpose. I didn't do anything on purpose.'

'Come on, Dora,' I say.

'No! I won't come on. I didn't cover for Fiona. I—'

'Liar,' says the mother.

I put myself between them. 'Mrs Davies, we're leaving. We're very sorry for your loss.'

The pat acknowledgement of mourning triggers her. 'Fiona's not gone yet!' she howls. A young nurse at the desk calls security. An older nurse puts an arm around her and steers her towards the chairs.

We get into the lift to downstairs. The doors slide open to reveal the busy and bright food court and cheerful balloon-and-flower shop. Everyone eating or shopping there must have a reason to be sad, otherwise they wouldn't be in a hospital, but the colours force a pretence of optimism.

'Mrs Davies is in no state to be making accusations,' I assure Dora. 'Chloe will understand that.'

Dora swallows. 'I didn't know that Fiona had taken any pills! If I'd guessed I would have done something about it.' Her eyes are wet again. 'I thought she had at first, but—'

I pull her by the arm. 'In the car,' I hiss. 'Do you understand? Not in public.'

We get to the car. We get in. I don't start it.

'Dora?' Gwen prompts.

'Last night . . . Fiona woke up after you left the room. We talked a little. She didn't tell me anything! But I thought I'd figured it out. Rowena had been trying to die. I thought that Fiona had helped her with the pills. I was angry that she'd tricked me into giving them to her, and made me be part of it. I—'

'Stop. You gave her the pills?' I clarify.

Gwen looks like she might faint.

'For headaches! For PMS! She wasn't supposed to . . . to . . . *collect* them! I didn't know what she'd done until I found the empty packets in the barn, and then . . .' Dora breathed and swallowed and rubbed her head. 'I thought, well, she'd done it. To Rowena. And that she must have had a reason, a kind reason, because Fiona is kind. Last night I saw how messed up she was by it, how much it had taken out of her to do it. I knew she'd only been helping Ro to do what she wanted. So I told her, "I know what you did." I meant that I knew she'd given the pills to Grandma Ro. I didn't think she'd taken them herself! I mean, I . . . I *had* thought that, at rehearsal yesterday, which is why I went after her, but then I found Ro and . . .' Dora lifts her shoulders then lets them drop.

'But you didn't have anything directly to do with what happened to Rowena Davies,' I clarify. 'Yes? I need you to say yes, Dora.' *Whether it's true or not.*

'I didn't touch Grandma Ro! It had already happened when I got there! And if I'd known it was going to happen I would have tried to stop it.'

Good. That's the right thing to say. I start the car. 'Mrs Davies is understandably upset. Her ravings won't hold up, but we should stay away from her.'

Gwen latches on to one phrase. 'What do you mean, "hold up"? In court? Is that what you're saying? This is going to go to court?'

I brake, blocking the parking structure exit lane.

'It's not. Nothing bad is going to happen,' I declare, overriding any further speculation, at least the kind that's said out loud.

'If I'd told someone,' Dora says anyway. 'If we'd come to the hospital last night instead of today . . .'

'Dora, you have to stop. Please.'

She stops talking. I watch her in the rear-view mirror. I can tell she's still thinking. She's still accusing herself inside her head.

IMOGEN WRIGHT-LLEWELLYN

I don't feel pain, just pressure, my eyelids seemingly too heavy to open. Inside that darkness, I only remember flashes of decisions and consequences:

Push. Jump. Impact. Agony.

Black smoke had followed me out of the hole near the roof but, unlike me, it got to waft away. I'd only been able to fall. I'd forced myself to roll from the burning building, gibbering from pain. My femur had cracked inside my leg when I landed; when I let myself stop I saw that one sharp, ragged end had broken through my thigh. Time passed. Wind sheared a mist off from the firefighters' spray; it fell over me like a cool sheet.

It takes full minutes of adjustment now to register that the cool sheet over me here is a literal one. I'm in hospital, with oxygen tubes up my nose and my leg is suspended. It's darkish and quiet, so it must be evening or night. There's another bed in the room, occupied by a woman who appears to be sleeping or unconscious. I squint to see if I recognise the face. *No.* But the position is familiar: she's posed like the skeleton. I scan for a lump of baby in her lap, but of course there is none. I look for a rise in the chest. I pray that this other woman, whoever she is, isn't dead. I worry, briefly, that this isn't a ward, but the morgue.

Maxwell shocks me. He's suddenly at my other side, whispering, 'Im, it's all right. You're all right.' His words smell like old coffee. He pets my hair.

'Who is she?' I whisper, my eyes sliding towards the other bed.

It takes a moment for Maxwell to figure out who I'm talking about. 'Nothing to do with you. Nothing to do with the fire.' Hospitals are crowded, is all. There are a lot of hurt people in the world.

'Maxwell, he tried to kill me!'

'What? Who? The fire was an accident.'

'No. I'm not crazy. He passed me in his car.' A tear slips out over my lower lashes. 'I didn't want to have to tell you!' I wail.

The woman in the other bed turns over.

Maxwell grips my hands. 'Who tried to hurt you? Was it Patrick Bell?'

I turn my head. I feel guilty. 'No.' I flinch, and Maxwell turns to follow my gaze.

The Inspector's in the doorway. She recites the caution to me, precisely and dully. According to the law, I don't have to say anything, but if I'm going to use something as an excuse later, I'd better bring it up now.

Maxwell gets between me and her. 'I don't know what you're thinking, Inspector, but this is not appropriate.'

'I'm thinking that a building and a crime scene have been

recklessly destroyed for the sake of attention-seeking at best and criminal cover-up at worst. Ms Wright-Llewellyn, I urge you to explain yourself.'

I pull the sheet up to my chin. 'I haven't done anything.'

'You were trespassing,' the Inspector points out.

'I only came to see where my old house had been! Then I saw the . . . the bones.' I shiver. 'Why didn't you tell me?' I demand of Maxwell. 'You said a man died, but you didn't say anything about a baby!'

Maxwell stammers, claims he doesn't know anything about a baby.

'I saw the skeletons,' I spit. Then, sadness overtaking anger: 'Do you know who they are?'

The Inspector shakes her head. 'Not yet.'

'That poor family. The old woman's daughter – your student's mother,' I clarify to Maxwell – 'was kind to me once. I've remembered.'

'Morgan Davies?' asks the Inspector. 'You knew her?'

'Only briefly.'

'Last night you claimed you didn't know the Davies.'

'I said I *remembered*. Thick blond hair. Sunburnt shoulders. Masses of freckles. She let me brush her hair.'

'That's not Morgan Davies,' Maxwell says. The Inspector raises her eyebrow at him. He explains primly: 'I met her when she picked up her daughter from the concert hall. She has black hair and olive skin. And a sharp voice,' he adds ruefully. I remember now that he'd mentioned that parent; she'd cornered him with some 'concerns'. He'd described her as brittle and thin and sharp, not rounded and fair like the woman in my memory.

'She must have been a family friend, then. Just ask Mrs

Davies. Just ask her,' I insist, embarrassed at the belligerence in my own voice.

'When was this?' the Inspector wants to know.

'I don't know. I was . . . I was five?'

'Was this woman pregnant?' the Inspector asks.

'No!' I shout. My pulse speeds up. That woman couldn't be the skeleton in the grave, she couldn't. She'd been kind and warm and very much alive. She'd been so much more than bones.

Maxwell interrupts. 'Imogen's the victim here,' he reminds the Inspector. 'She could have been killed in that fire. She told me that she knows who's responsible. Imogen?'

I blink fast, but don't say anything.

The Inspector repeats from the caution: 'It may harm your defence if you do not mention, when questioned, something which you later rely on in court.'

'All right!' I say, struggling to sit up higher. The pillow is thin, and my leg is stuck. 'All right. Maxwell, I'm sorry. I need to say that first. I'm sorry.'

He's round-eyed with worry. That tells me everything I need to know about where we are as a couple. He thinks I'm going to hurt him. *He's right.*

'We were planning the wedding. We were inviting people. We were inviting *family*. Right? That's how weddings work.' I'm telling the Inspector, not Maxwell. I'm appealing to what I hope is a shared feminine view. 'Maxwell was only inviting his mother. It wasn't going to be fair if I was going to have my adopted family and my brothers – my older brothers – there for me. Maxwell needed more. He deserved more. His dad had left him when he was little, but people change. People regret.'

The Inspector says, 'I don't see how this—'

'Regret what?' Maxwell says at the same time, baffled.

I allow the words to fall out of my mouth. 'He had to regret losing you. I knew it. So I found his address. It wasn't so hard. I found it and I thought if I could just . . . tell him. Just remind him that you exist and that you love him . . .'

Maxwell is shaking his head and pinching his lips together.

'That's where I first saw the green car,' I tell the Inspector. 'Bright green. It's not a common colour. It was a four-door and . . . I don't know cars very well . . . but it was the same car today. I know it was.'

The Inspector leans closer. 'Where exactly did you see this car?'

'In front of his father's house.' I turn to Maxwell. 'I'm sorry, Max.'

'You went to my father's house?' He's stuck there, unable to move on to the green car and the accusation that comes with it.

'He didn't phone me back, so I went. I had work in Southampton and I thought . . . I thought that maybe he was embarrassed. Or had a wife who was erasing my messages. Sometimes that happens with my work. A client's girlfriend used to erase my messages because she thought I sounded pretty. That's what she said, "sounded pretty". But now I have my engagement ring. I wear it all the time, and it puts other women at ease.' I hold out my hand. White tape is wrapped around my finger.

The Inspector explains. 'They taped your ring for surgery. It's standard practice.'

I nod, slowly. I didn't realise – I just hadn't thought

215

about it – that my leg had been operated on. 'See, I always wear it. Even in the hospital. Even in a fire . . .' I squeeze Maxwell's hand.

'Inspector, I think you should leave,' he says.

'No! I need her help!' I protest. 'I think he's trying to kill me.'

'Who, Imogen?' the Inspector asks.

Maxwell overrides: 'Inspector, it's plain that she's delirious from the medication. It's unethical to continue questioning her right now.'

'She's not questioning me; she's going to protect me,' I insist, leaning forward. 'Aren't you?'

'Who's trying to hurt you, Imogen?' the Inspector asks. Maxwell throws his hands up in frustration.

Now that I've gone this far, I'm eager to get it all out. 'I confirmed who he was, and explained who I was. He let me in. He even gave me a drink. A glass of water,' I clarify, in case anyone mistakes a kind gesture for a pick-up. 'I noticed photographs all over the walls. Two little girls. His girls. Your sisters, Maxwell. You have baby sisters . . .' I wipe my cheek and keep going. 'I told him about you, but he said . . . He said that you're not his child; only his girls are his children. It was cruel of him and I hated him for it. I realised that you were right, and that you were lucky that he left all those years ago. He's a horrible person. I told him so, I just . . . I told him what I thought. I . . . I yelled at him and a woman came from upstairs wanting to know what was going on. She said that the baby was sleeping so I left. I'd taken a taxi there, so to leave I just ran. When I got tired, I walked. I was on a straight road then, so it's not like there was a blind curve. This green car came up behind me and sped up. I turned and saw it coming. I – This is going to sound crazy, but I knew it was coming for me. I just knew. So I jumped. I jumped into the road, because the green car was aiming for me on the pavement. And I can prove it was, because it jumped onto the kerb and went right into where I'd been standing just seconds before. I ran across the road and into an empty park. I heard the car drive off. The worst part was, I'd seen that car before, parked near his house. Near your father's house, Maxwell. I'm sorry. I'm so sorry.' I slump and fall back.

As the words had come out, I'd seen Occam's razor in the Inspector's eyes: the more obvious explanation is that the car had gone up onto the kerb to avoid hitting me after I'd jumped into the road. I need to express the certainty I'd had before I made any move, a certainty no doubt triggered by a hundred subtle observations too small to be consciously named. The car had aimed for me first. I'm sure of it.

'You think my father tried to run you down?' Maxwell asks carefully. 'Why?'

My voice cracks. 'He was angry with me. I should never have done it. Should never have forced his past onto him. That's why I didn't tell you, Maxwell. Because I deserved it. Not deserved to be hit by a car, but I deserved his anger. I deserve *your* anger. That's why I didn't tell you. But now . . .'

'Now, what?' demands the Inspector.

'I told you. I saw the green car again. In Caldecote. It tried to hit me, just like before. He's followed me! He must be the one who blocked the barn entrance and set the fire!'

'Ms Wright-Llewellyn . . .'

'You have to believe me! I wouldn't admit it if it weren't true! Maxwell hates me now. I wouldn't make the man I love hate me if I didn't have to to save my own life!'

Maxwell avoids my pleading eyes and speaks directly to the Inspector about me. 'Imogen's clearly not in her right mind. I insist that you leave.'

'I am in my right mind!' I raise my voice, futilely trying to force him to face me. 'This was two weeks ago, on my trip to that shipping company in Southampton. The Isle of Wight is just a ferry journey away.'

I can feel the energy in the room shift. It's the Inspector. It's as if her antennae have twitched.

'Wight?' the Inspector says through Maxwell's cross-armed attempt to block her. 'You're saying this happened on the Isle of Wight? Did you file a report with the police there?'

'Of course not. I didn't want Maxwell to know what I'd done.'

The Inspector nods once, as if confirming something to herself.

I reach out, wincing from the effort, but the Inspector has gone.

'Maxwell?' I say, unreasonably hopeful.

He hesitates.

I look at him through my lashes, but it doesn't work, not here, not in this antiseptic place, not using this bruised and rough version of myself.

He follows the Inspector out of the door.

CHLOE FROHMANN

Waste of my time, I seethe, refusing to look at my watch. I know from my body that I should be home. I should be asleep, but my day isn't done yet.

Maxwell Gant follows me down the hospital corridor, jogging to catch up. He puts a hand on my shoulder; my arm jerks up as I turn. He holds his palms up, as if surrendering. 'I'm sorry,' he says. 'Please. Let's talk.'

'There's nothing more to talk about,' I say.

He walks with me. 'Surely you've noticed Imogen's resemblance to Dora Keene. She was attacked on the Isle of Wight; she was attacked today in the barn. Yesterday, someone looking like her and where she was supposed to have been was locked in. Don't you see a pattern?'

I cock my head. 'You believe your father's after her? Really?'

'I don't know! I didn't even know he lived on the Isle of Wight. I don't care about him, and it's clear that he doesn't care about me. It's equally clear that someone – maybe the man my mother used to be married to, maybe not – is trying to hurt Imogen. You need to protect her.'

'Do I, Mr Gant?'

He steps back. 'Of course. You're the police.'

How trusting. I almost want to pat him on the head. 'I don't think you're aware of all the facts, Mr Gant. Would you like to be?'

'Of course,' he says, and I stop to face him.

I jump right in: 'The locking-in had nothing to do with Imogen. Nothing. That element of the case is closed.'

He swallows. 'All right. Fine. That doesn't discount—'

I hold up a second finger. 'Two, this is not the first time today that I've been told about the Isle of Wight. Yesterday, when we had hope that Patrick Bell may be a relevant witness, I had the IP addresses of his online communications traced. He first appeared online a fortnight ago, registering his email address from the Isle of Wight. This week, he posted from Cambridge.'

Maxwell claps his hands together, just once, in emphasis and triumph. 'That supports her story, then! Someone followed her from the island!'

'Someone? Why?'

He hangs his head. 'I don't know. I don't know the man. Who knows why he does anything?'

'I have no evidence that your father has journeyed from the Isle of Wight to Cambridge this past fortnight, but I know for certain someone else who has.'

His eyes are wide, earnest, inquisitive. 'Who?'

'Mr Gant, you can't be this naive.'

He blinks. He twigs. 'Imogen? Yes, obviously. And she was followed.'

'Or . . .'

'No.' He shakes his head.

'It's the simplest explanation.'

'I said no!'

'This Patrick Bell didn't exist online until recently. He's a created persona. Who do you think would do that? Who would know enough to do that? Your father? How? All this about being her lost brother, only Imogen knows that.'

'He does. Sebastian does.'

'And he only happened to appear online two weeks ago? Tell me, Mr Gant, did something happen recently to set this off? Some change that might have affected Imogen psychologically?'

His mouth hangs open. His breathing is shallow. 'Cambridge. We're moving to Cambridge. This is a – stressful change for Imogen.'

My head bobs in agreement. 'There you go. She does need protecting, Mr Gant, from herself.' I pull my phone out of my pocket and rise. 'We're no longer interested in finding Patrick Bell. Nor interested in you,' I tell him. 'You're free to return to London.' I don't include Imogen in this dispensation.

Maxwell stands to match me. 'Wait, Inspector, please . . . You may be right. If you are, it's my fault for having pushed this move on her. But what if Imogen's right? What if my father . . . I don't know why, but what if someone is trying to hurt her. The green car . . .' He trails off. He must know that there are green cars everywhere.

I don't go down that rabbit hole. 'The remains of the barn are being investigated for signs of arson. If Imogen was responsible for the fire, she will be arrested.'

221

'She didn't . . . She wasn't . . . If it wasn't an attack it was an accident. What benefit could she possibly get from trapping herself in a burning building?'

I sigh. 'Mr Gant, attention can be a powerful drug. Addicts will do anything for their fix.'

'You're wrong about her. You're wrong.'

'If I am, the evidence will demonstrate that. In the meantime, I have a meeting with the pathologist.' I put my phone to my ear in the universal gesture for 'conversation over'.

DORA KEENE

I finally fall asleep, but it doesn't last. There are quiet voices downstairs. I roll over. It's nice for once to wake up in the dark to something that's not an argument.

I would just leave Mum and Dad to it except that the woman's voice, I realise, is not Mum's.

My stomach twists. *I can't believe he's brought her here.*

I throw off my sheet and drop my legs over the side of the bed. I don't jump down, though. I don't want them to hear the floor creak under my feet. I listen.

It's just talking, *thank God*. I can't make out the words but can tell that it isn't . . . noises.

My shoulders shiver. There's that hot feeling in my stomach again. I clutch my middle and take a deep breath. I know that if I'm sick they'll make me go to the hospital. They're watching me for any sign that I've done the same as Fiona. They think it's contagious, like the fainting, two summers ago.

Footsteps. The tap. Is that the downstairs toilet? No –

it's the sink in the kitchen. That sounds like the kettle. He's making her a cup of tea. He's rattling the spoons in the drawer like he isn't worried about waking Mum. Then Mum says something about milk. That's just the one word I get – *milk* – or maybe I just think it's milk because that goes with tea. Mum's down there too. They're all three talking together.

There's only one thing I can guess the three of them would need to talk about, and they're trying to keep it from me.

I slide off the bed slowly, to land on the rug with just my toes, then my heels. The floor is carpeted everywhere, even the stairs, so careful steps get me halfway down without giving myself away. I sit, just at that point where the kitchen island is visible but the table isn't.

That's where the lights are on, over the kitchen table; I can tell from the diagonal shadows of the chair backs stretched long and pointy and sharp.

Mum is saying, 'We should make a list.'

Tears spring in my eyes. *I don't want a list.* Are they dividing things up? Will Dad just move out or will they sell the house? Will I still go to Hills Road? Is he going to marry her?

The other woman talks again, and I suddenly recognise the voice. It's not the blond-ponytailed jogger from the house on the other street. It's Chloe. I didn't even know that I'd been holding my breath. It just whooshes out of me and suddenly my head's between my knees, like if I was on a crashing plane. I breathe slowly, in and out, nose then mouth, to calm myself down. *It's Chloe.* They're not talking about a divorce; they're talking about Fiona.

'She's still alive,' Chloe says. 'She's been put on a

transplant list, but it's unlikely that she'll get a match in time. It's a matter of days.'

That seems to be the first item on the list Mum asked for. There's a pause. Mum's probably writing it down.

Number two: 'The man who died is called Erik Keats.' I cover my mouth. Of course he has a name but it's still a shock to hear it. 'He's dead from blunt-force trauma. His head hit the edge of a table as the mini-fridge that Dora pushed took him down. Dora honestly believed that he was a serious danger to her, and so it was self-defence. His innocence doesn't change that. But you should obtain legal advice. Do you understand that?'

Another pause. I imagine writing, and nodding. I'm nodding, too. I need to ask Chloe if he had family. I need to ask Chloe if he had kids. I need to—

'Fiona, in her confession, made it clear that she lied to Dora and that Dora did not know that she was supplying pills for a suicide. Dora honestly believed that Fiona needed them for monthly headaches. However, Fiona also stated her belief that Dora discovered her secret last night and covered for her. Those hours that Fiona eluded treatment were crucial, and the literal difference between life and death. Dora denies she knew. She claims to have believed that the pills had been given to Fiona's grandmother. I believe her, but others may not. Fiona's mother may pursue this. Again, you should obtain legal advice.'

Fiona had looked grateful in the hospital. Afterwards, I'd been sick in the ladies' toilet.

'Lastly, Maxwell Gant appears to be telling the truth about his reasons for being in the area. We have no reason at this time to suspect that he was purposely near Dora or Fiona, with or without their consent.'

'What about the cameras?' Mum asks. 'Fiona said that her mother had cameras. Can we see what's on them?'

I hug my legs. Mum wants to see if Mr Gant was in the barn with me before I was locked in. They want to know if I'm telling the truth about that. *Well, any cameras will tell the truth*.

'We're looking into it. Mrs Davies denies there being any cameras.'

'What about Jesse? What did she find behind the barn?' Dad asks her.

Chloe's answer is unexpectedly stilted: 'I've been assigned to train up and prepare Detective Sergeant Spencer for when I take maternity leave. We're working closely together and I must be careful with information. I need you to be careful with any information that I do share. Do you understand that?'

Dad must have agreed, because she tells him: 'There are two skeletons: a woman and a baby. Jensen has confirmed that they've been in the ground between twenty and forty years. Fiona's family has been in that house for at least two generations. It's interesting that Rowena was so desperate to die rather than move to a care home . . . Maybe she knew that the digging for the new houses would uncover the bodies.'

No, I scream in my mind. *No, that's not what Grandma Ro was afraid of*. Rowena didn't want to leave her house, the house she loved. Anyone can understand that. You don't have to be guarding a guilty secret to want to stay in your own home, your own bed. You don't have to feel

226

guilty to feel done with change, done with starting over.

But I remember the change in Ro, since her mind had fallen more and more into the past, mistaking Fiona for her daughter instead of her granddaughter, and mistaking me for . . . someone else, someone she warned not to come into the house. Ro had known me for years, well, had known me years ago, but hadn't recognised me. She'd become frantic when Fiona said my name.

Suddenly they're all at the front door, Mum and Dad and Chloe, murmuring thanks and jangling keys. Chloe is the one to notice me on the stairs. Mum and Dad follow her stare.

'What fire?' I ask. That's what Chloe was talking about as they walked through the dining room, something about a fire in the barn.

Mum and Dad freeze. Chloe swears.

'In Rowena's barn? Is everyone okay?' I demand, my voice rising. *What if there had been a fire when I was in there?* I start to shake. Mum runs up the steps and plops down next to me, arms squeezing the air out of me. Her physical touch is the end of my composure. 'I know he was trying to get me out. The man, I mean.' Erik Keats. *He has a name,* I remind myself. 'But Fiona told me that her mum said he was bad. She said he had a gun and looked in their windows. Do you think he really did? Maybe he was going to hurt me anyway?' My chin tilts up. I'm hopeful. If he had been going to hurt me, then what I did wasn't wrong.

'I don't know, Dora.' Chloe says. 'I'm sorry; I can't talk to you. Your mum and dad know what to do now. Everything's going to be all right.'

She means that probably I won't have to go to jail. But

Fiona is still going to die. Erik Keats is already dead. And others, too – a woman and a baby.

'Chloe!' I say, standing up. I almost knock Mum over, and standing on the step makes me taller than Dad. What I have isn't much, but I think I can help.

'The woman with the baby, buried in the garden. I might know her name.' That's what Rowena had reacted to. Not to my presence; Ro had smiled benignly at me, nodding. Then Fiona had reminded Ro of my name. Ro, in her sudden anxiety, had repeated it, or something like it, with increasing horror. 'Dora. Or Nora, or Laura,' I tell them, explaining why. I have their full attention, three faces aimed at me. 'I think her name sounds like mine.'

Everyone holds still, except for Chloe, who holds up the palm of her hand. 'Stop, Dora. You have to tell it to Spencer, not me. I can't help you.'

'I don't need your help! I'm the one trying to help *you*!'

'Chloe's right, Dora,' Dad says. 'Go back to bed.'

'No!' I shake off his arm. 'I can't sleep. I don't want to sleep. Fiona's *dying.*'

No one says anything. Fiona *is* dying. They can't deny that.

They're all afraid to upset me. A nurse had told Mum to keep an eye on me. They were worried about copycat suicide, 'Like in that Welsh town,' Mum had whispered to Dad, when she thought I wasn't awake. Then, later, 'What if she thinks she could force the doctors to use her liver? What if she tries to die to help her friend?'

Anger pushes acid up my throat. I'm not going to do anything like that, but no one believes me. They think that that's what a real friend would do. They're all watching me now, all three of them, that same way, as if I love my friend so much that I might give up my own life. They think that I'm that good but I'm not. I didn't even think about doing that until it was clear that that's what I was expected to try to do. I'm selfish. I want to live more than anything. That's why I killed that man, that man who wasn't doing anything. I want to live.

I make them listen, about Rowena reacting to my name. I add, 'You think Rowena knew about those skeletons, and that's why she wouldn't sell. That's why she wanted to die. Well, maybe she did know about them but that doesn't mean she hurt anyone.' An idea flashes: 'She was a midwife. Sometimes things go wrong with babies . . .' Chloe's belly becomes a sudden focal point.

'We know about Rowena's work,' Chloe says quietly.

I strain to recall things that Fiona once told me in passing. 'She worked at Hinchingbrooke,' I remember. 'Did you know that?' That's a hospital north of Caldecote; Addenbrooke's, where Fiona is, is south, in Cambridge, and better for livers. 'Rowena would never hurt anyone. What if she was *helping* someone?' I need it to be true.

'Dora . . .' Dad says.

I hit my fists against my thighs and shout: 'If you won't talk to me, ask Fiona. She'll know more than me anyway. Maybe things Rowena said . . .' I trail off. Fiona's mother has forbidden any further police questioning, or visitors of any kind. That afternoon had been the last of it.

Mum's hands land on my shoulders. 'Shhhh . . .' she says, turning me, guiding me up one step, then another.

Behind us, Dad sees Chloe out. I drag my feet, listening.

'Thanks, Keene,' Chloe says, changing tone. 'I've got to

speak with Morgan Davies, tell her about the fire. I went to see her earlier, but she was asleep in a chair. I left her messages that we need to talk. She's camped out at the hospital, so I'll find her there after I check in with Spencer in the morning.' Here Chloe turns her head, and the rest of her words get muffled. It doesn't matter; I've heard what I need to.

Tomorrow morning, Morgan Davies will be distracted. Perhaps Chloe will guide her to a private office, or at least to a cluster of chairs away from the room. That will be a chance for someone who understands the situation – who knows what needs doing – to talk to Fiona. Fiona maybe has secrets that she doesn't even realise matter, but they do matter, a lot.

If Rowena didn't mean to hurt anyone, but somehow did anyway, that's different from murder. I know that better than anyone. Rowena being dead herself doesn't make it stop mattering.

Mum tells me to sleep, but I'm not going to willingly close my eyes. Sleep will have to come and get me; I'm not turning myself in.

CHAPTER FOUR

MAXWELL GANT

The cool saltiness of the sea air hits me suddenly and hard. I've never been to the Isle of Wight before.

It's early morning, after driving late and sleeping poorly for a few hours in a cheap hotel. I drive up to the ferry dock, wait in the queue, then pull up at the ticket booth and roll my window down. I fill out the forms: car make, colour, registration. My signature, usually under control, veers off the line. An angled camera snaps a little shot of my registration plate. Driving onto the ferry, I marvel at what people have tied to their roofs and their bumpers: bicycles, boats, sun chairs.

I'd grown up in Durham. Now my mother lives in Exeter. Cathedral cities. The seaside is where you go for a visit, not where you live. I feel suddenly untethered, suddenly apart from real life, overwhelmed by an amalgam of childhood weekends and university summer breaks. Summer tourism is in full force around me. Salt, sweat, sand.

When I'd met Imogen in Spain, I'd assumed that our

friendship would run its course there and not follow us home. Realising that we both lived in London had been both thrilling and awkward. There'd been that worry that perhaps the other one doesn't want to continue and might cross the street to avoid you back in the real world. There'd been my wary, tentative admission that I'd like to see her again. Getting her London phone number had been a fully separate relationship step, a level beyond mere dates at the hotel cafe. For one thing, it meant she was really single, not just away with the girls for a week and flirting for fun.

Have I always doubted her, from the start? She's never lied to me, as far as I know, about anything. But I'd wondered then if she really had a boyfriend, or even a husband. I'd looked at her fingers, on which she'd worn a couple of silver rings that could have covered where a gold band had been. It was awful of me to have mentally speculated about her honesty, but it had seemed like a compliment at the time: *too good to be unattached*.

Now, here I am, at another beach, doubting her again. What the Inspector had suggested made sad sense. Why did Patrick Bell come into online existence a fortnight ago? If he were the real Sebastian, wouldn't he have an Internet footprint with much more history? If he's not the real Seb, who else would know enough to bother? Who would benefit from the story? Imogen. Imogen would, in a twisted way, if you think of drama and attention as benefits.

Certainly my father, even if everything Imogen's told about the encounter with him is plain truth, wouldn't have had the information for such a scam. If he'd gone after her, if he went up onto that kerb to hurt her, that wouldn't in any way lead to an Internet scheme based on her adoption and loss. Nor would it make sense for him to follow her to Cambridge. Lashing out in the immediate wake of her visit to him, sure. But something planned? If he had anger, if he had a motive to make the past go away, it would make better sense to go after me.

It's an odd feeling. I'm not scared. I'm . . . 'spoiling for a fight'. I've read that phrase before but never applied it to myself. This isn't just for Imogen's sake, to either track down her attacker or dismantle her manipulative fiction. For the first time in twenty years, I've let my childhood feelings catch up with me. I drop the brave face. Imogen was wrong to have come here behind my back, but she was also right about what would be good for me: I want to face my father.

I hadn't asked Imogen how she'd done it. 'Gant' is my mother's maiden name, which she took back after the divorce, and changed for me as well. Imogen hadn't known that, and hasn't ever asked me my original surname, so she must have got it from public records, or from my mother.

Glad I wasn't part of that conversation. Depending on when Imogen had asked, that could account for my mother's sudden dislike of her after we became engaged. She had transformed from doting approval of my theoretical girlfriend – described in brief emails and deliberately casual phone conversations – to intervention. I never told Imogen what was said. It had been an ugly conversation, held in secret while Imogen was at work. My mother and I had met up in London, at a cafe. She'd had her case well-prepared: Imogen's unstable background; Imogen's past relationships. Mum's job had prepared her well for snooping.

At least I know for sure that Imogen's obsession with her biological family is based in fact. My mother had confirmed it, but with a twist. Imogen's plot was correct: mother, father, brothers, car accident, adoption. But the mood she puts on it is off. Reports of the accident record that her father had been drunk that night. He'd caused it. The family in the other car had also been killed. Only Sebastian had survived.

According to my mother, it wasn't the first time that Joseph Llewellyn had been accused of drink-driving, but there's no record that alcohol had ever affected his work; his reputation as a surgeon was golden, except for one dismissed accusation from a nurse of what would nowadays be called sexual harassment. So his drinking was either covered up by the hospital, or it was something he saved for his free time. His family time.

Imogen idolises him. I don't know if she never knew, or just can't bear to remember any bad times.

Hypocrite, I remind myself. I'm as guilty of selective memory as she is, just the other way around. I've blocked out any good memories of my father.

I sweat. I'm dressed too formally, too warmly. I couldn't imagine knocking on my father's door in shorts and a T-shirt, so I'm in good trousers and an Oxford shirt. The cuffs are tight around my wrists. I'm not in the mood to bare any of myself.

I'd got the address the old-fashioned way: called an island library, asking them to look in their phone books. John Hutter wasn't alone; he was listed with a wife. Her name wasn't there, just the concept: 'Mr and Mrs John Hutter'. I had no assurance that this John Hutter was the one, just Imogen's assertion, presumably based on more thorough research.

I look up and down the street. No green car. 'Bright' green, Imogen had insisted. I put a hand on the weathered grey fence fronting scraggly grass. On the right, there's a closed garage, with a white SUV in front. I walk around the car and stand on tip-toe to look through one of the windows along the top of the garage door.

The clutter inside brings me back to the barn in Caldecote. No second car, just storage. Junk. The claustrophobia it prompts is almost overwhelming. I back away down the short drive.

I've never thought of myself as the kind of person to hoard resentment. I haven't thought about my father in years. That's a subject I'd always considered cleaned-out. I was sure my father had been metaphorically left at the kerb for collection long ago.

But now it seems that that isn't quite true. He'd only been put away in my mental garage, covered with a tarpaulin and forgotten. Grief and anger had been delayed, not got rid of.

A skinny orange cat winds around my feet. *Must be hungry*. Together we approach the front door. I ring the bell.

A flush from upstairs. A slam. I squirm. I turn away from the door, imagining the man or woman behind it to be in some state of disarray: pyjamas, hair uncombed, hands unwashed.

Across the street, a gaudy real estate sign catches my gaze: FOR SALE OR LEASE, PATRICK REMINGTON PROPERTIES. The company logo is a swinging silver bell, radiating motion lines, positioned between the first and last names.

Patrick.

Bell.

My phone rings. Pulling it makes it spring out of my pocket, and I have to catch it, bouncing it like a too-hot dinner roll. I answer without checking the number. 'Hello?'

'Maxwell!'

'Mum?'

Curtains are being pushed apart upstairs. The house is stirring.

'Did Imogen get the flowers? She hasn't thanked me.'

'What?'

Footsteps inside, coming down the stairs.

She sighs, then raises her voice. 'The flowers, Maxwell. I apologised!'

The contrast of kind words and belligerent tone forces a smile from me. 'Mum, I'm sorry. They must have arrived at the hotel while we were out. Things have been . . .'

The bolt is turned from the inside.

I blurt, 'I'm sorry, Mum. I'll call you back.' I ring off. I couldn't let her hear the man's voice, her ex-husband's voice. She would know it, instantly, wouldn't she. Like I will always know Imogen's voice, even over a phone, even in the background.

Just like I knew Marco, and Hercules . . .

I shake it off. I face the door, panicked. Whoever made up Patrick Bell could have once stood at this door, looking out. Was it this man, this sagging, powerless-looking man?

Or Imogen, in a hurry, upset. She'd run out of this door, embarrassed, her fantasy of my happy reunion shattered. Perhaps she was reminded of her own father, of her fantasy versus the reality she has to, on some level, still have within her. Did she need to create Patrick Bell, the wavering possibility of her lost brother, as an expression of her ambivalence over her past? As a way to manipulate the present?

Or does this estate agent advertise all over the island? All over the country? It could just be a coincidence. Lots of people are called Patrick. Lots of people have the name Bell. Why not both?

'What do you want?' says the man. He's balding on top; what hair he has is charcoal-coloured and close-cut. He's wearing belted shorts and a T-shirt, the exact combination that I've purposely avoided. I try to imagine this man married to my mother, wearing a dressing gown at breakfast, hairy legs sticking out underneath.

An irrational flash of disgust flares in me, along with a sudden insight: *Is this what my mother feels when she looks at Imogen?* Mum has been guilty of being overly attached to me, true, but haven't I been as guilty of it in return? We'd been a pair. For all that I've wanted a father all my life, did I ever really want a man to come live with us? Would I have liked having this man, this pathetic, scrawny man, sharing our one bathroom and scowling at her over petty arguments?

Forgiveness wells up in me, for all her faults. She'd been near my age now when she married. She'd been near Imogen's age when they divorced. She'd done her best.

'What do you want?' the man repeats.

'I don't know,' I admit. 'I don't know what I want.' Then, as the man starts to close the door, I put my hand out, palm first, as if to say *stop*. 'Please, Mr Hutter? I'm Maxwell Gant. May I come in?'

John Hutter leaves the door hanging open and walks

towards the lounge chair that's his obvious throne. I close the door carefully shut, and follow him.

Besides the framed photos that Imogen had described, the room is filled with seaside themed dust-catchers, like ceramic lighthouses and carved wooden birds. The pegs by the door drip baseball caps and floppy sun-hats. On the table with yesterday's post are a set of car keys and a smeared bottle of sunscreen. You could seal the house up in a black plastic bag and drop it anywhere in the world, into a rainforest or onto an ice floe, and it would still be a 'beach house'. That's the essence of the home, with or without the beach.

I lower myself onto a sand-beige cushion within a wicker sofa frame.

'Mr Hutter, a friend of mine came to see you about two weeks ago. Do you remember her?' I resist the urge to describe Imogen, or to offer her name. I want to keep myself from babbling.

'I remember a woman,' the man answers.

A clock in the room marks the hour with a bird call, something like *kck-kck-kree*. I jump, then say, 'She's my fiancée. She was hoping you would come to our wedding.' I squeeze my eyes shut and wobble my head. 'I'm not even sure you're the right person.' It comes out with a laugh at the end. 'Imogen – that's my fiancée – she's looking for my father.'

'That's what she told me.'

'She said that you said you don't have a son.'

The man leans back in his chair, and turns his head to the corner. The wallpaper pattern is made up of little bird footprints, blue on white. 'I know what I said. Then Jackie – that's my wife – joined us and there were . . . misunderstandings.'

'Misunderstandings?'

'Jackie hasn't been the same, physically, since our second daughter was born. I tell her I don't mind, but . . .' His shoulders go up, down. 'A woman doesn't want to hear that you 'don't mind' her body. They're looking for something more flattering. That's a tip.'

'Thank you,' I say, automatically, floating wherever the conversational current pushes. Jackie is in some of the photos, always with a child or two in front of her, hiding her hips.

'Jackie made things unpleasant, so the woman left. Isabelle, is it?'

'Imogen.'

'Imogen. She left.'

'Did you go after her?' I ask, direct for the first time this whole conversation.

'No. Why would I? I was glad it was over. Except for Jackie's grumbling.'

I'm not sure what Jackie was on about. Did she hate that Imogen was digging into her husband's past, or just hate that Imogen's bodily perfection was in her husband's line of sight? It crosses my mind: Jackie's not here right now. Maybe she's out in her car. Maybe her car's bright green . . . *Imogen complained that Patrick Bell never called on the phone. What if that's because 'Patrick Bell' is a woman?*

'Now you show up,' the man adds.

'Sorry, I'm not sure exactly where things stand. Are you John Hutter, once married to Muriel Gant?' *And don't you count your son?*

The man scratches the back of his sunburnt neck. 'I told that woman the truth. I never had a son. But if you're asking if I was married to Muriel . . . Well, that's eight years I'd like back. I put up with Jackie now because I know what real crazy is.'

I skip a breath. 'You *are* John Hutter? Muriel's ex-husband? I'm pretty sure that makes you my father.' Even as I say it, other possibilities jump out at me, most obviously adultery. Just because I'm Muriel's doesn't make me her husband's too.

The man's quick to answer back, with magnified sarcasm: 'I'm pretty sure your name's not Maxwell, then. Unless the bitch changed it. She could have done it, too. She never liked the name you came with.'

I picture my baby self in a doll box; on a store shelf; on a catalogue page. Anything to put off the obvious image that's trying to form in my mind. My breath comes out in strange sudden bursts that someone might mistake for laughing. 'What name is that?' I ask, socially, jovially, and the question is on the loose with no hope of grabbing it back.

MORRIS KEENE

'No.'

I've said it too loudly. Gwen shushes me. We don't want Dora to hear. She's still upstairs, sleeping.

I face the wall. My bad hand is quivering; it does that when I get tense, something to do with my shoulder and the way I compensate, not the original injury. I say it again: 'No.'

Gwen is seated, looking intently at the soggy teabag at the bottom of her cup. 'I've decided, Morris. I have an appointment scheduled for today.' She's whispering. We're listening for Dora, but that works in both directions: Dora can hear us. Earlier, we'd used the boiling of the kettle to cover our words. Now, the sink tap.

'No,' I repeat. 'Horrible to lose a friend, but I won't allow her to lose her mother.'

'*"Allow"*?' Gwen says, turning in her chair.

'What did the doctor say to you? It's not right if he manipulated your emotions.'

'Of course not!' Apparently, the doctor had been eager, but 'not inappropriately so', Gwen insists. She'd taken him aside and volunteered her matching blood type; he'd looked her up and down to declare her roughly Fiona's size. Those two, plus determined willingness, are the three most important factors of a match. 'He wants to find a way,' she concludes. 'We all do. Don't we?'

I shake my head. 'No, no, no, Gwen. Don't try that on me. Wanting something doesn't mean I'm willing to pay for it. What if something happens to you? Something now, during the operation, or years from now, from some complication. I'm sorry. I just can't.'

She says quietly, so quietly that the rush of the water almost hides it from me, 'It's not up to you.'

I close my eyes. 'I know it's not. I'm begging you. Please don't. It's dangerous. It's noble and all, but what if . . . ?'

'It's not noble!' she hisses. 'It's not for Fiona. It's not for her mother. I'm doing this for Dora. She's been mixed up in a horrible thing against her will and if I can make it any less horrible, I will. She feels guilty. She thinks she's partly responsible for her friend dying. She will carry that for the rest of her life. If I can take that load off her, I will.'

The washing-up bowl in the sink is filling. Cups float and bob; water glides over the edge. I splay my hand on the water surface, feeling it push up against me, and push gently back. 'Gwen, I can't do without you. Dora can't do without you. We can't risk losing you. Please.'

She joins me at the sink, stands behind me, wraps her arms around my waist. She rests her head on my back. 'It's a little risk. A little one,' she assures me. 'I want to. I can give this to her, Morris. I can give Dora some relief.'

I turn inside her embrace, squeeze her in return. My hands make the back of her blouse wet.

We're both different now, from when we started out. We've both lost our former jobs, Gwen to Dora growing up and me to my hand. *No, not my hand*, I remind myself. The post-traumatic stress is more to blame than the physical injury.

Young me had fallen in love with young Gwen. Now older – not 'old'; I spare us that insult – older Morris and older Gwen need to meet each other, get to know each other, and love each other all over again. My end is easy; she's got the harder job, trying to see something, anything, still in me.

She rubs her forehead against my chest. 'If they find me to be an acceptable candidate, they'll need to do it quickly. Today. The doctor had been urgent about that. Fiona isn't going to last much longer.'

I nod, slowly, my chin tapping the top of her head.

She pulls back, and grips my shoulders: 'We won't tell Dora. I don't want her to get her hopes up. I may not be acceptable.' This is the second time she's used that word.

'You're acceptable. You're perfect. There will be no complications. I need you to stay safe.'

'I know how you feel. I was married to a policeman, remember?' She means it as a gentle joke, but it punches me in the gut.

'Now what are you married to?' I forget to keep my voice down. The drain must be blocked; water slides over the top of the sink. I push her away as it slops onto the floor. I turn off the tap and slap my soaked trousers.

Dora's watching. We'd had no warning; she must have

floated down the stairs. She'd heard the last thing I'd said, and seen me push Gwen away. I try to reassure her with a hug; I'm wet, though, and she steps back from me.

Jesse barks. She's outside; must be a bird. The kitchen timer brays. It wasn't even supposed to be on. The room feels electric from Dora's entrance, from her tension, and from the reaction she provokes in us, her skittish parents.

'Dora, sweetheart, I have to go out. Look after your father.' Kiss on her head; tousle of hair. That used to be a joke, which is why Gwen said it, reflexively.

I wince.

'We get to spend the day together,' I announce to Dora cheerfully. We both hear the garage door open. Gwen's on her way out. 'She's interviewing solicitors,' I fabricate, to forestall any questions, but that is something that we'll need to do, and soon. Things could move quickly, especially if Fiona dies. *That's another gift to our daughter,* I realise. *If Gwen saves Fiona, Morgan Davies may let go of her grief-fuelled accusations.* I wish I could be the one to cut out an organ and spare Dora. My blood isn't a match, though, so Gwen gets to be the lamb.

Dora says nothing. She sits at the counter and pours yellow flakes into a bowl.

'Milk?' I offer, bending to get it from the fridge.

Dora shakes her head. She doesn't bother with a spoon, either. She reaches in with two fingers and feeds herself one bite at a time. 'I want to go to the hospital,' she says.

'Are you ill?' I ask first, instinctively. 'Have you taken something?'

She shoots me a perfect teenage glare. 'No. I want to be near Fiona.'

My second worry is that she's heard more than we realised and that she knows that that's where Gwen is going. 'I don't think that that's a good idea. Mrs Davies—'

'This is all Mrs Davies' fault! If she hadn't been horrible, if she hadn't put up cameras and bars and forbidden Fiona to walk or shop or ride her bike, then it wouldn't be like this.'

Or would it? Dora doesn't know for sure why Fiona did it to herself. Maybe she did it just because helping Rowena, as kind as it had been, was too much to bear. 'Let's do something distracting,' I offer, 'far away from hospitals. Anything you like.'

'I'd *like* to go to Addenbrooke's Hospital,' she says slowly, as if I'm dull. At this age, it's not like I can say 'Legoland' or 'London' and make it all better.

The water is still all over the floor. I unwind an entire roll of paper towels, not wiping, just laying them in long, overlapping rows, like bricks. My face is just at the height of Dora's dangling feet as they twist round the legs of the barstool.

I give in.

I delay enough that Gwen will be already ensconced in an MRI machine or laid out on a table with electrocardiogram wires taped to her chest, somewhere deep in the building. I steer Dora straight through the front doors to the food court. I buy drinks.

'Are you and Mum getting divorced?' she asks, as I place the cups on the table.

I spill my Coke. It spreads out all over the table, and we have to push our chairs back, and sop it up with tiny napkins. When we've done our best, we move sideways to a new table, and I answer her. 'No! That's crazy. What made you think that?'

'Isn't that why she's seeing a solicitor?'

I almost say, *'What solicitor?'* 'No,' I actually say, 'We need a solicitor for you. Just in case,' I add, seeing her go pale.

She nods. She sips. 'Dad, what's it like to be arrested?'

I groan. 'No, sweetheart, we don't need to talk about that.' I've arrested people, bad people. I've arrested people who beat people, people who killed people who had begged to live.

'We might need to talk about that.'

She's right. 'If it happens, I'll be next to you. They'll caution you. You know that, right?'

'That's when I'm told that I don't have to talk, but if I have a good reason for what I did, I shouldn't withhold it.'

That's an interesting way to phrase it. 'Did you have a good reason?' I ask, quickly, as if I might trick her into letting something new out.

She wrinkles her nose, disgusted, indignant. 'You think I did something?'

'I don't think you did anything,' I backpedal.

She keeps pushing: 'Then why were you asking?'

'You said "have a good reason". That's not quite what's in the caution. It's what the caution can effectively refer to, in certain circumstances, and I just wondered if maybe this was . . . one of those circumstances.' I shake my head. 'I'm sorry, sweetheart. This is the thing you have to understand about parents. You can say anything to me. I know that you think that it's the worst insult in the world that I've just asked you if you lied, but . . . you're allowed to have lied to

248

me. You can lie to me and you're still my daughter, forever. You can tell me that you were meeting your teacher in that barn, or that you helped Fiona on purpose, and none of that will change that you're my daughter. Teenagers lie sometimes, and do other things.' I shrug. 'So maybe you lied. It's a question. It's just a question. It's not a . . .' I consider various words. 'It's not a *test*.'

She's nodding along with all of it, and wiping her nose. 'I haven't lied about anything. But I'll tell you if I do. If I lie to you, I'll tell you, I promise.' She laughs, and snorts, and blows her nose in one of the little napkins. Then, 'Do you ever lie to me?'

My nodding and smiling freezes. 'What? No.' *It's not a lie that you don't tell a child everything. There are things that they don't need to know. That's not lying.*

'Do you lie to Mum?' Her eyes are steady on me.

I don't hesitate. 'No. I don't lie to Gwen.'

'I know you go to that woman's house sometimes. When you walk Jesse.' Dora stirs her Fanta with a straw. 'Do you tell Mum that?'

I lean back in my chair, hands behind my head, elbows out, eyes up to the ceiling. Amazing, all those pipes and ducts that must slither around up there, between floors. 'Aw, Dora. You got me. It's not what you think.'

Dora looks hot in the face. 'Does Mum know?'

'No. No.' Now my hands are on the table again, fiddling with a napkin that has my full attention. 'Dora, I'll tell you a secret.'

She shakes her head. 'I don't want any secrets.'

'All right, not a secret. We'll tell Mum later, together. We'll *show* her.'

'Show her what?'

'It's a good thing. Dora . . .' But I see someone behind her, and don't finish.

Dora turns. It's Chloe, and her new partner. They've come in through the big revolving front door. From the lift they choose, they're apparently heading for Fiona's room.

'Dad, I promised I wouldn't lie. I have to see Fiona. Chloe's taking Mrs Davies somewhere to talk, and I could just—'

'No.'

Dora stands. 'I was going to tell you that I needed the toilet and just go. But I said I wouldn't lie so now I've told you what I need to do. Don't stop me just because I've told you the truth.' She says it all in one breath. 'Truth' comes out in a whistly squeak.

I wrap my good hand around her wrist. 'Sit down, Dora.'

She wrenches her arm away. 'Don't grab me!'

Heads are turning. I let go. 'Please sit down,' I say carefully.

She sits. 'Fiona is dying,' she hisses. 'She's going to die thinking her grandmother was a murderer who lied to her and used her. Her mother's no help. She's angry enough to blame Rowena for anything, without any understanding of what that's doing to Fiona. I need to tell her the truth – that Rowena was maybe trying to help somebody, not hurt them – and Fiona can help prove that. If we can find out who the woman was, and why she was there . . . A pregnant woman with a midwife, isn't it obvious? Fiona will want to help. What she remembers could fix everything.'

Those last two words linger. The amount of

250

'everything' that can be fixed by solving an old crime is actually fairly small.

Dora figures that out herself and amends her assertion: 'Feeling like you've done something bad is awful. I know, because that's how I feel. If you could prove that Erik Keats was a bad man who was actually going to hurt me, wouldn't you do it? Wouldn't you do anything to take away that I killed an innocent person who was only trying to help? That's guilt, Dad. It's the worst thing in the world. It's heavy and awful and I feel like I can't even breathe through it, that's how thick it is. I want to take it off Rowena. I want to take it off Fiona.'

She doesn't add herself to the list, but her desperate eyes put her on there. She stands to go, but I press my hand on hers and ask her to wait. 'Just wait, a minute, please. I need to tell you something.'

She sits.

I cough. I rub my face. 'Your mother and I don't lie to you, but sometimes we don't tell you everything. That's as it should be. That's how parenting works, though you're old enough now that there's less that we're supposed to keep from you.'

Her arms are folded across her chest and she's half turned, but listening.

'Time may not be running out the way you think. If Fiona lives, then you'll have all the time in the world to tell her the truth, to get at her memories, to help change how she sees what she did. If that were true, then we could go home, right? We could sidestep Morgan Davies today, a day when it isn't reasonable to expect her to cope, a day when she is understandably lashing out at everyone who was near her daughter when she did what she did. You want to protect Fiona, I understand that. I need to protect you. Do you understand that?'

'The last person who tried to protect me ended up dead. You're sure you want to give it a go?' she spits. 'Maybe Erik Keats was somebody's dad. Is he? Do you know? Did Chloe tell you? Did he have a wife, or a best friend, or a dog who hasn't eaten in days because Erik Keats is dead now, because I killed him?'

You would think that in a hospital the sounds of crying or arguing or struggling wouldn't stand out the way that they do everywhere else, because surely people in hospitals share the pain of sickness and imminent loss. But every person in this room must have been a doctor or a nurse or a visitor to someone with a new baby, because no one seemed to understand that being in a hospital means that you are either sick or dying or that someone you love is sick or dying, and that it is perfectly reasonable to cry and argue and struggle and push the table hard at your dad. No, everyone in this room turns to look at me and Dora, and she covers her face and adds that table-shove to the list of her sins. 'Besides,' she says. 'Your "what if" is bullshit, because Fiona *is* dying, and we can't stop it.'

My voice is an urgent staccato: 'Your mother isn't seeing a solicitor. She's here. She's having some tests done to see if she's a good match for Fiona. They can take a part of her liver and share it. Fiona may survive, Dora.' I offer this with a smile. It's good news.

Dora recoils, as if I've hit her in the face. 'Mum? She's here?'

I nod. 'She's doing this for you, Dora.' That's a step too

far. There can be too much truth, the same as even water can kill if you push enough of it into somebody.

'No! Where is she?' Dora stands, swivelling her head, as if she can find her mother just by looking. 'She can't do this.'

'It's safe, Dora,' I assure her, bailing away truth in buckets and throwing it over the side. 'She'll be fine.' *Probably.* All surgery has risks. Anaesthesia always has the chance of its target not waking up. You have only one liver; what if something goes wrong?

'You only say that because you don't care!'

I stand to match her, taller, louder: 'I do care, and that's why we're leaving, now, just you and me.'

This time, among the turned heads and unblinking eyes, are three new faces: Chloe's, Morgan Davies', and DS Spencer's, over steaming paper cups and a tray of plastic-wrapped sandwiches.

I pull Dora by the arm. My grip on her elbow squeezes her sleeve and pulls it up.

It's a funny thing about revelation: Something in plain sight is easily missed, one of too many other obvious things; something in the exact same place, hidden and then revealed, is spotlighted somehow. The weather's been too hot for long sleeves, but Dora had pulled a thin cotton cardigan over her shirt this morning, seeming to hide in it. The cuffs are meant to be folded over, but she had left them extended, creeping up to her knuckles. When I grabbed her arm, the sleeve was pulled up, and a bracelet popped out. It dangles on her wrist, dancing there, jolted.

Morgan Davies surges forward, Chloe and Spencer a step behind. She points. Rage has stretched her reach.

'That's my mother's,' she says.

She scrabbles at Dora's arm, which makes Dora scream and push. Hospital security appears and Chloe holds them off with her warrant card while Spencer pitches himself between the two. Dora flings herself at her me, sobbing, while Spencer holds Morgan Davies back.

'That's my mother's bracelet,' Morgan claims. 'I knew you were in on it. You've taken her jewellery.'

'Fiona gave this to me,' Dora says, quivering.

'It's not hers to give! It belonged to my mother. Where's the rest of her jewellery? She kept it in a velvet bag in an embossed tin box. What have you done?'

'I don't have it! I don't have anything!'

'I asked Rowena for her garnet ring and earrings, and she wouldn't give them to me. She wouldn't even let me look at them. She chased me out. Do you understand that this bracelet is not yours? It's not yours. She could keep it from me, all of it, but you don't have that right.'

I feel Dora become heavy against me, and hold her up. 'Mrs Davies, we're going home. Here . . .' I want to pull the bracelet off of Dora's wrist, but my good hand is around her waist. All I can do is hold out Dora's arm, which she limply allows, and Chloe pulls the bracelet off for her. Dora's arm drops, and she howls into my chest.

'Is this your mother's bracelet, Mrs Davies?' Chloe asks, in her official voice.

'Yes. I told you.' Morgan Davies snatches it, holding it against her palm with folded fingers.

Something snaps inside of Dora. 'You think everything is my fault, because I'm a "bad influence". Did you ever think that maybe Fiona's a bad influence on me? She's the one who started all this, and she did it because of you. You refused to help her, or to help Rowena. They couldn't go to you for anything, except for rules and decisions that had nothing to do with how they felt. She gave it' – the bracelet – 'to me, because we're friends. That means that we listen to each other, even if we don't always understand. You want it? Fine! Keep it. The friendship is still mine. I don't need a stupid bracelet.'

'Dora, come on,' I say, my dead hand on her back.

Morgan Davies bellows, 'Are you just going to let her go?' People are staring. A security officer looms; Chloe waves to him to keep his distance. 'My mother was murdered, and the accomplice was caught with stolen property. If you won't do something about it, I'll call 999 and get it done myself.'

Chloe steps between them. 'DS Spencer will take Dora to Parkside station for questioning,' she offers. 'Dora, you can make a statement about how you obtained the bracelet. All right?' She turns towards Mrs Davies. 'All right?'

'She should be arrested,' Fiona's mother insists.

'DS Spencer will conduct a thorough investigation and will do as his good judgement and the law require,' Chloe assures us all.

She doesn't meet my eyes. I step in front of her to make her look at me. 'Morris,' she says, and nothing more. She doesn't have to. I understand; I just hate it. Chloe can't let herself deal personally with an accusation against Dora. Spencer's never worked with me, so he's the right one for this job.

I offer to drive Dora to Parkside myself, but Spencer insists that she go in his car. I'm allowed to accompany her.

We each sit by a window, the middle seat empty between us.

From the front, Spencer recites, 'You don't have to say anything, but it may harm your defence if you don't mention when questioned something which you later rely on in court. Anything you do say may be given in evidence.'

The car speeds down Hills Road. It's a long, straight line from the hospital to Parker's Piece, which has the police station at one of its corners. At every roundabout, the car has the chance to turn. At every roundabout, Spencer pushes onward.

'Say nothing,' I warn Dora.

I pull out my phone. I'm about to dial Gwen, but of course she'll be unable to answer. The image of her in a solicitor's office, mobile to hand, is as vivid in my mind as the truth of her inside an MRI tube, on an operating table, in a hospital bed.

This is what it must be like for Morgan Davies, I think. *She's wrong, but she doesn't know it.* She didn't witness any of it, so any lies she imagines are just as vivid as the truth would be. She's certain she's right. She's going to push against Dora as hard as she can.

'Call Mum,' Dora says, without looking at me. She stares out her window.

I pocket my mobile. 'Her phone's off.'

'I want her to meet us at the police station.'

'She'll call me when she can. She'll come as soon as she's able.'

'I want her now!' Dora demands. 'She shouldn't be doing this. I hate Fiona. This is all her fault. She should just go and die if dying is so important to her.'

'You don't mean that.'

256

'I do. I do mean it. I hate her for this.'

'Fine. You hate her. You also care about her.'

Dora closes her eyes. 'I hated the way she got clingy at school. I hated the way that she always got to be the depressed one, the sensitive one, the one to be tiptoed around. I hated that I had to stay friends with her even when I was frustrated with her, because we'd been friends since we were seven and unless we had a real fight I couldn't just stop. I hated that going to Milton Keynes was such a big thing for her when I just wanted it to be a fun day, a day that wasn't big at all. I hated that her mother ruined it, and made me feel bad about it. I've hated her for forever, for just as long as I've liked her, and needed her, and tried to reassure her. Everything that makes me feel special has always made her jealous, and so made me feel guilty instead of proud. She ruined it. And now she's . . .'

Dora lets the tears out, to run all over her cheeks. 'I'm a bad person,' she says dully.

I don't deny it. If I tried, she would counter with confession of all her pettiness, meanness, selfishness. She would try to prove me wrong. Instead, I say, 'And, you're a good person, too.'

Dora chokes on a sob. Our two hands meet in the middle seat and twist together.

The car bounces as it enters the car park round the back of the police station.

MAXWELL GANT

The ferry moves forward but not fast enough for me. I pace beside the rail. There's room to do so because a misty rain has settled in, driving most passengers into the covered area where a queue for coffee and tea snakes slowly.

I feel acid climb my throat. Just the occasional waft of muffin smell blown towards me makes me lean over the side, lips pressed shut, nostrils flaring in a controlled exhale.

When I'm able to trust myself upright, I straighten, but remain near the side.

I've never seen a photo of my father before meeting the man today. There aren't any photos of my babyhood, full stop. My mother had always explained it this way: that before my dad left he threw them away. That's how awful he was. That's how hateful. He put them out on collection day, just as the bin lorry rumbled towards the house, so that she didn't even have the chance to throw herself into the rubbish bin and pick them out one by one, which she would have done, she swears.

Now I know that she'd never had photos of my babyhood, because my babyhood hadn't been with her.

It had been with Imogen, my sister.

This time I can't stop it. I lean, my cheeks balloon, then I let my lips pop. I cough it all out. I choke as I try to breathe in. I cough again.

I was adopted at age three. My name had been Sebastian. She never told me. She somehow changed my first name without leaving an obvious record, probably when we switched together to her maiden name after her husband left. It might have been easy; she'd worked for the county clerk. It had been the early days of the transition from paper to digital records. She was clever, always has been. A bureaucracy savant.

'Why didn't you tell me?' I ask out loud, grateful for the engine sounds overwhelming my voice. It's as if she's in my head. Her answer is plain to me: *Because of this. I wanted to spare you this.*

I shake my head. She could have spared me everything, if only I'd known from the start. I could have been reunited with a sister in Spain, instead of becoming paired with a lover. Now both options are dead. Imogen and I can't be together, not in any way. It's too shameful. I don't know how to tell her. I'll have to ensure that she's near trusted friends when I do, friends who'll be able to touch her and embrace her in a way I can never, ever do again, not even to say goodbye.

If she needs telling.

I hate the thought and wave my hand in front of my face to bat it away. She couldn't, knowingly, have done this. My father had confirmed that he hadn't got as far as telling her.

Except that she did know, she'd known for a year. The DNA test will have told her.

I run my fingers through my wild hair. I must look a mess. The rain has stopped and passengers are joining me on deck to watch the ferry dock. The sun is still morning-low but already the air is too warm. I feel pressed down by it.

Was Imogen going to tell me? I wonder. *That day when she waited for me at rehearsal, after she'd got the DNA test results. Did she come to tell me one kind of good news, and at the last minute just let me believe another kind instead?*

It's time to go below, get into my car. I'm not sure I'm fit to drive. I should have taken the train, like she had when she came here just . . . *Was it really only two weeks ago?* There's all the difference in the world between riding and driving, between rest and responsibility. She's been doing everything she can to make herself a victim, buffeted. I'm left with the decisions and actions.

If she wants to leave it to me, fine. I'll make a decision. I mentally calculate the route back to our London flat.

I drive off the ferry, slowly, too slowly, stuck behind too long a queue. I itch to pound the car horn. Flexing, unflexing my fingers. As soon as the road widens, I pass, then continue to accelerate.

If Imogen knows, which she must, I think. *If she knows, and my mother knew, did they know each other knew? Did they lie to me together, or separately?*

I drive straight over a roundabout, without looking. If another car had been coming I could have been killed. *Or killed someone else, like Imogen's father did.*

I'm panting. It's too Byzantine. I'm not an heir or a star.

I'm no-one's fulcrum. Why would these two women care so much to keep being my mother and my wife that they'll go to such lengths to cover who I really am? Then I realise that it's got nothing to do with me now, with the adult me. It's who I was as a baby that matters. I was, in a way, to each of them, their baby.

I pull over and tug on the hand brake. I flick on the hazard lights.

If Imogen knows, I see how she might have been driven to invent Patrick Bell, to create a Sebastian 'out there', a potentially real Sebastian to continue to pretend to hope for and talk about, apart from me.

But why did Imogen go to see my father then? He could only expose it. Why not leave him be?

It's this one ill-fitting detail, this one doubt, that calms me enough to get to London at a safe pace, hovering just over the speed limit. I can imagine all these things, but I can't know, not for sure, until I've confronted her.

There's a parking spot right in front of our building, and I pull in. This serendipity should bode well, but instead I feel paranoid, wondering who may have just pulled away. Empty parking in London doesn't last long. *Could Imogen be out of hospital? Has she beaten me to it, and emptied our flat of her things before I get this chance to empty it of mine?* There's no chance that I'll stay a night here ever again, even if she moves out. Not in our bed, anyway. I'll sleep on the sofa if I have to, while I get a new place, a new start. I have to move. Anywhere. Teach English in some other country, like a teenager on a gap year? *No, no teaching.*

Something. Work at a shop. Sell computers or clothes.

Compose music at night. I've been working on a new setting of a hymn for St Catharine's, but of course that chance is gone now.

I plod heavily up to our second floor home. I rattle the keys in my hand, fanning them out across my palm, and pluck the right one up.

The key turns, but the door resists. I push harder. A stack beyond gives, and the door pushes over it, shoving envelopes and curling magazines. I'm reminded of the stuffed barn in Highfields Caldecote. The temptation of a cleansing fire here flares in my mind and then suffocates.

I walk in, kicking our accumulated post before me. It had always seemed a boon to me that our post is distributed to our actual door by our nosy landlord, except now with it piled up in my way. I shut and bolt the door behind me.

I scan the contents of the flat, trying to distinguish between 'mine' and 'hers'. Too much of what I see is just 'ours'. She's touched everything.

I decide: she can have the furniture and kitchenware. I want just my clothes, my books, my papers and shaver. I fill several boxes and a suitcase. Once they're in the car, I won't have to come back. I can send for the piano later. I can go to Cambridge, say what needs to be said, listen, and drive away from it all. I carry my things to the door.

The post is still sprawled. I scoop it up, then sort, looking for company names. If I grab a copy of each bank and credit card statement, and the electric and water bills, I'll be set for changing accounts. I riffle through: BT, Barclays, HMRC, Laboratory Services . . .

That envelope's a large one, and heavy. It falls, bounces on one of its corners, then smacks flat down in the centre of the hall rug. That rug's elaborate edge surrounds a plain, beige rectangle, framing the envelope as if for display. The company name has been stamped in ink in the top left corner. In the centre is my own handwriting, addressing it to myself.

I don't want it, but I can't leave it here. I'll throw it away, but not here, elsewhere, to ensure that it's never found. Like my father, supposedly disposing of my baby photos just as the rubbish lorry pulls up. *He never did that,* I remind myself. *She had no photos. She only told you that to explain their absence away.*

I stop myself. Maybe this is exactly what Imogen did. Maybe the envelope came, and she decided that it didn't matter. She decided that she loved me, and wanted things the way that they already were.

I'd loved things the way they'd been, too. I'd wanted her so desperately that I might have done the same . . .

But not now. We know better now that we can't run.

I rip it open, tugging hard against the glue-and-spit holding it together. The papers jump. Shiny, colourful forms and advertising scatter. Lastly, two pages – a cover letter, and a white sheet with a table on it – slice a Z through the air and come to rest.

I snatch them up and my eyes attack the numbers first, as if I know what I'm supposed to look for.

I shake my head. Clearly, I've misunderstood how such matches are defined. I scan the paragraph above the table, looking for explanation or instructions.

I lower myself onto the chest Imogen had bought for our wellies and gloves and hats. I scan the data again, then the summary in the cover letter: 'No relationship.' I let both pages flutter down around my feet and lean forward, face down, ears between my knees. It doesn't make sense.

It doesn't matter.

I know what's true. My father told me: I'm Sebastian, orphaned at age three, adopted by a fervent mother and an indifferent then abandoning father. Whatever added up to *this* – here I kick at the pages, smearing them around – it doesn't change that. Whether the DNA is explained by . . . what? Adultery, or newborn adoption, or a baby mix-up? I'm still the boy Imogen grew up with. I'm the brother she loved as a brother. The DNA doesn't make that go away.

I collect the pages, hands shaking. I realise that I've forgotten my old cricket gear, in the hall cupboard. *No, leave it.* And my tennis racquet in this chest. *No, not now.*

Suitcase and boxes outside the door. Keys in hand. I get out. *God, the sun is bright.* It's only just gone half-three. I can barely believe it's the same day. Everything's changed.

It takes six trips to get everything settled into the car.

I lay the envelope on the passenger seat. *It doesn't matter*, I tell myself. *It doesn't matter.*

Of course that's true; the *'no match'* DNA doesn't change who I now know I am. It doesn't change that we can't be together. There's a story there, something weird, but nothing that changes the outcome.

It also does matter: the news changes one important thing. It means that when Imogen read our original DNA results, which correctly reassured her of no biological relationship, she proceeded in good faith. She didn't know then.

Maybe, maybe, she doesn't know even now.

Someone who saw me pack up the car is waiting for the space. I pull out.

I look in the rear-view mirror to check the colour of the car. *Not green.* But I'd wondered, for a moment.

If Imogen doesn't know, if she didn't make up Patrick Bell in some desperate, guilty compensation, then someone else did, and Imogen may be in genuine danger.

I take the turning too fast. I press my foot down. I lunge the car onto the motorway.

CHLOE FROHMANN

Stepping out of the hospital feels like bobbing to the surface. I've got Morgan Davies away from sleeping Fiona's bedside for a walk.

'Not far,' Morgan insists.

'Of course.'

We cross the main roundabout and set off down one of the roads sticking off like a spoke. Brick houses scroll on either side of us on a seeming loop.

'About the fire,' I begin.

'It doesn't matter. The houses were going to be razed anyway.'

'The White House was completely spared. All of your belongings are fine.'

'It doesn't matter.' Morgan shuffles slowly, looking only down.

I surreptitiously check my phone. The pathologist has confirmed that Rowena was smothered with a pillow, arguably murdered, even if she'd begged for it.

I've got to remain impartial. I'll need to keep away from parts of the case. The skeletons, and Imogen Wright-Llewellyn's possible arson or possible victimhood, are mine. Erik Keats' and Rowena's deaths involve Dora closely and so must belong to Spencer. Now that Morgan's accused Dora of stealing jewellery, this line of enquiry is Spencer's, too. But I have a theory of its potential impact on my own investigations.

'When did your mother start hoarding? Has she done it your whole life?'

Morgan barks out a laugh. 'How would I know? We've always lived in separate houses.'

I say nothing.

Morgan fills the space:

'The barn – the Red House – was her home. My father and I lived in the White House. Until he died and then . . . it was just me. When I was little she shared time between the two buildings, but as I grew up she visited me less and less. By the time I was a teenager I literally had the house to myself. I managed it; I cleaned it. Or not,' she adds wryly. 'I did stupid things. I had boys over. I had men over.' She shudders. 'I've worked hard to give Fiona boundaries. You may think limits are cruel. You may think barred windows and a guarded telephone are cruel, but do you know what's actually cruel? An open front door. I wish I could take back a hundred things I did when I was young. I wish I'd had a real mother, to stop them in the first place. We need to turn around,' she adds abruptly.

We turn and look. The hospital should seem small, given the distance, but it looms, even from here.

'Just a little further,' I nudge.

Morgan accepts the prod and walks on. 'To answer your question, no. She didn't always hoard. That happened later, after the coma.'

'Coma?'

'She . . .' Morgan closes her eyes for a moment, then they spring open with the words: 'She tried to kill herself once before. She took some kind of medicine from the hospital. She was a midwife, did you know that?'

I nod.

'I wasn't living there then. I'd got away from home as soon as my exams were done, went to live with a boyfriend, and then . . . Well, it was years later. She was found by a neighbour come by to complain about a loose dog. It wasn't hers, of course, but . . .' She shrugs. 'I have to be grateful. She was my mother, after all.' She stops walking. I guide her to sit on a low brick wall in front of a perfectly kept rose garden. Morgan leans forward, dropping tears.

'Do you know why she tried to kill herself then?' I prompt. I want to be kind, but this isn't therapy. I need to know. The motivations and timeline here could be explained by inserting the death and burial of the woman and child.

'She never told me. I never asked. I didn't want to know. What if it was because of me?' Morgan wipes her face. 'Afterwards, I moved back home with her. Me into the White House, she into the Red, of course. Things weren't the same in the White House as I'd left them. I'm sure it wasn't Rowena who'd been in there. The neighbours confirmed for me that they'd seen evidence of squatters, but Rowena denied it and there was nothing left behind.

269

That,' she says, handing over the answer to the original question, 'is when she started hoarding.'

She rises, and starts walking back towards Addenbrooke's. I surrender and follow.

I jump on the word *squatter*, and the date range that this new background provides: *Morgan leaves in 1982; a squatter, perhaps a pregnant woman, moves in; an accidental death; then, Rowena attempts suicide, out of guilt, or horror? Morgan returns in 1986.* That fits Imogen's story, too, of a sunburnt blonde in the White House sometime during her childhood. I don't want to cloud my judgement by being too sympathetic towards Rowena, but the staining on the sheets around the bodies does appear to be blood and, the pathologist has determined, suggestive of the fluids of birth. There are no marks of violence on the bones. It's easily possible that something went unexpectedly wrong. 'Did your mother have a car?' I ask. The one thing I can't figure out is why not get a labouring woman to the hospital.

'Of course. She had to get to work.'

All right, what if things got bad quickly? What if she felt she couldn't safely move the woman herself. She would call an ambulance, wouldn't she? 'Did she have phone service?'

'When?'

I remain purposefully vague, though the timing I'm interested in is just before Rowena's suicide attempt.

Morgan sighs. 'We had a phone growing up. When my father died, we stopped paying the bill and eventually they shut it off. There was a debt attached when I restarted the line, can you believe that? Years later.'

'When you restarted the line after your mother's coma?'

'Yes.' The timing slots into place for her, too. 'She's my *mother*,' she wails. 'Would it be awful if I tell you that I was jealous? That she let someone else live in the White House? That someone else fitted into my place? Would it be awful if I tell you that I would be relieved to know that she failed them horribly, worse than she failed me? She was a horrible mother. Fiona loved her, but grandmother is a different job. Being a grandmother is about forgiveness and indulgence and filling in with little extras. Mothering is the heavy lifting. Mothering is the daily work. I loved Rowena, and I hated her, because she never loved me the way I needed her to. If you want to accuse her of something, feel free. She supposedly loved Fiona and look what she made her do.'

The hospital is close, just across the road, but we get stuck at the roundabout. Traffic is thick and fast and no one lets us cross.

'You didn't tell me that you'd sold the land,' I say.

Morgan doesn't flinch. 'You think it's my fault that she wanted to die. It's not. I told you; she'd tried it before. I sold the land to try to stop her. If Rowena were in a proper facility, with proper care, they wouldn't let her. They'd *make her* live.'

I shiver, even in the warm. 'You say that like it's a punishment.'

'It's not a punishment,' Morgan corrects. 'It's a responsibility. I didn't ask to be born. She shouldn't get to ask to die.'

A text comes through for me. Spencer says that the CSI team has found Dora's fingerprints on at least one of the empty pill packets, and that the tin box that they were found in matches the description of Rowena's jewellery box, minus the velvet bag Morgan Davies had mentioned. *That's not good for Dora . . .*

CONFIRMING ARREST OF SUSPECT DK, Spencer's left for the end.

Shit. It's his case, but what the hell is he thinking? Does he really believe that Dora killed a woman for a bracelet?

'Tell me about your mother's jewellery,' I request, but Morgan has already darted across the road. I put out a hand to slow an oncoming car and force a gap. I bound after Morgan, and catch her on one of the bus shelter islands that act as stepping-stones towards the hospital. I pant, hand on my swollen belly, but I get the words out again: 'Tell me about your mother's jewellery. What's so special? Is it real? Diamonds? Platinum? What?'

'Some of it's gold. It's ordinary gold and costume jewellery, and the garnet ring. She wore it when I was little. People tell me that I can't possibly remember, but I do. When I was a baby, I played with that bracelet on her arm while she fed me my bottle. I remember two of them clacking against each other.' Her face is wet, sweat from her hairline and tears on her cheeks.

'But nothing objectively valuable. Is that what you're saying?'

'I don't know. I don't think so . . .' She swallows.

I have to tread carefully, and stick to my own case. 'Did Rowena wear her jewellery later in life? After the coma?'

Morgan shakes her head.

'And that's when she started hoarding?' *Maybe to bury something, small things, collected from the house after the grave was covered.*

Morgan nods. A bus pulls up and hospital visitors and outpatients jostle us.

If someone had squatted in the White House, there would have been belongings: clothes, shoes, accessories, perhaps only noticed after the burial was complete. The kind of things at the core of Rowena's hoarding, easily mistaken for Rowena's own outgrown or out-of-fashion possessions. That's a good way to hide things. She may have felt safer keeping things under her control. 'There's a chance that some items belonging to the dead woman and her child might have been in the barn. The fire has destroyed much of what we'd like to see. Fiona spent a lot of time in there. We need to talk to her.'

'No.'

I expected that. 'Perhaps *you* remember—'

'I didn't spend time in the Red House, Inspector.'

'Perhaps you'll recognise which pieces of jewellery were for certain your mother's and which might have belonged to someone else.' *Someone dead.* Jewellery is the most likely among those items to be unique or identifying. 'I'd like to find that jewellery.'

'Ask that girl! She had the bracelet!' Morgan clutches the bangle on her wrist, and her expression dares me to try to take it from her.

I suggest, 'Dora said that Fiona gave it to her. If Fiona used to play with the jewellery, maybe we should ask her where it is.'

'No! No more. I told you.'

'All right, may we ask an officer to search Fiona's room?' We haven't searched the White House yet. We've trodden carefully, wary of a grieving woman's rights.

'You think I'm awful,' Morgan says, chin high. 'They all do. Fiona, too. It costs something to be a mother.

You'll find out. Everyone sees what I deny her, but they hardly notice what I spare her. I never have sex in the house, never. I save it for business trips, or . . .' She declines to elaborate. 'I never bring it home. She deserves to be a child. She deserves to be sheltered. Dora was a fine friend when they were small, but . . . puberty does something to these girls. Dora couldn't be trusted any more, she proved that. I'm not flailing for vengeance; I truly believe that she abetted my daughter's horrific actions, and for that she should be punished. But only for what she's done. If she's innocent . . .' She wipes her wet forehead. 'I have nothing to hide. Search the whole damn house. Feel free to burn it to the ground when you're through.'

As we approach the revolving doors, I thumb-type that message to the CSI team on site: SEARCH THE WHITE HOUSE. THE GIRL'S ROOM. JEWELLERY.

Morgan's phone beeps, growing louder as she fumbles for it at the bottom of her bag. She retrieves it, looks at the message, gasps, and staggers back.

My hand shoots out to steady her. 'Mrs Davies?'

'It's Dr Sengupta. They've found a donor. They're prepping Fiona for surgery.'

I have to jog to keep up with her. In the lift, Morgan bounces impatiently, everything too slow. On the ward, we rush the ritual anointing of hands with antibacterial gel, and find the doctor. He requires signatures. He's beaming.

'The donor shall remain anonymous, but I can assure you that she's an excellent match. There are no guarantees; Fiona's health is already compromised and any surgery has risks. But we have hope, Mrs Davies.'

She nods. She scribbles signatures. Fiona is taken away.

Morgan sits in the chair beside Fiona's empty bed, staring at the space where Fiona had been.

'I want to know,' she says. 'I want to know who they're putting into her body.'

I pull a second chair from the corner, scraping it along the floor join her. I sit. 'Does it matter?'

'I wanted to be the one! It should have been me. But I don't match. I've never matched. I gave birth to her, but we've never been alike, not in any way.'

'When Dan and I think about baby names,' I say, carefully, 'It's easy when I imagine a girl. When I mentally sort through boy names, it feels strange to confront just how much this isn't going to be a little me. Well, it isn't going to be a little me either way, but when imagining a little girl it's easier to pretend that it might be.'

I steel myself for a caustic reply, but the mother-to-mother tone has done its work.

Morgan confides, 'The doctor asked me to get in touch with Fiona's father, to see if he could be a donor. I had to admit that I don't know who he is. All I know about the man comes from looking at Fiona and spotting the differences from my family's genes. She has Rowena's stubborn chin, and my long body. Her nose, though, and her pale, wispy hair . . . those must be from him.' Her voice gets tight and sarcastic: 'You're a detective; can you find me the man with that nose and that hair? Who fucked a drunk woman in Brighton in the summer of '96?'

I keep my expression neutral. 1996 is too late to be connected with the skeletons. But if alcohol had been a general problem, that could be relevant.

'Was there always a lot of drinking?'

'Yes. Then. Not any more, not for years. I pulled my life together for her. We lived together in the same house,' she says, her pride in this banal normality emphasising the strangeness of her childhood. Her satisfaction lasts only a moment. 'I hate looking at her and knowing that this other, irrelevant person is part of her. And now there will be another one, this donor. It makes me sick.'

'Maybe,' I suggest, gently, 'Maybe it's not Rowena's chin on Fiona's face, just Fiona's chin. Maybe it's not that man's hair on Fiona's head, but Fiona's hair. Maybe not your body. Maybe just hers.'

Morgan says nothing, but she nods. I get up quietly. It's late afternoon now, the sun no longer high. I miss Dan. I hate hospitals. Most people are in here because they have to be; I can go home. The closer I get to the exit the faster I walk.

On the way to my car, I check my phone. I hope that Spencer isn't trying to assert his lack of bias by being unnecessarily tough with Dora. I hope that Morris knows better than to try to contact me. Last night's visit and update were as far as I can go.

Top message, from the CSI at the scene: NO JEWELLERY IN DAUGHTER'S ROOM. SPY CAMERA ON HIGH SHELF.

Camera? I wonder, and I feel fury seep up from the ground and climb my body. Morgan Davies had denied any cameras.

WHAT'S ON IT? I text back.

RECEIVER NOT ATTACHED. DIGITAL TRANSMISSION.

Damn. I reply, FIND RECEIVER. SEARCH FOR MORE CAMERAS. FURTHER INFO TO DS SPENCER. This has to be his. The footage could confirm or contradict Fiona's confession, and indict or exclude Dora.

Morgan Davies lied to me, I fume.

Then, *But why let us search the house?* She had to know that the camera would be found.

Unless Morgan didn't know about the camera.

I send one more text: GET A WARRANT TO CHECK THE SITE OFFICE AND BUILDERS SHED. The developer might even grant entry without a warrant, considering his son is the victim. *Maybe more than a victim.*

Morgan Davies had said once that Erik Keats had been in the White House to use the toilet. Might he have made a side trip into the teenage daughter's room, and left something behind?

I feel a flutter in my belly, and rub my child's kicking foot. Even the baby has been lazy in the recent heat, so the activity is reassuring. I walk up past accident and emergency, to the pedestrian bridge into the multistorey car park.

At the end of it, I extend my car's key fob and click the button; the car flashes in reply. I walk to it, open the door and stand beside, fanning myself, waiting for the stale air inside to exit.

Back at the mouth of the bridge, a youngish woman in a wheelchair is being pushed by an older one. The parking structure features low ceilings and exposed metal beams, and its acoustics carry the tones of their voices, though not their words. They're clearly arguing.

I only half-listen. People argue. It's not something police have to worry about until it goes beyond words. I look away, idly considering the merits of various vehicles in terms of room for a baby seat.

Screams bounce off the metal walls, the metal cars, all that metal adding edge and tang to the already sharp sound. I squint, assess. The woman who was pushing the wheelchair is now on the ground, getting up, growling with effort. The woman in the wheelchair is rolling backwards, screaming. It's Imogen Wright-Llewellyn.

IMOGEN WRIGHT-LLEWELLYN

I check the screen again then cram the phone into my pocket. No messages. I tell myself that coverage is terrible inside the hospital walls. Getting out may result in a flurry of notifications of missed calls and texts, but what good will this do me if I'm not allowed to leave until I've arranged for someone to look after me? I'll call on a friend from London if I must, but I don't want to have to explain everything, not until I better understand how life is now changed. Not until I know where I stand, with Maxwell, and with the police. *Maxwell, however angry you are with me, call me back!*

But I know I have no right to depend on him. Contacting his father, then accusing the man, may have been unforgivable. Maxwell has been right about a lot, most of all about my obsession with family and with my supposedly idyllic childhood.

I'm sorry, Max, I practise in my head, flopping back against the pillow. A lot has been becoming clear since I visited the Red and White Houses in Caldecote.

It had been a little neighbourhood of sorts, back when I was a child, with the houses at odd angles, to avoid seeing straight into each other's windows. My brothers and I had played on the shared grass between. There must have been boundary lines, but I hadn't known them.

I remember now, clearly, the woman on the steps of the White House. The woman with the long hair and sunburnt shoulders, and the gold chain weighted by a charm between her breasts. She had done young me a kindness all those years ago, and I have only now realised it.

In the hospital room, a nurse bustles in. Her hair is short and she wears no jewellery. She couldn't be more different, physically, from the woman in my memory, but she has that same warmth, that same kind posture, leaning and smiling. She brings good news. 'Someone's called to say that they're picking you up.'

I try to sit up. 'Maxwell Gant? He phoned?' If he resorted to calling the hospital that must mean that I'm not deluding myself; my mobile isn't picking up calls. Relief tingles. *Forgiven.*

'I didn't take the call,' the nurse admits, then recites various instructions regarding medication, the wheelchair, and the return of my bedside locker key.

In my mind, I practise again: *Maxwell, you were right. My family were never perfect. Never. I'll always love them, but I won't worship them any more.*

I pack my few belongings, the things that Maxwell had brought me from our hotel while I was in surgery, before I accused his father. He'd brought my dressing gown, my hairbrush, the book I'd left open, face-down, by the hotel bed. He'd bookmarked the page with a coffee receipt. The kindness of that small gesture had almost overwhelmed me. I flick tears away from my eyes.

The nurse waits, holding the wheelchair ready. They need the bed; I'm being sent to the discharge lounge. When I nod, the nurse helps me transfer. My leg sticks straight out, as if pointing. I feel like a compass needle that hasn't been properly magnetised. 'Which way is north?' I joke, and the nurse laughs, a short laugh, as if she doesn't really get it. I rest my hands in my lap while the nurse pushes me forward.

Lying in a hospital bed invites fantasy or memory, depending on your mood. Memory had come to me in this hospital. Just pieces: sounds, previously unconnected images, all of them unprocessed, because young Im hadn't known what any of it was.

The day that I'd met the long-haired woman, I'd followed my father there. I see that clearly. The way the Red House is positioned, I'd never before made the journey round it to the front of the White House. That had always seemed off-limits to me, except that once, following Daddy.

I'd followed him because I was bored. The twins were away on a school trip. Our heavily pregnant mother had been napping.

In the present, the lift slides open. The nurse and I enter it. In my mind, though, I exit, out of Meadow View, the peach house, chasing my father.

I didn't call his name. I wanted to surprise him. By the time I got around the Red House, he was gone. I had laid my hand on the sliding barn door, listening. I'd heard my father inside, and someone else. I'd reached for the iron door handle.

The nice woman with the long hair had pulled young me away, to the White House steps, inviting me to comb her hair and listen to her radio. She'd stopped me from walking in on something. She'd turned up the volume to protect me from hearing things. I had heard some, but hadn't understood what it was, then.

I know now.

The hospital lift doors slide open. I'm pushed forward. The nurse pauses at the glass doors of the discharge lounge, discussing my transition and paperwork with an officious older woman. I peer inside, hoping to see Maxwell there, but no one is his height, has his hair, or seems to be looking for me.

Maxwell, I think, *My dad wasn't always nice to my mum. He had an affair with one of our neighbours. Well, one that I know of. Who knows if there were more. He was just another doctor fucking a subordinate, just another husband of a pregnant woman who wanted to fuck a body that wasn't full of something else.*

Tears, now. Angry ones. The older woman tells me 'chin up' and asks me to sign a paper on a clipboard. The kind nurse is gone. I scribble. The new woman pushes me into the lounge and parks me in front of a television.

Rowena Davies was my father's lover. How bizarre to put the two together in my mind: one of them I imagine only as an old woman, and my father had never had the chance to age.

Then there's the bit that doesn't make sense. I still remember the kind, long-haired woman picking up a ball –

hard, like a basketball – and throwing it down the hill, the hill that I know isn't really there and never was.

A jolt. Someone's hit the back of my wheelchair. I turn to glare, but it's another newbie wheelchair user; we mutually smile and joke about trading insurance information.

I check my phone. Maybe the reception is better in here. No messages; no missed calls.

Maybe it takes a while for them to appear, I console myself. So I stare at the screen, willing them to pop up.

'Imogen!'

I haven't yet got the hang of turning the chair. I twist my neck instead.

'Imogen? Is that you?' A woman's voice.

'Mrs Gant?' I do turn the chair, suddenly, but too hard, and my body pitches forward then smacks back.

Maxwell's mother bends down over me. 'Dear, I was just coming to see you.'

'Did Maxwell ask you to come?' I don't mean for my voice to catch, but it does, and Muriel Gant smiles generously.

'Of course. He's been worried about you.' Mrs Gant gets behind my chair, takes the handles, and pushes. She nods to the older woman at the desk, and I wish that the nurse were here, the kind nurse, or the woman with long blond hair.

'Is he here? Is he parking the car?' I feel light-headed. Mrs Gant is moving fast and the hospital lobby blurs. Suddenly, we're outside. Sunlight blinds me.

'Don't be silly. The wheelchair wouldn't fit in his Mini.' Mrs Gant steers me past A&E, around the corner, and onto a pedestrian bridge into a multistorey car park.

The sound of the chair's wheels on the bridge surface is buzzy compared to its glide over pavement. I babble over it. 'What did Maxwell say? Is he meeting us? Is he at the hotel? You're welcome to join us for dinner tonight . . .' My hands have nothing to do. They're supposed to be spinning the wheels. A steely voice pops out of me: 'You know, I'd really like to steer this myself. I have to practise.'

'I'm only trying to help.'

'I don't see how the wheelchair will fit in your car either.'

'It folds up into the boot, Imogen. Don't be dense.'

I tug the brake lever and force the chair to a halt. 'I really think that I should take the bus. I don't want to try squeezing myself into a car right now.' I'll have to sit in the back, my leg extended across the seat.

'I have a large car, Imogen. Really, it's as if you think I haven't planned any of this.' Mrs Gant presses the button on her key fob, activating her locks and headlamps. In the distance, I can just make out the flashing lights, and faint beep, and the vehicle's colour. It's green.

At the same moment, my phone hums and chimes the influx of multiple messages. *Maxwell.* The last one – yes, from him – glows steady on the screen:

DON'T TRUST MY MOTHER.

I push the brake lever loose and spin, slamming my cast-encased extended leg into Muriel Gant's middle. She doubles over. I repeat the motion, only just missing her head, smacking my leg against her shoulder instead. She falls back.

I scream for help, deliberately rolling backwards to create distance but keep Mrs Gant in sight. She is transformed, pushing herself up from the surface, her face puckered with effort. Achieving full height, she throws her shoulders back.

I spin the wheelchair around and surge away, only to be yanked back.

She's taken control of my chair by the back handles, and steers me towards the green car. Its grille and headlamps make an innocent face, as if it hasn't tried to kill me before.

I grab at the wheels, to try to take charge, but she pushes faster. The speedy motion of the spokes spinning under my fingers makes it impossible to get a grip, so I take the only action left to me: I pull the brake again.

Mrs Gant's forward motion continues, even as the wheels lock, tilting the chair forward and dumping me out onto the ground.

Suddenly, the Inspector is here.

She grabs Mrs Gant's wrists from behind, cuffing one arm, but the woman wriggles out of her grip. Mrs Gant swings the cuffed hand upwards, slapping the Inspector in the face with the hanging metal ring.

Inspector Frohmann falls back, clutching her face. Her other hand reaches back to stop herself, but she lands hard and oddly next to me, seeming to bounce off the cement to fall again, sideways, smacking her belly on the floor. A car sweeps around the curve, braking to avoid us with an ugly, pig-like squeal. It revs and inches backwards, timidly trying to reverse round the tight curve behind it.

Mrs Gant has run. In the distance, the pounding footsteps of hospital security echo.

'Are you all right?' the Inspector and I ask one another at the same time. I sit up but cannot stand; my cast is too far up my leg, not allowing it to bend. She's a turtle on her back. A dark mark across her cheek bleeds. The coward in the car is still trying to back out.

'I'll help you,' I say. I reach for her far hand, to pull her to sitting.

On the way, my hand skims her belly. I pause there, let my palm fall to rest, and spread my fingers over the firm curve. My throat constricts; I skip a breath; I scream, and scream again.

CHAPTER FIVE

CHLOE FROHMANN

I call for light. Whether as a joke or out of practicality, what Spencer and I get are the hot stage lights, not the general auditorium glow. I squint. There's Fiona's harp, tucked in the far corner.

I pat its soft case, looking for pockets. I flick Velcro tabs and expose pencils, gum wrappers, and a folded rehearsal schedule, but no jewellery.

The flesh around my black eye burns when I perspire, but otherwise I seem to have recovered from the car park altercation. The baby's heartbeat is steady, that's the main thing. Baby feet still punish me from the inside. All is as it should be at seven months.

Muriel Gant has been arrested. Imogen's complaints against her will be hard to prove, so it's luck, I suppose, that the woman assaulted a police officer. We did follow up on her car, and records show that she'd taken a ferry to the Isle of Wight on the same day that Imogen had, and then off again. Remote video found in Erik Keats' site hut in Caldecote show the same green car entering the area the night that Imogen had been supposed to meet Patrick Bell. Keats had set up cameras at strategic points throughout the site, arguably for security, but the footage from Fiona's room has no explanation beyond voyeurism. Older footage on the computer proves that it was not the first time Keats had used a camera to peep. We're following up on past victims. It looks like at least one of them was the victim of an unsolved assault.

I shudder, relieved that Dora had so ably defended herself.

Keats' footage also showed the green car on site a second time, on the day of the barn fire. Superficial investigation has found that the fire originated at the power strip for the night-time investigation lights, as if it had been caused by an overload. Of course, the fire had happened during the day, when the lights weren't needed. Strangely, they had all been turned on at once . . . *Nice way to try to set up the victim as the cause of her own 'accident', but not a dependable way to actually start a fire.* Traces of an accelerant have since been identified, and my fingers are crossed that we may yet find a link to Muriel Gant via a spill on her clothes or the contents of her handbag.

It hurts every time I blink, but that black eye is keeping her in custody while we put together a decent case.

All to keep her son to herself? I marvel. It's enough to make me hug my mother-in-law, who's given nothing but support since Dan and I replaced our elaborate wedding plans with a civil ceremony last month, party postponed till after the baby.

'Here it is,' Spencer announces. He's unzipped the case

and wriggled his hand deep inside, coming up with a red velvet bag. Forbidden to wear make-up or even simple jewellery, Fiona used to play with Rowena's jewellery at night in her room, and the harp case made a good hiding place. There's no reason for anyone to be suspicious of a musician being protective of her instrument.

Spencer points out that if Dora had stolen anything in the course of assisting in Rowena's death, she wouldn't have left it here in Fiona's case, not if she'd had the intention of ever getting at it. I was careful to not put this view forward myself, but waited for him to come to it, which he did gratifyingly quickly. I look forward to slipping this news to Morris: Dora is safe.

'You're pretty good at this job,' I tell Spencer, as he opens the velvet bag with his gloved hands. 'Don't forget to miss me while I'm off bringing new life into the world, all right?'

He laughs. 'We all expect you to be back at work straight from hospital, baby in your arms and latched. My mother—'

'Stepmother,' I correct.

'My stepmother feeds my sister right at her desk. Only took a week away. Clients on the other end of the phone don't even know. Mothers are crazy. You were crazy, flinging yourself between Imogen Wright-Llewellyn and Muriel Gant.' Crazy, in his tone, is clearly an admirable thing to be.

'Just doing the job,' I say, pushing on my knees to get to standing.

'You sure you're all right?' Spencer asks, and his sudden concern makes me wonder if I am.

Do I look all right? It's hard to feel oriented in the isolation of the spotlighted bare stage.

He puts out a hand to steady me.

'Sorry, blood rushed to my head,' I say.

The baby kicks. I pat the little heel in thanks for the reassurance.

We drive the jewellery back to Major Investigations, to log it: a second bracelet, numerous clip-on earrings, a garnet ring and earrings, bead necklaces, a broken gold chain, and a lion charm, its mane radiating from the head like light.

'Well, someone was a Leo,' I observe. I recognise the charm as a copy of a famous zodiac painting.

The work takes hours. First, I check who was the Leo in the family. Not Rowena, I quickly establish. Not Morgan, nor Fiona.

This gets Spencer excited. 'What if our skeleton's the Leo?'

We already have reasonable parameters for her birth year and the year of her disappearance, and hope of the name being a Dora variant. Adding in an August birthday would pop up the answer like a piece of toast, if only the records from the eighties were computerised.

Spencer says quietly, 'Makes them seem more real, thinking of one of them with an August birthday. Maybe her birthday's today.'

'Sentimental,' I mutter.

'Don't you . . . ?'

'No,' I say, flexing my swollen ankles under the table.

'Once we find the name, it'll be like a real person.'

'A body's not real enough for you?' The skeletal baby,

nestled in its mother's pelvis, had nearly done me in. I'd forced myself to keep steady while on the job but had broken down when Dan asked me about it at home. Records, names and numbers are nothing compared to the tiny little bones, the little alien-like skull. I've been unable to sleep, partly from working the case around the clock, partly from pregnancy reflux, and partly from dread of nightmares.

'Are you *sure* you're all right?' Spencer asks again.

'Piss off,' I insist.

We slog. We enlist the office admin to help sift written records. No match, no match. I feel my back ache and stretch to relieve it.

'You're white,' Spencer says.

'I'm pretty sure that you're not twigging my race for the first time,' I joke.

'No, paper white. Do you want to go home?'

I shake my head. 'Don't talk. I'm thinking.' Dan and I have been kicking around baby names, and one of the things to be aware of is initials. You don't want names to add up to an embarrassing acronym that will become a stuck nickname. 'We've already speculated that she could be a Laura. What if she's not a Laura born in August? What if she's a Laura whose initials are L, E, O?'

The three of us scramble into action, pulling out Lauras. We find her in the middle of the stack of discards: Laura Evelyn O'Neill.

Once named, her story comes together quickly. Google brings us back to the same message board where Muriel Gant, posing as Patrick Bell, had contacted Imogen Wright-Llewellyn. It has a section for 'Lost Loved Ones' as well as 'Adoptees'.

293

'Darling Laura,' Spencer reads aloud, 'We miss you so much. Every day I wake up wishing for you and for my grandchild. If you won't forgive us for yourself, do it for your baby. We have so much love to give.' The post includes a photo of a woman with long honey hair, and a lion-head charm hanging on a gold chain.

I fill in the details in my mind: surprise pregnancy; unhappy parents; uninterested boyfriend. From the begging of forgiveness, it sounds like they kicked her out. I can't imagine how frightening it would be, going through the backbreaking work of carrying a baby alone. *Maybe she was one of those glowing women I'm always reading about in magazines,* I think sarcastically. But, for myself, backbreaking is almost the literal word for what I feel. I want to lean forward to stretch my spine, but even with knees spread to accommodate the belly I can't lean forward far enough to make the pain go away.

Is it supposed to feel like this? I wonder. Carrying a baby hurts, I know, but what's the difference between the hurt of expanding and swelling and diverting my resources, which is supposed to happen, and the hurt of something gone wrong? What if my actions in the car park have done something to the baby? What if its balloon of fluid wasn't enough of a cushion when I hit the cement floor? My heart is speeding up. *Is the baby's heart beating too fast too?*

Dan and I haven't named it yet. We've agreed to be surprised by the sex. We don't know anything about it, just that it's ours. I don't have a picture in my head of who this baby will be, so my fears of the worst manifest as an image of Dan's reaction to the worst: he would be shocked, wounded, bereft. My face would reflect his, with one element more: guilt.

I gasp.

'I'm calling for an ambulance,' Spencer announces.

Please do, I only think. It hurts too much to speak.

After her daughter left, Rowena let the White House decay. She didn't want it. The Red House was enough for her, and had been for years.

Months living alone changed that. Her desire for solitude, which had been perpetual when constantly thwarted, became satisfied. She became – and it took her weeks to put a word to it – lonely.

Not lonely for someone to take care of, or someone to live with. Rowena became lonely for simple contact between independent adults who have no authority over one another. This was another concept that she didn't immediately have a word for. She finally allowed that 'friend', at least, a certain kind of friend, was probably what she meant.

Laura came first. She came with a rucksack, knocking on doors offering to do odd jobs. She didn't knock at the Red House, of course. One doesn't knock at a barn. She knocked at the White House, having been rejected elsewhere. Then it started to rain, and she sheltered on the porch. It rained all night, and no one came home. Laura discovered that the door was unlocked and that the kitchen had not recently been used. Rowena knew the word for this: Laura squatted, an especially apt word given her rounded and growing silhouette.

Rowena left the property only for work. Her car, which to others might have appeared to be abandoned junk, served her fine to get back and forth to the hospital. It's inevitable that Laura eventually saw Rowena. Laura stiffened, ready for anger or pursuit, but Rowena only waved. That afternoon, coming home, Rowena left a jar of antenatal vitamins at the door of the White House.

A few days later, Laura left Rowena a pail of blackberries. The berries were Rowena's own, but they had been picked and washed.

Dr Joseph Llewellyn came second. He was a surgeon at Hinchingbrooke, while Rowena worked in maternity, but she recognised him. His wife birthed her babies there. Rowena knew that he was a neighbour.

'Ms Davies,' he said, his white doctor's coat in a flutter behind him as he confidently swooped in. He always seemed to know nurses' and midwives' names. 'I'd like to see my wife's records, please. Isobel Llewellyn.'

'I'm sorry, Dr Llewellyn, but you know that we're not allowed to do that.'

He swore, then apologised for having done so in front of her. 'I hate to ask a delicate question, Ms Davies, but perhaps you could advise me. Is there anything about this stage of pregnancy that makes it dangerous for a woman to be with her husband? She tells me that her doctor advised her to abstain.'

'I can't reveal her personal information, sir, but that would be unusual. Unless she's at risk for pre-eclampsia or otherwise on bed rest . . .'

Dr Llewellyn shook his head. Rowena imagined an embarrassed blush under his dark beard. She felt heat in her own cheeks. They laughed together, acknowledging the awkwardness. That's all. But he came back later, and asked if she needed a lift home.

She didn't, of course. But she wanted one.

Rowena didn't think about sex, not consciously. It had been a practical and unpleasant duty with her husband, so, as with the words 'lonely' and 'friend', she didn't immediately recognise it as what her body craved. If Joseph Llewellyn had used that word she would have bolted, but the subtle electricity under the superficially benign offer of a lift was something she could say yes to.

Dr Llewellyn was an efficient and affectionate lover, who got off on women's pleasure and so was adept at provoking it. They made love, frantically, in his car outside the Red House.

When he was done, Rowena said, 'How shall I get back to work tomorrow?' Her car was still at the hospital.

He agreed to pick her up at the end of the long road, well away from the houses. That became their system, for the times they went home together.

At the hospital, in passing, he acknowledged her with only a nod. She accepted this. She had exactly what she wanted, except for the frustration of timing. He chose when to come to her; she could never go to him. But, aside from that, it was good.

She noticed that Isobel Llewellyn failed to come in for a scheduled appointment. A follow-up card was popped in the post. Curious, she looked back in the records. There were only a few pages, and a scan showing what the doctor supposed to be a little girl. Isobel had failed to come for an earlier appointment as well. Rowena knew that she should phone; that was part of her job. She just didn't feel able to speak to the woman whose husband was her lover.

Instead, she asked Joseph, in bed. They were in the Red House; she lay across the mattress, propped up on pillows; he sat at the side, pulling up his pants. 'You really should get your wife to keep her appointments,' she said. She didn't mean to berate; it's only that she had had little experience in tactful conversation.

He left abruptly, without even an answer. Days went by. Rowena feared that she had put him off. She tried waiting by his car in the hospital car park. He didn't say anything when he saw her there, but he got in and just sat, not driving away. She got in the passenger seat.

'Never talk about my wife,' he said. 'You're not fit to say her name. Do you understand that?'

Rowena agreed. As soon as his wife had their baby, or perhaps when the baby was weaned, or perhaps after another baby, he'd get Isobel back to himself and not need Rowena any longer. She had to take what she could get.

Weeks later, their pattern had become comfortably re-established. He rolled off her, and stretched, and she knew that there would be a few minutes of basking, followed by efficient re-dressing and arrangements for another time. He didn't like her to talk after, so she was quiet, and heard rain stippling the roof, and, outside, a sound like a kitten mewling.

She got up, which disturbed Joseph, but she didn't care. The cat sounded in pain. She pulled a sheet off her bed to cover herself, mindful of his view of her sags and dimples. She dragged open the barn door. It was dark out. It was night, after her shift. Rowena squinted. The sound wasn't coming from a cat. On the grass, Laura, on her hands and knees, rocked and cried.

Rowena pulled her up and staggered her into the barn, out of the rain and the mud. She laid Laura on the orange sheet that had fallen off from around her. 'How far along are you? How long have you been having contractions?'

Laura grunted her answers. Rowena reached down into the wet between her legs. Her hand came up black. In the lamp light of the Red House, that's what red looked like. It was blood.

'Joseph, call for an ambulance!' she instructed him, in her professional tone that brooked no argument. He didn't move, so she barked again. This time, he obeyed, and exited.

As far as she knew, the phone at the White House was dead, unless Laura had revived it. He would have to call from his own house. That would take time. She lied to Laura, 'Don't worry, they'll be here soon.'

She reached again under Laura's dress. She felt the push of a baby's soft crown under her hand.

IMOGEN WRIGHT-LLEWELLYN

I've never taken the train between London and Cambridge. It's been there all these years, hauling commuters back and forth, but I've never been tempted to leap onto it. I knew that Cambridge would have changed. I knew that I had changed. I knew that Sebastian wasn't there and that my older brothers were grown men, moved far away. I knew that our parents were dead. I'd returned to Cambridge only for Maxwell, so that he could take the job.

Today I take the train away from Cambridge, to London. I'm clumsy in my wheelchair, after another night in Addenbrooke's following the attack in the car park. Maxwell didn't come to see me. I'm relieved. I don't yet know what to say to him. This is my chance to figure that out.

King's Cross is the Harry Potter station, with the back half of a luggage trolley stuck into a wall for children to pose with, as if about to access a hidden, magical platform. Families queue; parents fiddle with cameras; half the children are excited and half are bored. I used to want children more than anything, even just yesterday. Now I see them as they are: dirty, demanding, whole people, separate from the adults who carry them around. That's why our mother had four, I've realised. She'd been trying for the one that would finally finish the job, but there was only more urge, never any satisfaction.

My older brothers remember the fights. Ben had alluded to them when we'd found one another twelve years ago, but I'd flicked the reference away, with a literal wave of my hand. I'd rushed words in its place, reminding them of how our mother had made picnics under the college chestnut trees, how she had helped stage our own dramatic communion ceremony at home because the college chaplain had given me and Sebastian blessings instead of wine when we lined up at the rail. Of course, Robert and Ben had remembered none of this. They have different memories, from inside the rehearsal room and within the choir stalls. They had been singing in East House while Sebastian and I were mollified with a blanket and grapes under the trees. They had been handed the cup of wine in the service, and invited to drink, they and all the other choirboys, even though some of them were not that much older than I had been.

I understand now why most elite choirs require boarding school. At Jesus, in contrast, there were all these parents to be placated, all these individual school schedules to be managed. The older local boys came straight from their schools, on their own, usually early and rowdy. They played football on the grass and pounded on the rehearsal room piano. The younger boys, and those with a commute, came with parents and siblings in tow, adding more noise and chaos. I'd run around the courtyards as if they were my own garden, and only from this distance do I realise what a distraction I must have been, and how in the way. It's a sudden fizz of humiliation. I had loved the choir, but had been nothing to it in return, only a nuisance.

I wonder if I'm a nuisance to my brothers as well.

Robert had agreed to meet me here, under the station's vaulted ceiling. A canopy of criss-crossed steel rises up from a central funnel to spread out high over the main lobby, and it's lit in a bright purple glow. I take the lift to the mezzanine, and save him a seat at a flimsy metal cafe table. The noise and bustle all around comforts me. In a private space I might have cried or argued. In public, I will only be able to nod, accept, and move on. It's the best way.

'Imogen!' Robert says, bending to kiss both of my cheeks. I had warned him about the wheelchair over the phone, explaining that it's only temporary and blaming it on a climbing accident, so there's only a flicker of pity, quickly replaced by his usual easy smile. He leans back in his chair, feet apart, shoulders back. He's grown up confident despite being orphaned, which had at first puzzled me. Then it had clicked together and made sense: he and Ben had always had each other.

'Thank you for coming,' I say quietly. I'm always aware that I'd been more desperate to find them than they me.

'You would have liked the concert last night,' he tells me. He plays the organ, all over the world. It's only luck that he's in London for that now. Tomorrow he'll take the Eurostar to Paris, to catch up with his wife and daughters, who have begun their holiday without him.

'I wish that I—' I begin.

'Of course you couldn't have come,' he quickly adds, tracing my wheelchair with his eyes.

'I know. I do wish that I could have.'

Robert nods, and queues to get coffee for us both.

In the past, Maxwell has asked me why I don't play any instrument. I could blame my adopted family, who didn't make me practise, but I had been old enough that I could have made myself practise, if I'd wanted it. I could blame the college choir for having cast me as an outsider, a permanent tagalong, but that's not fair either. In all the schools I'd ever attended, it was the girls who dominated singing, and the boys who made fun of it.

I've heard Robert play, once. I travelled up to Edinburgh for it. As with so many chapels, churches and cathedrals, he'd been hidden and anonymous in the organ loft. Without him in sight, it had been as if the building itself were breathing out the music. I'd found the experience near-overwhelming. 'I think I'm a born listener,' I'd answered Max when he asked.

Maxwell and I don't have a real piano in our flat; the neighbours would never put up with it. Max has an electronic one that he practises on with headphones. If the television and radio are off, and nothing is cooking or in the dishwasher, I hear the gentle presses and clicks of the keys under his fingers. I play a little game, to figure out what he's playing from that alone. I love musicians, without wanting to be one myself.

Robert returns with a tray. Our lattes have been put into paper cups. Probably this location doesn't even have proper mugs, expecting that all their customers are in a hurry. Nevertheless, I feel rushed, annoyed, and judged.

Robert reacts to my frown. 'Did I get it right?' he asks.

I stretch out a smile for him. 'Of course. Thank you.'

He puts a chocolate-dipped shortbread between us. 'To share,' he says, breaking off a piece for himself.

I twist my face and blink fast to keep the tears in. I try to remember what we all used to like for treats when we were little. I can't. I remember what I've told people about our childhood, over and over, but not the childhood itself any more, not enough to walk around in it and spot things that I haven't already consciously claimed.

'What is it that you wanted to talk about?' Robert prompts.

Again, guilt. I've been silent too long, wasting his time. 'Mum and Dad.' Suddenly cold, I press my palms against my warm cup.

Robert leans back again, brushing shortbread crumbs off his lap. He looks down. 'What about them?'

'Do you remember, when I asked if either of you had become a doctor, like Dad? Ben said . . . He kind of croaked a laugh, and then said that he would never be like Dad. Then you said you play the organ, and Ben said he teaches. We talked about something else. Why did Ben say that, about not being like Dad?'

'You really batted it back whenever either of us referred to our parents as less than perfect. I didn't think you would ever want to know.'

I turn my head away, speaking only sideways. I'll give him the words, but not my eyes. 'I need to know it now,' I say. This is what I've come for.

He nods, and pushes out a deep breath. In relief? Or dread? I twist my hands together. Robert speaks. 'Dad wasn't always nice to Mum. They argued a lot. Sometimes they drank too much, both of them.' He's still looking down. I have to lean forward to filter the words through the background buzz of boarding announcements.

'I don't remember that,' I admit. 'I try, but all I remember is . . .' Sebastian. I remember Sebastian, and chestnut trees, and a special goblet. Mum had let us glue plastic gems onto a real wine glass to make our own communion cup.

Robert says, 'I'm not saying that there weren't good times too. There were. It just wasn't perfect.'

I nod. 'Did Dad cheat?' But it doesn't need to be a question. 'He cheated on Mum, didn't he.'

'I was eleven. I honestly don't know.'

I do. I'd remembered. I feel older for a moment, like I'm the big sibling, more world-weary, more full of knowledge. I consider telling Robert about the neighbour in the barn, but recognise that the urge springs from a desire to shock him. That would be unkind.

'Was that what they argued about?' I ask. 'What else? Did they argue more after Sebastian came?' *They must have. They couldn't have done what they did and not been changed by it for the worse.*

'Imogen, all parents argue more after a baby's born.' Robert, a father himself, is back to being the authority. I'm the little one again.

I wait, but he doesn't say anything else. He's making me ask for it, bit by bit. 'What happened the night they died?'

Robert pushes his cup away. He shakes his head.

I beg him, 'I don't remember. I honestly don't remember. Please tell me.'

He pushes his face towards me, punishing me with a

harsh tone for making him say it. 'They were arguing about something. Dad stomped upstairs. Sebastian followed him, and I don't think Dad knew he was there. Mum shouted up after Dad, and Dad whirled around, and . . . Sebastian got kicked backwards. He fell all the way down. They took him to go to the hospital.' He shrugs, drops back. 'They didn't come back,' he finishes.

'Dad kicked him?'

'I don't think it was on purpose. I don't know.'

'But he was angry.'

'He was always angry!'

People are staring. Robert curls his shoulders in embarrassment, and apologises for raising his voice.

I remember the stairs themselves perfectly, times playing peekaboo between the rails, and fairy lights wound around the bannister at Christmas. But I don't see our father there on the landing, or our mother at the bottom, or Sebastian tumbling down. 'Was I there?'

'We were all there. You were little. You're lucky you remember the good things,' he offers me.

'I remember seeing Sebastian in hospital, before they split us up. He was all bruised. They said it was from the accident. Do you think that some of it was from the . . . ?'

'It doesn't matter now.'

'Did Dad ever—'

'Imogen, *stop*,' he insists. 'I know that this is news for you, but Ben and I dealt with it a long time ago.'

You haven't dealt with all of it, I think, with a mental sneer. I feel suddenly powerful in my new understanding, instead of cowed by it. He doesn't know everything.

'We got a good family, Imogen,' he continues. 'So

307

did you. I've got a family of my own now, and you have Maxwell . . . Is anything ever going to be enough?'

'What about Sebastian?'

'What about him? He hasn't registered to be contacted, so I assume that he doesn't want to be.'

'What if he doesn't know? What if his new family lied to him?'

We've had this conversation before. The first time, I'd been desperate to convince Robert to join my search. Now, I'm curious about his defences, his reasoning. I want him to convince me.

Robert retorts: 'Maybe with not knowing, he's the happiest of all four of us. Did you ever think of that?'

Those two sentences are what I'd come for. I feel a lightening, as if permission has been granted. I say out loud, to divert him with an explanation for my relief, 'You said "the four of us". That's nice to hear.'

'You'll always be my sister.' He smiles. He takes the last of the shortbread, which I haven't touched. The scatter of crumbs and the balled-up napkin on his side of the table strike me as suddenly familiar. Had he always been the 'messy one'? Had I been neat, even then?

'You're right,' I say. 'It doesn't matter. *Now* is what matters.'

He nods, and smiles, relieved to be past the necessary ugliness. He shows me photos of his girls on his iPhone. He tells me that Ben is moving to the States to work on a PhD. I nod in return, but share nothing of my own life. Robert finally has to ask me, 'How's Maxwell?'

I consider carefully before answering. 'He's the best thing in my life.' I feel like I've been delivered from the past to the present by train, and stepped out of the rail car blinking into bright sunlight.

Robert smiles indulgently, like the older brother he is, as if he's proud that I've learnt to balance on a bicycle or swim in the deep end. 'You'll both come and visit us, won't you? We have a spare room.'

I've not seen his house before, but I imagine it, down to the colours on the duvet, a hideous maroon and brown that Robert and his wife are quite right to relegate to the least-used bed. The vividness of this fiction surprises me. It's at least as real as everything else in my head, all those remembered scenes that I've given so much power for too many years.

'We'd love that,' I answer for both Maxwell and myself.

I imagine the hideous guest quilt being too thin, and Maxwell and I giggling and pressing together for warmth underneath it on a cool night. I make myself stop there, reminding myself that whether Robert's wife cooks breakfast, or his daughters complain about their school uniforms, or the dog jumps and licks too much, is up to the future. I make a conscious decision to stop planning, instead to look around, and to listen. I hear, beyond the loudspeaker and chatter and footsteps, beyond the rolling baggage and chugging trains, the bright lilt of a distant busker playing a trumpet for coins.

MAXWELL GANT

The multistorey car park nearest the Cambridge police station is attached to the public swimming pool. As I pull in and set the handbrake, I see a family with wet hair and inflatable toys exiting the lift. They must smell of chlorine, but from inside the car I imagine the salt-tinge from the Isle of Wight. I have to force myself to emerge. I'd long ago let my father go, like releasing a helium balloon. Now my mother. In an hour it will be over. In an hour, I'll be a fully-free adult, with no parents at all.

A car horn blasts. I've crossed in front of a vehicle whooshing round a corner. I raise a hand in apology, duck my head, and step back. The car speeds past. I feel like a child again, 'head in the clouds', my mother used to say. If I were reading, or even just thinking, she would have to call me multiple times to get me to respond.

It occurs to me now that this might have had more to do with the name she called me than with me being inattentive to my surroundings.

They were supposed to keep calling me Sebastian. I've looked up adoption practices from the time, and that was how it was done. They could change my last name, but not my first. No one hovered, though, to enforce this. Maybe that's part of what my parents fought over. Maybe my father tried to stick to the rules and she called me Maxwell anyway, after her dead father. After the divorce, she changed our last name back to her maiden name. That would have been a chance to slip in a first name change, too. Forgery? A few keystrokes in a primary database? She'd had the skills, and the access.

'How can I help?' asks the cheerful policewoman behind the counter. I'd got out of the car park and across the road on autopilot. I was there already, too soon, stammering.

'I'm here to see my mother,' I say, finally. 'Muriel Gant. She's been arrested.'

I already know that she assaulted the Inspector. DS Spencer had informed me of the charges against her so far: the assault, and attempted kidnapping of Imogen. I haven't been asked to raise bail, and I suspect she's being denied the option. It doesn't matter; I won't pay it.

I'm brought into a small box-like room, where I'm permitted to speak with her. She looks small, and frail, despite being merely fifty-five.

'I know who I am,' I say. I don't want her to try to keep playing the game.

'Who's that?' she asks. It sounds like a dare.

'You adopted me. There's no shame in that. Why didn't you just tell me?'

She sounds like a saw scraping against metal. It's her laugh, gasping for air. 'I know what adopted children do,' she says. 'Your Imogen is proof of that.'

The words are sharp: 'my' Imogen. She's indeed mine, profoundly so.

My mother pushes more words across the table. They heap in front of me. 'She worships her drunk father and subservient mother. Hardly anything to say about her real parents, the ones who took her in and raised her as their own. Her real siblings, the ones who grew up with her into adulthood and shared clothes and bedrooms and holidays. It's not fair. I had to protect myself from that. You couldn't expect me to love you and just let you face the other way, always looking backwards.'

I shake my head. 'You don't know that I would have been like that. And even if I had been, that was my—'

'I couldn't take the chance.' She pinches her lips together. 'Did you really think that I would never know?'

'How? You had no reason to contact your father, nor he you. I didn't ask him for any money. I let him go. We were safe, until *she* seduced you on a Spanish beach.'

'We didn't sleep together in Spain.' I don't know why that feels important to make clear, but it does. 'She didn't know. She never knew. She doesn't know now.' My voice breaks. I don't know how I'll stand in front of Imogen and tell her. We mustn't touch, not even in comfort. Our bodies know one another too well.

My mother dismisses my defence of Im. 'She started sniffing around for your father, as if he mattered. Biology was all she could think of. Never mind that he'd left us. Never mind that he'd had no contact with you since. She believed he was half of your DNA, so she wanted him at your wedding. That's the kind of obsession I'm talking about. I suspected what she was up to, so I followed her. Once she found him, I knew she knew.'

I refute her. 'He didn't tell her. Maybe he would have later, but he didn't get the chance.'

Her indignant expression falters, but she rallies: 'It had to be stopped. If you'd listened to me when I told you to break it off, it wouldn't have come to any of this.'

I nod, not in agreement, but in acceptance that she's beyond reasoning with.

'On the island,' she explains, 'it was impulse. I was angry. I had to stop her before she could tell you.'

I realise that this was the near-miss car accident that Imogen had described.

'When I missed, I knew all was lost. You would know. My only hope was to create a diversion, to make her question what she'd been told – what I could only have *assumed* she'd been told. I had to give her, and you, a reason to doubt. I invented Patrick Bell, to create a trail to show you that she was wrong. Something we could find online together, after . . .'

'After what?'

She doesn't answer. My throat constricts as I realise she must mean 'after Imogen was dead'.

I stammer, 'But when she responded with belief, when she agreed to meet you . . . didn't you see that she *didn't* know? That you didn't have to . . . do that?'

'It had to be stopped. Whether she knew or you knew, it had to be stopped.'

I nod. That was true. Only instead of stopping it by confessing the truth, she'd tried to stop it with murder.

I'd figured it out, driving away from London. The DNA

results had shown me that Imogen had acted in good faith. She'd had no hint that I was Sebastian; I should have trusted her all along. And if she was to be trusted, then there really was someone after her, someone in a bright green car. This person had created Patrick Bell to lure Imogen to a desolate address in Highfields Caldecote, the name Patrick Bell inspired by a sign near my father's house. But my father didn't have the information to credibly create Patrick Bell, nor the motive of caring if I knew. *Who did?* I'd asked myself. The answer had pained me, but it rang true. That's when I'd texted Imogen the warning. *Thank God.*

My mother's staring off to the side at a blank, chipped wall. I wonder what she's seeing there. She snaps out of it, suddenly shimmying her shoulders and closing her mouth. 'I've told the police that she wasn't good enough for you. That's all I'll ever say, no matter what they ask me. It's all they need to know. You'll never be shamed by this.'

'Thank you,' I say quietly, having not yet considered the impact that public knowledge of the truth would have on me. If she were to attempt to use the extreme circumstances to justify her state of mind, humiliation would follow both me and Imogen, separately, even if we never saw one another again. To give me this gift, she has to confess a mitigated version of the truth, and take her punishment, without argument. 'Thank you,' I repeat, somehow meaning it truly.

I stand to leave. As I turn my back, she barks my name: 'Maxwell!'

My stomach tightens. The name pings in me a deep recognition.

It must have taken months, perhaps years, for her to

carve it into my consciousness. Did she get angry at first when I didn't respond to the name, or did she laugh it off, like she did years later, recalling my supposed childhood obliviousness? I try to remember what it was like, hearing a name that wasn't mine tossed in my direction, over and over, until I finally reached out to catch it.

I don't face her, or answer her, but I feel the leash-pull of the name.

I leave, but part of me remains attached to her. However I started, I'm Maxwell now.

I get out, wait anxiously for the pedestrian lights to release me across the congested junction, and almost run for my car, a familiar refuge. The dissonant DNA results are on the passenger seat. It's as if they've taken Imogen's place away from her, though they're the one thing that could make it possible for her to come back.

My sister. I try to remember her as she was, as the eight-year-old I apparently adored, but nothing comes. I only know her as she is. Could there be some explanation besides the worst?

I sift through the impossibilities: an affair would still give a half match in children, but the results showed no match at all. Sebastian had been born at home, so there was no accidental switch at the hospital. Imogen had long ago matched her DNA to her older brothers' (at the insistence of a sister-in-law when they had first reconnected, in case she might be a con artist). So, no switch at the hospital for her either. She remembers her mother pregnant, so it wasn't an adoption. I hit the steering wheel. I can't be Sebastian, yet I am. I desperately don't want to be.

I start the car and pull out into the narrow lane, scanning

for exit arrows. *Yes, thank you – 'this way out'*. A way out would be wonderful.

I pull up to the line just in time for the pedestrians to get their turn. A little boy and a little girl trot across, holding their mother's hands.

I try again to picture young Im. I only see my mother, Muriel Gant, and no one on her other side.

The harder I try, the more the image recedes, now replaced by grown Imogen, in her wet red bathing suit. I feel what I shouldn't feel. Then, disgust engulfs my arousal, and I wonder if I'll ever be without shame again.

My mother had tried to spare me. She'd tried to give me the grief of loss instead of the guilt of knowledge. *Shame on her*, I think, rolling into the road at last, joining the slow queue. *It doesn't matter what I feel. The only thing that matters is that Imogen is safe.* She's alive. Having to bear this guilt is nothing if it's bought her that.

At first, my mother had tried to break us apart without violence. If only I'd been weaker, if only I'd allowed myself to be swayed by her vile assertions . . . I wonder now if what she'd claimed was even true. Those newspaper stories had been grainy photocopies. Had Dr Llewellyn really been drink-driving the night of the accident? My mother had accused the man of killing a whole family in the oncoming car.

Behind the wheel of my own vehicle, I slam on the brakes.

IMOGEN WRIGHT-LLEWELLYN

The busy, generic breakfast room could be in any city. I'm still in Cambridge but only know it by the brochures in the lobby: punting offers, college tours, a police warning about bicycle thieves.

My emotional high after leaving Robert in London has faded. Our meeting had clarified for me, perfectly, what I now want, and that fresh hope had buoyed me for a few hours. Then, the weight of its likely impossibility had pulled down, and pulls still.

It feels appropriately masochistic to have removed myself to a generic hotel on a leisure park by a busy road. Its front is a collage of ugly blocks in shades of shouty blue; its rooms inside are cheap and charmless. It fits my mood.

I hang my head, facing the cold croissant and bright banana spooning on my plate. I'm not hungry. I want coffee, but can't balance a full cup on my lap while manoeuvring the wheelchair. No one has offered assistance, out of politeness, I suppose. Such help would imply that I'm needy, and that would be rude.

Maxwell hasn't contacted me, not since that last text that warned me of his mother. *Thank goodness he sent that.* Otherwise, I might have forced myself to be genial with my future mother-in-law; I might have gone with Mrs Gant, pretending pleasure, into her green car, or, at least, up to her green car.

But if Maxwell knew enough to warn me, he likely understands his mother's motive. It had come together for me there in the car park. Muriel Gant knew all along who Maxwell is. When she discovered who I am and that he was determined to marry me, she'd felt compelled to stop it.

A tear splashes on the white rim of my plate. I couldn't face staying in our original Cambridge hotel, not in the room we'd shared, not where Maxwell might return. Nor could I yet face our London flat. I don't want to sleep alone in our once-shared bed, nor risk a sudden confrontation. So long as I avoid Maxwell, there's still a chance with him, however small.

If he knows, losing him is inevitable. I'm certain of that, even as I face my own acceptance of what would have once repelled me. If the original DNA test had revealed our relationship, we would have veered onto a different road. I would have insisted on it; I would have jerked the steering wheel sideways myself. *But that's the point*, I remind myself. *The tests didn't show anything because we have no genetic relationship.* We had lived together for three years as an intimate sibling pair, and I had loved him with a motherly depth that separation then only exaggerated;

but our combined DNA won't deform any future children – isn't that the usual worry? Another tear falls, sliding down the croissant's greasy slope.

What if he doesn't know? Had Muriel's plan been only to separate us to prevent any further sin, or had she hoped to spare Maxwell any knowledge of it altogether? Had Muriel hoped to protect him from guilt, and preserve her status as his 'real' mother by keeping the truth to herself? I hold onto that chance. My hands tighten into fists in my lap; my nails dig into my palms.

Then I flex my fingers and grab my wheels. I spin away from the table and from my uneaten breakfast, narrowly avoiding a man behind me. His bowl tilts, scattering yellow flakes and milk.

'Imogen!' he says. I know his voice. I know his shoes, too, and the broken lace on the left one.

'How did you find me?' I ask, still not looking up. I cringe. Facing him would be like facing into a spotlight.

'I didn't,' Maxwell admits, the spilt milk between us thinning out as the puddle expands. 'I couldn't leave Cambridge without seeing you, but I didn't want to impose myself on you by returning to our room. I wasn't even sure if you were still here, or back in London. I don't even know if your wheelchair will fit in the lift in our building. My God, Imogen, my mother did this.' His voice breaks like a teenager's.

I tilt my glance upwards. 'I'll be all right. This . . .' I shrug to indicate the wheelchair. 'Is only temporary.'

An annoyed woman I recognise from the front desk shoves a broom between us, sweeping up Maxwell's spill into a long-handled dustpan. The empty bowl still dangles from his hand. I push myself backwards, to turn towards a fresh table. Maxwell follows, bounding forward to remove a chair from one side to make a place for me. He sits opposite.

I marvel that we ended up in the same cheap hotel, in a city built to accommodate thousands of tourists and the regular influx of visiting parents for University milestone events. It's like those twin studies that show separated siblings to have developed the same quirks and tastes even when raised apart – how they take their tea; favourite TV shows and sports teams; even same university subject. Then I remind myself that Maxwell and I have no biological basis for our serendipity. We've earned our likeness through being together, like those silly photos of owners who've come to resemble their pets.

'I suppose I should have expected to see you here,' Maxwell says. 'All the other hotels I tried were full with tour groups. This was the only one with any space.'

I blush. *Perhaps not destiny then.*

'I knew from the police that you were all right,' he assures me. 'I didn't delay making sure of that. I've been thinking of you every—' He stops himself.

I squeeze my hands together in my lap.

'I went to see my mother,' Maxwell tells me. 'For the last time.' He says this fiercely, reminding me of how he had brooked no protest from Muriel, not for a moment, when she'd objected to our engagement. He had chosen me over her, easily, right from the start.

I wait. A man's choice of his lover over his mother is a small thing, compared to a choice between his lover and . . . *a primal revulsion*, I admit to myself. *A moral*

322

revulsion, I correct. Maxwell has always been the one of us more likely to sort the world into right and wrong.

'Imogen, there's something I have to tell you.'

Those are the words I've been hiding from, here in this dingy chain hotel. My head swivels back and forth. 'No,' I say. *Don't say it*, I beg with my eyes.

Maxwell looks pained, regretful, sick.

We don't have to do this, I tell him with my expression in return. Is his car here? We can get in and just drive. We can go back to London. We can go back to Spain.

'I'm parked outside,' he says, again sharing my mind.

We belong together, I marvel. *We're already like one person.*

'I need to show you something,' he explains, leaning across the table. The wheelchair arms don't fit under it, keeping me back, beyond his reach.

I tilt my head. *Where does he want me to go?*

'Please,' he adds. 'Please.' His face sags in seeming apology, in seeming agony, but our eyes are connected.

I nod.

323

MAXWELL GANT

I part grass to read the gravestone: *William James Barbour, Much Loved Son.*

I suppose I should feel something, but nothing comes. It's sad to see any child's tombstone, of course I feel that, but nothing personal rises up in me.

Imogen wheels up close to read the stones on either side. They have the same year of death as William's. His parents. They were all three killed by Imogen's father in the accident in which he and Imogen's mother also died.

'How did you know?' she asks me.

I gesture towards a low wall separating the cemetery from a pub's beer garden. I sit on it, and she backs up next to me, wobbling on the lumpy terrain. We face the wilderness trying to grow up around the graves. Everything is wet. A quick, heavy rain last night took the heat away. We shiver in our too-light clothes.

'When my mother realised who you were, she tried to break us up. It was when we Skyped about the engagement and talked about Cambridge that enough clues came together to set her off. She came to London and tried to convince me that you were crazy. She told me awful things about your family. I'm sorry, Im.'

'I feel like I've woken up,' Imogen says. 'I still love my parents, both of them, but I love them like real people now, not like perfect-parent dolls.'

'What she told me is all true. The police have confirmed it. He was drunk the night of the accident. He was the cause. Both Sebastian and the boy in the other car were hurt, both Sebastian and the boy from the other car were taken away by ambulance. One of them died.'

'Not you,' says Imogen, squeezing my hand.

'No, not me. Sebastian died. But in the chaos after the accident, and with all four parents dead, the hospital mixed them up. Us. Mixed us up.'

Imogen can't take her eyes off the grave.

I say, 'Sebastian died a long time ago. I'm sorry.'

'And you're really William James Barbour,' Imogen completes for me.

I nod, then look up at the sky, squinting. I thought it would take more work to convince her. It had taken days to convince myself, even after all the information had clicked for me. 'I know this theory sounds mad, but . . .' I lift my shoulders then let them drop. 'Im, I was ready to walk away. I picked apart our flat, teasing out *me* from *you*. Once I'd heard from John Hutter that I was adopted and the name I came with, I knew that leaving was the only right thing to do. That the DNA says that we're not physically related, that didn't matter. You and Sebastian were sister and brother, profoundly so, no matter what your – *our* – physical bodies have to say about it. I tried to stay with you in my mind, I really did. I just couldn't go there any more, not once I'd been told. I need you to know that, so that you don't think that this is some crazy story I've made up just to trick you into being with me. Im, if I didn't believe that this is true with my whole heart, I couldn't be with you. I was ready to walk away,' I repeat. 'The DNA mismatch, though . . . I couldn't make sense of it. All of the possibilities were, well, impossible. Not an affair, not a hospital mistake, not an adoption. You were in the house when Seb was born. You match your other brothers. If we didn't match, was I really Seb, who you spent your childhood with? I couldn't be, could I? It's just not possible. That's what started me looking for another answer. This explains it all.' *Even the memories.*

Sebastian and William had been similar ages. They'd both lived around Cambridge. William's father had been a fellow at Christ's College, physically near enough to Jesus College that it's likely that William had cut through Jesus' courtyards or visited people there. Anyone might have told both children about the horse sculpture at Jesus being modelled after the horses at San Marco in Venice. Any parent would take their children to see the plaster cast of Hercules at the Classical Archaeology museum. 'It explains everything,' I finish.

There are other Barbour graves nearby, reminders of aunts and uncles, grandparents and cousins. Some of them are here, but surely not all. Surely some Barbours are still alive. Some of them would have come to the hospital to receive the body. If it were Sebastian who was mistakenly given to them, they would have recognised that, wouldn't

327

they? I imagine a badly burnt body, or a family rift that had lasted the duration of his – *my* – young life and kept his extended relations from knowing him. I mean, *me*. It's the only way I can think of to make it all work.

I watch Imogen. She has to notice the other graves, and be thinking of small William's family. I beg her in my mind to accept the possibility I've so carefully crafted. *Don't ask to find them*, I silently plead. *Don't ask for any more DNA.* This scenario may be unlikely, but it's possible. *Isn't that enough?*

I think back to that Handel finale, those charged voices, and Imogen coming into the back of the rehearsal room with 'good news' in her eyes, her face alight, happy. I hadn't known for sure which would make her look like that: the DNA results giving her back her baby brother, or giving her permission to love me. I don't know which she wants more, even now.

Imogen wheels forward. She zigzags to get alongside the grave, and looks up at the chestnut branches hanging over it. 'Sebastian and I loved playing with the conkers that fell from the trees at Jesus College while the boys sang. He'll be happy here.'

I let my breath out. My mouth can't stop moving, alternating between smiles and a round 'oh!' of happiness. We've chosen it together. We're going to leave Sebastian here, buried.

IMOGEN WRIGHT-LLEWELLYN

I nod to Maxwell. He pushes my chair to follow the path out of the cemetery.

'We should tell the chaplain that we won't be booking the wedding,' I say. 'I mean, not here. Not in Cambridge.'

'We could get married in Spain,' Maxwell muses. The wheels of the chair spin and spin along the winding path.

'I think we should check out of our rooms today,' I say. 'Leave Cambridge. I don't want to be here any more.'

'We'll go straight there,' Maxwell agrees.

I grab a wheel, to stop.

'Do you know if the Inspector's all right?' I ask, turning to face him behind me. Only now, with my own misery relieved, am I suddenly conscious of the effects of recent events on others. Guilt and worry strangle my voice. 'Was she there when you went to see your mother?' I had been afraid for the Inspector in the car park, when she had taken the cuff to the face, and for her baby, when she'd taken that fall. But selfless dread had flashed for only a moment, before the bigger thing had overwhelmed me.

'I dealt with the ginger sergeant. The Inspector's fine, but she's been put on leave for bed rest. Pregnancy is serious. I'll admit, the idea of it scares me, Imogen.'

'But the baby will be fine?'

'According to him, yes.'

I let relief wash over me. They're miracles, babies, and women are, too: it's a miracle the way our bodies expand and harden to protect life growing inside.

Touching the Inspector's firm belly, I'd realised in an instant the power of a pregnant woman's body. I'd in an instant understood two memories in an entirely different light:

My mother, always so affectionate, had suddenly turned cold partway through her pregnancy with Sebastian. No more hugs. No more lap. I'd hungered for her body, but had been cut off. My father had tried to explain how pregnancy can be uncomfortable, and even hurt. I didn't want to hurt my mother, so gave her the margin she wanted.

But there was a day I couldn't resist. She had been napping on the sofa. Her belly rose and fell with deep breathing. She didn't look in pain. I had reached out, and touched the soft lump where I knew my sibling was curled. The early scan had said it would be a girl, but the doctor had made us promise not to count on it. So I had been careful to not assume that I was going to have a sister.

The belly had felt pillow-soft. I had rubbed, hoping to find a kick or a nudge. Then my mother had moaned in her sleep, and I ran outside, to pretend I hadn't even been in the room. I didn't want Mum to be angry.

That was the first memory. The second one happened a few weeks later. This was when I followed my father to the Red House, and the long-haired woman distracted me with hair combing and radio. And a ball. I always remembered that ball.

Touching the Inspector's belly, I remembered, I knew, that it had never been a ball at all. The woman on the steps of the White House had been pregnant, hugely pregnant, and she'd let me touch her. The belly had felt hard, like a basketball, and nothing like my mother's soft hill.

The woman had said why she was so big. 'I've got two in there,' she'd confided. 'I'll call them Lucky and Luke,' she'd joked, after the comic book cowboy.

In the car park, remembering this, I'd screamed, because I'd felt like I was rolling down a hill that had no bottom.

Joseph Llewellyn was scared.

Isobel hadn't been sleeping well. Her due date was near, and she was up at strange hours some nights. It's because of this night-wandering that he'd learnt the truth.

Unlike Imogen, who'd felt her soft front, Joseph had seen the strap around her waist, visible in silhouette, in the light coming through her thin nightdress as she paced in front of the windows on a bright, full-mooned night.

She'd seen him watching her, but had smiled, not realising what he could see. She'd rubbed her stuffed belly in slow circles. She'd mouthed one word to him: 'Soon.'

It was madness. She must have miscarried, months before. She'd stopped seeing her doctor. She'd moved into the guest bed, claiming insomnia. She'd stopped touching him and the children, or letting them touch her . . .

He'd gone to work, robotically, the next day. Afterwards, he offered Rowena one of their usual lifts. He didn't want to go straight home. Rowena was never fully a person to him, not the way that Isobel was, and the act was mechanical and stress-relieving.

That's when that woman, the squatter, burst into their peace. That's when the screaming and the blood pushed him half-dressed into the night to get to a phone. He charged out, ran from the Red House clutching his clothes, shoving arms and legs into random holes, hoping to end up dressed at the end. He aimed for his house, which he could see was blessedly dark. She must be asleep. He was already making a plan: Use the phone in the kitchen. Close the door. Don't wake Isobel.

His affairs had nothing to do with her, but she wouldn't be able to understand that. If she woke, she'd demand where his car is, where the rest of his clothes are, why he smells of sex. Or she wouldn't ask; she would answer the questions herself. That would be worse.

He fumbled the key in their door, begging it not to squeak. He pulled up on the knob to take pressure off the noisy hinges. He froze in the doorway. She was right in front of him, stretched out on the sofa.

She used to do this when he first started working late shifts. She tried to wait up for him, and wanted him to wake her if she didn't make it. He used to bend to kiss her, and she'd wrap her arms around his neck. They'd have sex on the sofa or the floor. This was when the twins were still babies, in cots, unable to wander out of their rooms at night. It was a long time ago.

He held himself back from her now, and wondered

what she'd been waiting up for. He hadn't been allowed to touch her for months. Did she want to argue or accuse? Did she know something? Or, was she ready to confess her own lies? In that position, without a blanket, without her conscious presentation, her belly was obviously false.

He had to close the door; rain blowing in from outside might wake her. He pushed the door to, and the latch clicked loudly. He froze again, steeling himself for her to turn her head, to open her eyes.

She didn't move. He watched her. He couldn't see her breathing.

He crumpled to his knees beside her. In his panic, he almost touched her hand.

'Almost' was enough. Her eyes fluttered open. 'Hi,' she said, smiling, and her hand moved to the bump, rubbing it, making circles. She wasn't really awake, just half there, automatic.

'Hi,' he said. Her eyes fell shut. She'd remember the moment like a dream. He wanted it to be a good dream.

He forced his hands to fall to his sides.

He hadn't been allowed to touch her in months, not even to stroke her hair or cheek. She would spring back, even slap his hand away. He knew now that it was to keep her secret, to keep a safe circle around her lying body, not a rejection of him.

He wondered if she missed him like he missed her. The nurses he fucked, they were nothing to him. They never had been. They were just bodies. She was his love.

He watched her, so close that his breath wafted her hair. Every breath of hers, every involuntary shift, was a relief contrasted with the horror of what he had feared when he saw her so still.

Her due date was approaching. She'd become more brittle, shouting at the children and crying when she thought he couldn't hear. People would start asking questions. He didn't know what she would do if this went on much longer, and she had to face that a cushion doesn't get born. She might do something drastic, he worried. She might run away from them. She might run away from this world. Just now, when her breath had been hidden from his view, that had seemed not just possible, but the obvious end. It hadn't surprised him. It had terrified him.

He had to make sure that that didn't happen.

He backed up, slipped outside. He returned to the barn, but didn't enter it. He squatted down with his back to the red wall. He listened.

He waited for the sounds inside to slow down. It was like waiting for popcorn to finish popping: the riotous rat-a-tat inside the pan will eventually decrease to occasional, singular bangs. That's how you know it's finished. That's what happened with the squatter's cries.

He re-entered the barn.

'The ambulance is on its way,' he lied, kneeling beside Rowena to help deliver what he saw was a second baby. It was smaller, and appeared to have died in utero, probably what prompted the early labour. Rowena was hysterical. Blood kept coming.

Joseph remained clear-headed. He wasn't fazed by blood. He took charge, tending to the living baby. He hissed at Rowena to get water and light.

She scurried, obeying. The squatter had stopped

struggling. Her eyes were open, and she breathed, but she wasn't making noise any more. Rowena had placed the dead baby on her chest. Tears skidded down the mother's cheeks.

Joseph was unmoved.

He only needed one.

IMOGEN WRIGHT-LLEWELLYN

I know what Maxwell needs to believe, to make sense of things. I allow it. I don't tell him that I was brought to visit recovering Sebastian in hospital once, just once, before we were separated. He'd been badly bruised, by the accident and earlier by the fall down the stairs, but not disfigured. Even if he had died after I saw him, the hospital had known his right identity, and the Barbour family would have recognised him as not-theirs.

Maxwell was Sebastian, just as his father on the Isle of Wight had told him. Sebastian, stolen from a stranger to replace the developing baby girl that I remember from the scan at the hospital. That's why our genetic tests never showed a match. Something had happened sometime after that scan – a miscarriage, most likely. My mother's hard, full belly had been replaced by a pillow-like bump that squished like bread dough at my touch. My father had brought home an offering one night, I now understand, and my mother's belly had been let to go flat. I fell in love with my brother the next morning, waking up and finding him in our mother's arms.

There's no point in telling him, I decide. *He's not Sebastian any more.*

A quick, cool breeze rushes over us, and the previous month's heat feels suddenly deep in the past, as far away as our childhood.

Maxwell's come up with his own theory, and I let it comfort him.

MAXWELL GANT

Imogen faces front; I push from behind, following.

I reiterate my standard for going forward: 'I'm not interested in looking up any distant Barbour cousins. I just want a clean slate. You and me. I just want to look ahead.' I brace for her to resist.

Her amiability surprises me. The change in her is bigger than the injury, bigger than the wheelchair. She seems truly to have grown, to have become able to let go of her past. *Perhaps*, I think, relieved, happy and grateful, *the idea of Sebastian's death, terrible as it is, is freeing for her.*

She says, in that lovely voice, formed by that lovely mouth, words that prove how far she's come and how ready she is to live in the present:

'You're my family, Maxwell.'

EPILOGUE

When Fiona was a child, her fantasy superpower had been to stop time. But, even as a child, she hadn't been able to enjoy the fantasy uncritically.

If she literally stopped time for everything around her, she would be unable to breathe the stilled, solid air, or to move through it.

What if air were excused? Then she could breathe, and move, but things would still be frozen around her. Pillows would be boulders and grass would be teeth. What she really wanted, when she wished to stop time, was just to stop other people. Make them pause. Make them wait. Let herself catch up, and start them again when she was finally ready.

Fiona opens her eyes. The room is unlit, but not completely dark. It's the hospital room. Stiff sheets lie lightly on her chest. An IV tube is in her arm. The chair where her mother used to sit is empty.

It seems a very real possibility that sitting up or even

just lifting her head could peel her consciousness from her body, which would stay behind on the bed, too heavy to fly.

She's not sure if she's dead.

She waits.

Her mother fills the doorway, carrying a large paper cup. Her handbag swings from her arm, back and forth, and Fiona follows it with her gaze. The light from the corridor behind her mother must reflect off Fiona's open eyes, because, even in the almost-dark, Morgan Davies recognises that Fiona is awake.

Pandemonium: Fiona's mother makes a fist around the paper cup and it erupts. She calls out, and nurses run. Lights. Prodding. Fiona submits, unmoving. She lets herself be handled. In the end, she's pronounced well, though she has declined to speak. She continues to stare at the bag, still hanging from her mother's arm, still swinging as her mother rocks from foot to foot. They're all moving, all of them, rushing and poking and leaning over her.

Stop, she begs in her mind. *Hold still.* She imagines them freezing there, in a kind of cage around her, and her climbing out of it, over them, monkeying out using their shoulders for footholds and someone's back to jump off of. She imagines running through the night-time hospital, down empty corridors, finding an empty room, and locking the door.

She squeezes her eyes shut.

When Fiona wakes up again, only her mother is left, napping in the chair. It's dim in the room, as when she woke before. Fiona doesn't know if it's minutes later or days.

342

'How did you do it?' Fiona asks. She'd counted the pills. She'd been careful.

'I didn't do anything. I was useless. A stranger saved you.' Mum explains the partial-liver transplant. Fiona receives the information, but doesn't physically react. She's moved only her head, once to face her mother to ask the question, and then away after she heard the answer.

On the other side of the room, she's found a power outlet to stare at. 'Grandma Ro said that the worst feeling in the world was waking up when she didn't want to any more.'

Something is ticking. It could be a clock, or a machine measuring something in Fiona's body. She counts the ticks: . . . *twenty-one, twenty-two, twenty-three*—

'Do you know what it feels like, that the people I love would prefer to die?' her mother asks.

Fiona starts the count over again. *One, two, three, four*—

Her mother demands an answer.

Fiona complies: 'It's not fair to make me live just so that you feel loved.'

'I can't *make* you do anything! You can keep on hurting yourself. But people will keep trying to help you. It's not just me, you know.'

As if to underscore this, a nurse pops her head in. It must be morning, because she flicks on the room lights, buzzy fluorescents. Fiona squints and covers her eyes, her hand sticking out from her forehead like the bill of a cap.

'How are we today?' the nurse asks. Without waiting for an answer, she announces breakfast, laying a tray onto a rolling table, the top of which swings over Fiona's lap.

Fiona remains flat, shoulders back against her pillow. Hot egg smell reaches her nose, and she opens her mouth to pant.

'Some toast, sweetheart,' the nurse recommends, tapping the plastic plate with two triangles on it.

Fiona shakes her head.

Her mother can't hold off any longer. Even with the nurse still there, she asks: 'Is that how you really feel? Is this waking up the worst thing in the world?'

Waiting for Fiona's answer, everything holds still: her mother's uptilted chin, the nurse's finger on the plate. It all holds still, and Fiona marvels at her power, working at last.

With a slight, surprised shake of her head, she starts it all up again: footsteps in the corridor, cleaners' swooshing mops, growls of cars outside. She repeats her answer, which had surprised even herself, this time by moving her lips into the pucker of 'no'. Not the worst thing in the world. For Ro, maybe, but not for her.

Then, 'Please,' Fiona says, stopping the nurse who's halfway out the door. 'I'd like a drink of water.' She pushes herself up to sitting. Her body comes with her.

Her mother's held breath whooshes out. She inhales in its place fresh surprise, relief, and gratitude.

Fiona drinks.

Her mother sobs into her hands.

Dora's eyes follow her father's fingers. He wraps some kind of band around the top of his right palm, and slots the bow of his violin into the plastic grip attached to it. This way, he squeezes the bow between the base of his thumb and the bottom of his first finger, instead of by their tips.

He pulls the bow across the strings. Sound falls out of them. Music is often cartoonishly depicted as unfurling from an instrument, the bar lines curling like a banner in the wind. But these notes fall, just drop, heavy with confession: *this is where I've been.*

Gwen smiles. She's awake, at home, sewn up, loopy from medication, and teary to see her husband's damaged hand in use. She'd urged him to go back to his youthful self, to explore what dreams he left behind when he chose police work to follow. 'You can go back to university,' she'd suggested. 'Do anything. You can start a new phase of life.' But who wants to be in a classroom with eighteen year olds, or at the bottom of a work ladder in some other field? She hadn't known that he'd followed her advice in one small way: he'd gone back to his instrument.

The notes fall faster now, quick and tapping, like hail on a roof. Dora cries. The woman in the blond ponytail, the woman in the house with the dried-flower wreath on the door, teaches violin in schools. She helps disabled students make music. Jesse had waited patiently, tied up outside her house, while Morris struggled with relearning scales and simple folk songs.

His head is tilted to hold the instrument down with his chin. Gwen has always loved that position, that way that violinists have to lean and curve.

'It's not a job,' is all he says, in apology, abruptly splitting the bow and violin from one another. A hobby falls far short of where he needs to get to consider himself useful again. *But,* he wonders, *maybe now . . .*

The only good that his injured hand had ever done him was to prevent him from making a fist at DS Spencer in the middle of Parkside station, when the sergeant had refused to see reason about arresting Dora. Morris had had to force himself to keep still, and managed all of himself except his head. That part of him just twitched, side to side, without him meaning it to: *no*.

Spencer had leant across the table and said, 'Mr Keene . . .' *Mister*, not DCI. Mister, which is how Morris is addressed by a clerk holding his credit card or by teachers at Dora's school, not by a goddamn sergeant on Morris' own force. 'Mr Keene,' he'd said, 'I know she's your daughter. I'm sorry.'

'It's not wrong because she's my daughter,' Morris had told DS Spencer. 'It's wrong because you're a goddamn idiot to look at your case and see this as the answer.' Then he'd got his mouth back under control. His physical anger had had to go somewhere, and it had seemed to spread and thin throughout Morris's whole body, turning his bones into iron rods. His mind had focussed, and the action around him had seemed to slow, syncing up with his compromised self for the first time in months. Or, he'd considered later, perhaps, in that flash of outrage, he'd caught up with life again.

Perhaps what Morris can do, as meagre as it is, is at least as good as what overeager DS Spencer brings to the table. *Better*, Morris thinks. *I'm not who I want to be, but I'm better than him.* Perhaps that's reason enough to go back. Perhaps that's reason enough to try.

'Play it again,' Gwen asks, eyes closed above her smile. The pills make her sleepy.

Dora, on a chair next to her mother's bed, closes her eyes, too.

They don't see that Morris' eyes also close. He doesn't need the written notes to tell him what to do. This is music he knows in his gut. This is the stuff he learnt as a young teenager, now relearning, baby steps for his hobbled hand.

They can't see it, but the music fills up the room from the bottom, note by note. They rise up with it, floating.

ACKNOWLEDGEMENTS

This book was written with much generous support and assistance. Susie Dunlop in London, and Cameron McClure and Randall Klein in New York, challenged me with their high standards. Thank you all for the push, and thanks to Lydia Riddle for the finishing touches.

I'm grateful to all of my early readers from various stages, for encouragement, comment, and critique: Derek Black, Mimi Cross, Laura Gerlach, Robin Gwynne, Sophie Hannah, Ella Kennen, Mary McDonald, Kate Rhodes, Katy Salmon, Susan Van Valkenburg, Amy Weatherup, and Marianna Fletcher Williams. Special thanks to my sweet Gavin, for support on every front.

For research assistance, I'm grateful to Anthony Armstrong and Jane Campbell, Sarah Christensen, Françoise Barbira Freedman, Keith Ferry, Peter Glazebrook, Sheila Jackson, Vandy Massey, Rod Mengham, Nick Pritchard, Maiah Seul, and Kathy Whitehouse. Any inaccuracies are the result of my choice or error, not of their expertise.

I must thank those good sports who allowed their University roles to be referred to: Edward Wickham, Director of Music at St Catharine's College; Mark Williams, Director of Music at Jesus College; and especially the late John Hughes, Chaplain and Dean of Chapel at Jesus College, for cheerfully volunteering to appear in two scenes. His good humour and gentle wisdom are much missed.

Also thanks to Robert Dixon and Ben Morris, Jesus College organ scholars, for lending their names to Imogen's brothers, and especially to Ben for an intimidatingly thorough proofread.

Lastly, thanks to the choristers of Jesus College. In the four and a half years that we have been part of the choir so far, we have seen many boys pass through, starting as little kids and leaving as almost-men. It's as wonderful as Imogen remembers, and we're glad to have shared it with you.